Praise for Amanda McCabe

"…the immensely talented Amanda McCabe."
—*Romantic Times BOOKreviews*

"Amanda McCabe…has a tremendous knack
for breathing robust life and gentle humor into her
lovable characters."
—*Romantic Times BOOKreviews*

"Miss McCabe's talent for lively characters and
witty dialogue is always a winning combination."
—*Romantic Times BOOKreviews*

A Notorious Woman
"Danger, deception and desire are the key ingredients
in *A Notorious Woman,* and Amanda McCabe skillfully
brews all these potent elements into a lushly sensual,
exquisitely written love story."
—*Chicago Tribune*

"Amanda McCabe has woven a tapestry of deceit
and danger set in the romantic streets of Venice
that will keep the reader up past their bedtime.
A Notorious Woman will appeal to all of us
who enjoy suspense and historical romance all rolled
up into one book. Awesome, first-rate tale!!"
—*Cataromance*

"Suspenseful and full of surprises."
—*Romantic Times BOOKreviews*

"Will you kill me now, Emerald Lily?" he said roughly.

He slid his clasp to her hand, drawing her arm straight as he peeled back her sleeve to reveal the small blade strapped to her forearm. She had forgotten it was there, forgotten all but his kiss. She pulled her arm away, shaking the sleeve into place. "If I wanted to kill you tonight, you would have been dead long ago."

"So, why am I not? What is it you want?" His accent, usually so faint, so lightly musical, was hoarser, rougher. He stepped back from her, wiping his lips with the back of his hand as if to erase the very taste of her.

Marguerite turned away, wrapping her arms tightly around herself. She forced herself to laugh mockingly. "La, *monsieur,* I only desired a kiss! A kiss from a handsome man, is it so much to ask? So odd to you that it must be madness?"

He stood there in silence, just watching her, as if to say he knew her too well now to believe that. To believe that her only motive could be a stolen kiss in the moonlight.

His voice lowered to a whisper. "You know well this is not over."

Ah, yes, she knew that all too well. This, whatever it was, would not be over until one of them was dead.

* * *

A Sinful Alliance
Harlequin® Historical #893—April 2008

A Sinful Alliance

AMANDA McCABE

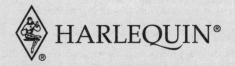

HARLEQUIN®

TORONTO • NEW YORK • LONDON
AMSTERDAM • PARIS • SYDNEY • HAMBURG
STOCKHOLM • ATHENS • TOKYO • MILAN • MADRID
PRAGUE • WARSAW • BUDAPEST • AUCKLAND

ISBN-13: 978-0-373-29493-0
ISBN-10:   0-373-29493-X

A SINFUL ALLIANCE

www.eHarlequin.com

Printed in U.S.A.

DON'T MISS THESE OTHER
NOVELS AVAILABLE NOW:

#891 KLONDIKE FEVER—Kate Bridges
Robbed at gunpoint, chained to a drifter, Lily thinks life can't get
any worse—until she realizes that she's shackled to the one man
she's never been able to forget!
*Don't miss the continuation of Kate Bridges's thrilling
Klondike series!*

#892 NO PLACE FOR A LADY—Louise Allen
Miss Bree Mallory has no time for the pampered aristocracy!
She's too taken up with running the best coaching company on
the roads. But an accidental meeting with an earl
changes everything....
Join Louise Allen's unconventional heroine as she shocks Society!

#894 THE WANTON BRIDE—Mary Brendan
With disgrace just a breath away, Emily ached for Mark's strong
arms to comfort her. Yet she held a secret—one that would surely
prevent *any* gentleman from considering her as a suitable bride....
Can Mary Brendan's hero's passion overcome Emily's fears?

Prologue

Venice, 1525

Her quarry was within her sight.

Marguerite peered through the tiny peephole, leaning close to the rough wooden wall as she examined the scene below. The brothel was not one of the finest in the Serene City, those velvet havens purveying the best wines and sweetmeats, the loveliest, cleanest women—for the steepest prices, of course. But neither was this place a dirty stew where a man should watch his purse and his privy parts, lest one or the other be lopped off. It was just a simple, noisy, colourful whorehouse, thick with the scent of dust, ale and sweat, redolent with shrieks of laughter and moans of pleasure, real or feigned. A place for men of the artisan classes, or travelling actors here for Carnival. A place where the proprietor was easily bribed by women with ulterior motives.

She had certainly been in far worse.

Marguerite narrowed her gaze, focusing in on her prey. It was him, it must be. He matched the careful description, the sketch. He was the man she had seen in the Piazza San Marco. He did not look like her vision of a coarse Russian, she would give him that. Were they not supposed to be built like bears, and just as hairy? Just as stinking? Everyone in France knew that these Muscovites had no manners, that they lived in a dark, ancient world where it was quite acceptable to grow one's beard to one's knees, to toss food on to the floor and blow one's nose on the tablecloth.

Marguerite wrinkled her nose. *Disgusting.* But then, what could be expected from people who lived encased in ice and snow? Who were deprived of the elegance and civility of France?

And it was France that brought her here tonight, to this Venetian brothel. She had to do her duty for her king, her home.

A bit of a pity, though, she thought as she watched the Russian. He was such a beauty.

He had no beard at all, but was clean shaven, the sharp, elegant angles of his face revealed to the flickering, smoking torchlight. The orange glow of the flames played over his high cheekbones, his sensual lips. His hair, the rich gold of an old coin, fell loose halfway down his back, a shimmering length of silk that beckoned for a woman's touch. The two doxies in his lap seemed to agree, for they kept running their fingers through the bright strands, cooing and giggling, nibbling at his ear and his neck.

Other women hovered at his shoulder, neglecting their other customers to bask in his golden glow, in the richness of his laughter, the incandescence of his skin and eyes.

And he did not seem to mind. Indeed, he appeared to take it all as his due, leaning back in his chair indolently like some spoiled Eastern lord, his head thrown back in abandoned laughter. He had shed his doublet and his white shirt was unlaced, hanging open to reveal a smooth, muscular chest, glimmering with a light sheen of sweat. The thin linen hung off one shoulder, revealing its broad strength.

No lumbering Russian bear, then, but a sleek cat, its power concealed by its grace.

Oui, a pity to destroy such handsomeness. But it had to be done. He and his Moscow friends, not to mention the Spanish and Venetian traders he consorted with, stood in the way of French interests with their proposed new trade routes from Moscow to Persia, along their great River Volga and the Caspian Sea. It would interfere with the French trade in silks, spices, furs—and that could never be. It was even more vital now, after the king's humiliating defeat at Pavia. So, Nicolai Ostrovsky would have to die.

After one last lingering glance at that bare, golden skin, Marguerite turned away, letting the peephole cover fall into place. She had her task; she had done such things for France before, she had done worse. She could not hesitate now, just because the mark was pretty. She was the Emerald Lily. She could not fail.

There was a small looking glass hanging on the rough wall of her small room, illuminated by candles and the one window. She gazed into it to find a stranger looking back. Her disguises often took many turns—gnarled peasant women, old Jewish merchants, milkmaids, duchesses. She had never tried a harlot before, though. It was quite interesting.

Her silvery blonde hair, usually a shimmering length of smooth waves, longer even than the Russian's, was frizzed and curled, pinned in a knot at the back and puffed out at the sides. Her complexion, the roses and lilies so prized in Paris, was covered with pale rice powder, two bright circles of rouge on each cheek and kohl heavily lining her green eyes.

She was not herself now, not Marguerite Dumas of the French Court. Nor the lady who had strolled, modestly veiled and cloaked, through the Piazza San Marco in the bright light of day, watching Nicolai Ostrovsky in his guise as an actor. An acrobat, who juggled and jested and feinted, always hiding his true self behind a smile and the jangle of bells. Just as she did, in her own way.

Voila, now she was Bella, a simple Italian whore, come to Venice to make a few ducats during Carnival. But hopefully a whore who could catch Nicolai's eye, even as he was the centre of attention for every woman in the place.

Marguerite stepped back until she could examine her garb in the glass. It was scarlet silk, bought that afternoon from a dealer in second-hand garments. It must have once belonged to a grand courtesan, but now the gold embroidery was slightly tarnished, the hem frayed and seams faded. It was still pretty, though, and it suited her small, slender frame. She tugged the neckline lower, until it hung from her shoulders and bared one breast.

Hmm, she thought, examining that pale appendage. Her bosom was good, she knew that; the bubbies were not too large or small, perfectly formed and very white. Perhaps they were meant to compensate for her rather short legs, the old scars on her stomach. But they seemed a little plain, compared to the other whores'. Marguerite reached for her pot of rouge and smeared some of the red cream around the exposed nipple. There. Very eye-catching. For good measure, she added some to her lips, and dabbed jasmine perfume behind her ears. Heavy and exotic, very different from her usual essence of lilies.

Now she was ready. Marguerite lifted up her voluminous skirts, checking to see that her dagger was still strapped to her thigh, its point honed to perfect sharpness.

She smoothed the gown back into place and slipped out of the small room. The corridor outside was narrow, running behind the main rooms of the house, the ceiling so low she had to duck her head. It was also deserted. But even here she could detect the sounds of laughter and moaning, the clink of pottery goblets, the whistle of a whip for those with more exotic tastes. Marguerite hoped that was not a Russian vice. Baring her backside for the lash would surely reveal the dagger.

She turned down a small, steep flight of stairs, careful on her high-heeled shoes. The low door at the foot of the steps led out of the secret warren into the large, noisy public room.

It was like tumbling into a new world. Noises here were no longer muffled, but loud and clear, echoing off the low, darkened ceiling. Smoke from the hearth was thick, acrid, blending with the perfumes of the women, the smell of flesh and sex and spilled ale. The wooden floor beneath her feet was sticky and pockmarked.

Marguerite stood for a moment in the doorway, her careful gaze sweeping over the entire scene. Card games and dice went on by the hearth, serious play to judge by the great piles of coins on each table, the intent expressions on the players' faces. There was drink and food, plain fare of bread, cheese and prosciutto. But whores were the first commodity, any sort a man could fancy. Short, tall, fat, thin, blonde, brunette. There was even a young man clad in an elaborate blue satin gown. He was quite good, too, with smooth skin and silky, black hair. 'Twas a shame he couldn't do something about that Adam's apple.

Marguerite surveyed them dispassionately, her competition for this one night. She knew she was beautiful, had known it since she was a child, taken to Court by her father.

She was not vain about it. It was merely an asset to her work, particularly at times like this. She was fairer than any of the others here, even the boy in blue. Therefore she should be able to catch Nicolai's attention.

Her competition was less now, anyway. Many of the women who had clustered around him were scattered, sent by the proprietor to see to the other patrons. There were just the two on his lap, half-dressed in their *camicias,* wriggling and giggling. Marguerite straightened her shoulders, displaying her bosom in its red silk frame, held her head high, and sauntered slowly past the Russian and his harem. She let her train trail over his boots, let him smell her perfume, glimpse her white breast, her half-smile. Once past him, she glanced back and winked. Then she went on her way, seeking a cup of ale.

Now—well, now she waited. In her experience, a touch of mystery worked better than fawning attention, which he obviously got enough of anyway. She sipped at her ale, carefully examining the room behind her in an old, cracked looking glass hanging on the wall. The two whores were still on his lap, but she could tell his full attention was no longer on their full-blown charms. He sat forward on his chair, watching *her,* a small frown on his brow. She turned slightly toward him, her pretty profile displayed. A slight impatience made her fingers tighten on the cup. He had to come to her before anyone else did! She flicked lightly at her lips with her tongue, and tossed her head back.

Whatever the secret charm, it worked. She turned away again, and in a few moments she felt him close to her side. How warm he was, yet not in a heated, lascivious, overpowering way, as most men were. More like the summer sun in her childhood home of Champagne, touching her skin with light fingers, beckoning her ever closer. He smelled like the summer, too, of some green, herbal soap behind the salty tang of sweat and skin. Of pure man.

She swivelled toward him, smiling flirtatiously. He had eased his shirt back over his shoulders but his chest was still bare, and he stood near enough that she could see the faint sprinkling of wiry blond hair against his skin. Gold on gold.

"Good evening, *signor*," she said, every hint of a French accent carefully banished.

"Good evening, *signora*," he answered, giving her a low bow, as if they were in the Doge's palace and not a smoky brothel. His eyes were blue, she noticed. A clear, sky-like expanse where anything, any wish or desire or fear, could be written.

And they watched her very carefully. The laughter he shared with the other women was still there, but lurking in the background. He was a wary one, then. She would have to be doubly cautious.

For an instant, as that blue gaze met hers steadily, unblinking, she felt a prickle of unease. A wish that she had worn a mask, which was ridiculous. The heavy make-up was disguise enough, and he would not see her after tonight.

Marguerite shoved away that unease. There was no time for it. She had to do her task and be gone.

"I have not seen you here before," he said.

"I am new. Bella is my name, I have just arrived from my village on the mainland to work for Carnival," she answered, gesturing for more ale. "Do you come here often, then?"

"Often enough, when I am in Venice."

She laughed. "I would wager! A virile man like yourself, I'm sure the pale, choosy courtesans of the grand palazzos could never keep you satisfied." The ale arrived, and she handed him one of the goblets. "Salute."

"*Na zdorovie,*" he answered, and tossed back the sour drink. "Venice is truly filled with the most beautiful of women, *signora.* Lovelier than any I have ever seen, and I have travelled to many lands. But I do prefer company more like—myself."

Marguerite glanced toward the boy in blue. "Yourself, *signor?*"

He laughed, and she was again reminded of summer and home, of the warm, sparkling wine of Champagne. "Not in that way, *signora.* Closer to the earth." She must have looked puzzled, for he smiled down at her. "'Tis a saying from my homeland."

"You are not from here, either."

"Nay. I can see where you might mistake me, though, given my excellent Italian," he said, giving her a teasing grin. "I am from Moscow, though many years removed from that place."

"Ah, that explains it, then."

"Explains what, *signora?*"

"The virility. For is Moscow not snowbound for much of the year? Much time to spend in front of the fire. Or in a warm bed."

"Very true, *signora.*" His arm suddenly snaked out, catching her around the waist and pulling her close. For one flashing instant, Marguerite was caught by surprise and instinctively stiffened. She forced herself to go limp, pliant, arching back against his arm.

Through her skirts and his hose she felt the press of his erection, hard and heavy. "No ice tonight, I see, *signor.*"

"The Italian sun has melted it away—almost."

She smiled teasingly up at him, twining her arms about his neck. His hair was like satin spilling over her fingers, cool and alluring. She tangled her clasp in its clinging strands, inhaling that clean, warm scent of him. "I'm sure *this* Italian sun could finish the job completely, *signor.* You would never feel the touch of ice again."

In answer he kissed her, his lips swooping down on hers so quickly she had no time for thought. She could only react, respond. His kiss was not harsh and bruising, but soft, gentle, nibbling at her lips, luring her to follow him into that sunshine and forget all. For a moment, she *did* forget. She was not Marguerite Dumas, not the Emerald Lily. She was just a woman being kissed by a handsome man, a man who ensnared her with a blurry, humid heat, with his scent, his strong arms, his talented lips. She pressed closer to him, so close the edges of her being melted into his and she couldn't tell where she ended and he began. His tongue pressed into her mouth, presaging an even more profound joining.

Overwhelmed, Marguerite eased back. She needed her own ice now, the cold thoughts, precise actions. Not this, this—*lust.* This need. The Emerald Lily did not have needs, especially not carnal ones. Nicolai Ostrovsky was a task, nothing more.

Why, then, was it so very hard to remember that as she stared up into his pale blue eyes?

She made herself smile. "You *are* hot tonight, *signor.*"

"I told you the Italian sun has made me so."

"Then come with me, *signor,* and I'll cool you off—eventually." She untangled her clasp from his hair, reaching down to take his hand. His fingers held hers tightly, holding her prisoner as she led him toward that small doorway she earlier emerged from.

They climbed the narrow stairs, Nicolai ducking to avoid the rafters overhead. The quiet enclosed them again, the loud, bright world shut away, and Marguerite felt her heart thud in her chest, felt her skin grow chilled. The time was almost upon her.

At the entrance to her little room, Nicolai suddenly reeled her close to him, spinning her lightly around to press her to the wall. Marguerite's heartbeat quickened—had he discovered her, then? Was she caught in a trap of her own?

He did not slit her throat, though. He merely held her there, pressed against her in the half-light, staring down at her with those otherworldly eyes as if he could see into her soul. Her sin-riddled soul.

"Where did you come from, Bella?" he said softly. His accent was more pronounced now, the edges of his words touched with some icy Russian music.

Marguerite smiled at him. "I told you, from the mainland. This is our most profitable time of year, but one has to be in Venice to make the coin."

"Have you been a whore long, then, *dorogaya?*"

She laughed. "Oh, yes. Decades, it seems."

"Miraculous, then. For you still have your teeth, your clear eyes…" He reached down to trace the underside of her naked breast, the soft, puckered flesh. His thumb flicked lightly at the rouged nipple, making her shiver deeply. "Your smooth skin."

"I was born under a lucky star, *signor.* My father always said so," she said, still trembling. And that was one true thing she said tonight. Her father *had* told her that when she was a child, holding her up on his shoulder so she could see the clear, bright stars in the Champagne sky.

But then her star faded, and here she was in a Venetian brothel. Bound up with this beautiful puzzle of a man.

"A lucky star on the mainland," he said.

"Just so. You must have been born under an auspicious sign yourself, to be so handsome." She spoke teasingly, but it was also true. Such beauty and charm should belong to no ordinary mortal. He was blessed. Until tonight.

This was a fateful hour for them both, then.

"If we are both so fortunate, then, Signora Bella, why are we *here?*" he murmured, as if he truly could read her thoughts. "A whore and an actor, who must both sing for their supper. Can we even afford each other?"

"I am not so expensive as all that," Marguerite said. She went up on tiptoe and whispered in his ear, "Not for you. I think we are alike, you and I, whores and actors both in one. And we do love our homelands, though we don't want to admit it."

He pulled back, staring at her as if surprised by her words, but she wouldn't let him go. She caught him closer, kissing him with every secret passion of her heart.

"You didn't come from any human land," he muttered roughly against her neck, his lips trailing a fiery ribbon of kisses along her throat, her shoulder. "You come from an enchanted fairy realm, and you'll surely vanish back there at the dawn."

"'Tis hours until then," Marguerite gasped. "We have to make the most of the night."

Nicolai captured her breast in his kiss, laving the pebbled, rouged tip with his tongue until she added her hoarse moans to the others of the house. That hazy, hot passion descended on her again like a grey cloud, and she felt so weak, so warm and yet shivering. Through that fog, she felt him reach down and grasp her hem, drawing her skirt up.

The cold draught on her bare leg brought sanity crashing down around her. *Non!* He could not see her dagger, or all would be lost. She pulled away, laughing. "I said we had all night, *signor!* We don't have to rut against the wall." She drew him toward the small cot tucked beneath the room's one window. Later, when her task was done, she would escape through that portal, vanishing over the rooftops of Venice. Not to any fairy kingdom, but to a curtained gondola where "Bella" would disappear for ever.

She lightly pushed Nicolai, unresisting, on to the sheets, standing above him for a moment, studying him in the moonlight. His golden hair spilled around him on the rumpled, dingy linen. *So handsome—so unreal.* He smiled wickedly up at her, a fallen angel.

"So, we can rut on a bed like civilised beings?" he said.

"Exactly so." She leaned over him, tracing the muscled contours of his chest with her fingertips. The arc of his ribs, the flat, puckered discs of his nipples. So glorious, like a map of some exotic, undiscovered country. She felt the pace of his heartbeat, racing under her caress. "We can savour each moment. Each—single—touch." She kissed his nipple, tugging its hardness between her teeth, tasting the salt of his skin.

Nicolai shivered, and she felt the pull of his fingers in her hair, the shift of his body under hers. He was so hard against her hip, his whole body taut as a bow string. *Oui,* he was under the spell of desire now. She couldn't let herself fall prey to it, too.

"How much will this cost me?" he said tightly.

Marguerite eased up his body until she lay prone atop him, pressed close. "Your soul," she whispered.

Then she acted, as she had before. As she was trained to do. She drew up her skirts and snatched the dagger, in the same smooth motion rising up from his chest and lifting the blade high. She had a quick impression of his eyes, silver in the moonlight, his body laid bare for her to claim. She had only to plunge the dagger down into that heartbeat, and an enemy of France would be gone.

But those eyes—those inhuman, all-seeing eyes. They watched her steadily, not even startled, and she was captured by their sea-like depths.

Only for an instant, one quicksilver flash, but it was enough to lose her the advantage. Nicolai seized her wrist in a bruising grip, tightening until her wrist bone creaked and she cried out. Her fingers opened convulsively, and the dagger clattered to the floor. He swung her beneath him, pinning her to the bed. No lazy, debauched, lustful actor now, but a swift, pitiless predator. Just as she was.

Marguerite was well trained in swordplay and the use of daggers and bows, in courtly fencing and rough street brawling. She knew tricks and dupes to compensate for her small size and feminine weakness. Yet she also knew when she was truly defeated, and that was now. She knew what it was she saw in those eyes. It was doom.

As she stared up at him now, she felt strangely calm, as if she was already hovering above her body, watching the scene from the rafters. Her victim became her murderer, and it was no less than she deserved for her sins. This day had been long in coming. If only she could not die unshriven! She would never meet her mother in heaven now.

But she *did* see her avenging angel, rising above her in the darkness. He scooped up her dagger, examining the blade while he held her firmly down with his other hand, his strong body. She felt the full force of that lean strength; the smooth, supple muscles that held him on a tightrope or in a backflip now held her easily in place.

He stared at the dagger, so thin and perfectly balanced. So lethal. The small emerald embedded in the hilt gleamed. "Why me?" he said roughly. "Why try to kill a poor actor?"

"You are not a poor actor, Monsieur Ostrovsky, and we both know it," she said in French. "You have secrets to equal my own."

"What *are* your secrets, *mademoiselle?*" he answered in the same language.

Marguerite laughed bitterly. "It hardly matters. I have failed in my task, but I take my secrets to the grave."

"Do you, indeed? Well, that might be a long time from now, *mademoiselle.* I have the feeling that fairies, like cats, have many lives. You are young; I'm sure you have some to go."

Marguerite stared up at him, baffled, but his face gave nothing away. He was as beautiful, as cold, as the marble statues in the piazza. Her passionate lover was gone. "What do you mean?"

"I mean, *mademoiselle* whatever-your-name-is, that this is not your night to die. Nor mine, though you would have had it otherwise." The dagger arced down, but not into her heart. It sliced into her skirt, cutting away thick strips of silk. Holding the blade between his teeth like a corsair, he bound her hands and feet tightly, with expert knots.

"What are you doing?" Marguerite cried, bewildered. This was not how the game was meant to be played! "I would have killed you! Do you mean you won't kill me? You won't take your revenge?"

"Oh, I will take my revenge, *mademoiselle,* but not on this night." He tied off the final knot around her wrists, so firm she could not even wriggle her fingers. "It will be some day when you least expect it."

Once she was trussed up like a banquet goose, he leaned down and pressed one gentle kiss to her lips. He still tasted of herbs, ale and her own waxen rouge. And he still smelled of an alluring summer day. *Quel con!*

"I just can't bring myself to destroy such rare beauty," he whispered. "Not after your fine services, incomplete though they were. *Adieu, mademoiselle*—for now."

He tied the last strip of silk over her mouth, and opened the very window Marguerite had planned for her escape. As she stared, infuriated, he gave her a wink, and with one graceful movement leaped through the casement and was gone.

Marguerite screamed through her gag. She arched her back and kicked her legs, all to no avail. She was bound fast, caught in her own scheme. And the *cochon* didn't even have the decency to kill her! To follow the code all spies and assassins adhered to. At least French ones.

"Have his revenge," would he, the beautiful, arrogant Russian pig? Never! She would find him first, and finish this task, no matter what. No matter how far she had to go, even to the frozen wastes of his Russia itself.

For the Emerald Lily never failed.

Chapter One

The Palace of Fontainebleau, January 1527

Marguerite Dumas walked slowly down the corridor, gaze straight ahead, hands folded at her waist, her face carefully blank as she ignored the whispers of the courtiers loitering about. In her fingers she clutched the summons of the king.

She had known this day would come. A new assignment. A new mission for the Emerald Lily. If only this one ended better than the last, that night in Venice!

Marguerite paused at the end of the corridor, where a shadowed landing became a narrow staircase. Here, there was no one to see her, and she closed her eyes against the spasm of pain in her head. It was no illness, but the memory of Venice, the thought of the handsome Russian *encule*. The coppery, bitter taste of humiliation and failure.

The king had said nothing when she returned to Paris with her report of the Russian's escape. He had said nothing when he sent her back to her "legitimate" duties as *fille d'honneur* to Princess Madeleine, her ostensible reason for being at

Court in the first place. There she had languished for months, walking with the other ladies in the gardens, reading to the princess, dancing at banquets. Fending off the advances of useless, arrogant courtiers.

They could do her no good, those perfumed popinjays who pressed their kisses on her in the shadows. Only one man was useful here, King François himself. And he maintained his distant politeness, merely nodding to her when they happened to pass in the garden or the banquet hall.

Marguerite knew the whispers, that she and the king had been lovers who were estranged now that he was involved with the Duchesse de Vendôme. If they only knew the truth! They would never believe it. Not of her.

She scarcely believed it herself, in these days of quiet leisure in the princess's apartments. Had she truly ever been sent to the far corners of Europe, to defeat the enemies of France? Had she once used her wits, her hard-learned skills, to find a secret victory over those who would defy the king? It did not seem possible.

Yet at night, alone in her curtained bed, she knew it was true. Once, she had had adventures. She had won a place for herself in the wider world. Had one mistake, one instant's miscalculation, cost her all she worked for?

It had made no sense to her that she would be dismissed in only a moment, when now more than ever her special skills were needed. Since the king's humiliating defeat against the forces of the Holy Roman Emperor at Pavia, since his two sons were sent to Madrid as hostages, dark days had descended on France. Her enemies were becoming ever bolder.

Marguerite *knew* she could be of use in these new, dangerous games. Why, then, was she relegated to dancing and card playing? All because of the Russian, damn his unearthly blue eyes!

But those days seemed to be at an end. She held the king's note in her hand, so tightly the parchment pressed her rings into her skin. It was time for her to redeem herself.

As she climbed the narrow, privy staircase, the sounds of hammering and sawing grew louder, more distinct, shouting of the king's new mania for building. Since his return from Spain in defeat, François had thrown himself into a frenzy of remodelling, of making his palaces ever grander.

Fontainebleau, one of his favourite castles thanks to the seventeen-thousand hectares of forest ripe with deer for hunting, was his latest focus. Since the Christmas festivities, so muted without the presence of the Dauphin and his brother, work was begun in earnest. The old keep of St Louis and Philipe le Beau was being demolished, replaced by something vast and modern.

Marguerite lifted the hem of her velvet skirt as she stepped over a pile of rubbish. A shower of stone dust from above nearly coated her headdress, and she hurried to the relative safety of the great gallery.

This was one of the few rooms in the place to be almost finished. A long, echoing expanse of polished parquet floor swept up to walls of pale stuccowork, inlaid dark wood in the panels of the *boiserie*. A few of the many planned flourishes of floral motifs, gods and goddesses, fat little Cupids, were in place, with blank spaces just waiting to be filled.

At the far end of the gallery, leaning over a table covered with sketches, was King François himself. He was consulting with one of the Italian artists brought in to take charge of all this splendour, Signor Fiorentino, and for the moment did not see her. Marguerite slowed her steps, studying him carefully for any sign of his thoughts and intentions. Any hint that she was truly forgiven.

François was very tall, towering over her own petite frame, and was all an imposing king should be, with abundant dark hair and a fashionable pointed beard. His brown eyes were sharp and clear above his hooked Valois nose, missing nothing. After Pavia and his captivity, he seemed leaner, more wary, his always athletic body thin and wiry.

But his famous sense of fashion had not deserted him. Even on a quiet day like this, he wore a crimson velvet doublet embroidered with gold and silver and festooned with garnet buttons, a sleeveless surcoat of purple trimmed with silver fox fur to keep the chill away. A crimson cap sewn with pearls and more garnets covered his head, concealing his gaze as he bent over the drawings.

"There will be twelve in all, your Majesty," Fiorentino said, gesturing toward the empty spaces on the gallery walls. "All scenes from mythology, of course, to illustrate your Majesty's enlightened governance."

"Hmm, yes, I see," Francois said. Without glancing up, he called, "Ah, Mademoiselle Dumas! You surely have the finest eye for beauty of any lady in my kingdom. What do you think of Signor Fiorentino's plans?"

Marguerite came closer, peering down at the sketches as she tucked the king's note into her tight undersleeve. The first drawing was a scene of Danaë, more a stylish lady of the French Court in a drapery of blue-tinted silk and an elaborate headdress than a woman of the classical world. But her surroundings—broken columns and twisted olive trees, her attendants of fat cherubs and even more fashionable ladies—were very skilfully drawn, the scene most elegant.

"It is lovely," she said. "And surely the dimensions, the way the scene is framed by these columns, make it perfect for that space there, where the afternoon sunlight will make Danaë's robe shimmer like a summer sky. You will use cobalt, *signor,* and flecks of gilt?"

"You are quite right, your Majesty! The *mademoiselle* has a most discerning eye for beauty," Fiorentino said happily, clapping his paint-stained hands. Perhaps he was just glad he wouldn't waste expensive cobalt.

"*Bien, signor,*" the king said. "The Danaë stays. You may commence at once."

As the artist hurried away, his assistants scurrying after him, François smiled at Marguerite. Try as she did to gauge his thoughts, she could see nothing beyond his courtly smile, the opaque light of his eyes. He was even better at concealing his true self than Marguerite herself.

"Shall we stroll in the gardens, Mademoiselle Dumas?" he asked lightly. "It is a bit warmer, I think, and I should like your opinion on the new fountain I have commissioned. It is the goddess Diana, a great warrior and hunter. A favourite of yours, I believe?"

"I would be honoured to walk with you, your Majesty," Marguerite answered. "Yet I fear I know little of fountains."

"Egremont will loan you his cloak," he said, gesturing to one of his attendants, who immediately presented her with his fur-lined wrap. "We would not want you to catch a chill. You have such important work, *mademoiselle.*"

Important work? Was this truly a new task, then? A chance for the Emerald Lily to emerge from hiding? Marguerite was careful not to show her eagerness, settling the cloak over her shoulders. "Indeed, your Majesty?"

"*Oui.* For does my daughter not depend on you, since the death of her sainted mother? You are her favourite attendant."

"I, too, am very fond of the princess," Marguerite answered, and she was. Princess Madeleine was a lovely child, charming and quick-minded. But she was hardly a challenge. She could not offer the kind of advancement Marguerite's ambition craved. The kind she needed for her own security. She thought of the stash of coins hidden beneath her bed, and how they were not yet enough to gain her a vineyard, a life, of her own.

"Indeed?" François led her down the stairs and out into the gardens, now slumbering under the winter frost. They, like the palace itself, were in the midst of upheaval, their old flowerbeds being torn up to be replaced by new plantings, a more modern design. For now, though, everything was caught in a moment of stasis, frozen in place, overlaid by sparkling white like an enchanted castle in a story.

François waved away his attendants, and led her down a narrow walkway. The air was cold but still, holding the echo of the abandoned courtiers' voices as they lingered by the wall.

"It is most sad, then, that my daughter will have to do without your company for a time," the king said.

"Will she?"

"Yes, for I fear you must journey to England, *mademoiselle*. And the Emerald Lily must go with you."

England. So the rumours were true. François sought a new alliance with King Henry, a new bulwark against the power of the Emperor.

"I am ready, your Majesty," she said.

François smiled. "*Ma chère* Marguerite—always so eager to serve us."

"I am a Frenchwoman," she answered simply. "I do what I can for my country."

"And you do it well. Usually."

"I will not fail you. I vow this."

"I trust that is true. For this mission is of vital importance. I am sending a delegation to negotiate a treaty of alliance with King Henry, and to organise a marriage between his daughter Princess Mary and my Henri."

Marguerite considered this. Despite flirting with English alliances in the past, including the long-ago Field of the Cloth of Gold, which was so spectacular it was still much talked of, naught had come of it all. Thanks to the English queen, Katherine of Aragon, aunt of the Emperor, England always drifted back to Spain. Little Princess Mary, only eleven years old, had already been betrothed to numerous Spanish grandees as well as the Emperor Charles himself, or so they said.

"What of the Spanish?" Marguerite asked quietly.

"I have heard tell that Henry and his queen are not as— united as they once were," François answered. "Katherine grows old, and Henry's gaze has perhaps turned to a young lady who was once resident of the French Court, Mademoiselle Anne Boleyn. Katherine may no longer have so much influence on English policy. Since the formation of the League of Cognac, Henry seems inclined to a more Gallic way of seeing things. I will be most gratified if this treaty comes to completion."

Marguerite nodded. An alliance with England could certainly mean the beginning of brighter days for France. Yet she had dealt with the Spanish before. For all their seeming piety and austerity, they were just as fierce in defending their interests as the French, perhaps even more so. It was said that in their religious fervour they often employed the hair shirt and the scourge, and it seemed to sour their spirits, made them ill humoured and dangerous as serpents.

"The Spanish—and Queen Katherine—will not let go of their advantage so easily as that," Marguerite said. "I have heard Katherine seeks a new Spanish match for her daughter."

"That is why I am sending you," François answered. "I have assigned Gabriel de Grammont, the Bishop of Tarbes, to head the delegation, and I am sure he will do very well. As will his men. But women can see things a man cannot, go places a man cannot, especially one as well trained as my Lily. Keep an eye on the queen, and especially on the Spanish ambassador, Don Diego de Mendoza. It is entirely possible they have plans of their own, of which Henry is not aware."

"And if they do?"

François scowled, gazing out over his frozen gardens. "Then you know what to do." He drew a small scroll from inside his surcoat and handed it to her. "Here are your instructions. You depart in two weeks. I will have dressmakers sent to you this evening—you must order all that you require for a stay of several weeks."

With that, he turned and left her, rejoining his waiting attendants. They all disappeared inside the château, leaving Marguerite alone in the cold afternoon. There were no birds, no bustle of gardeners or cool splash of fountains, only the lonely whistle of the wind as she unfurled the scroll.

The words were brief. The king's kinsman, the Comte de Calonne, was to be part of the delegation, along with his wife Claudine. Marguerite was ostensibly to serve as companion to Claudine, to accompany her when she called on Queen Katherine and attended banquets and tournaments.

But Marguerite knew well what was *not* written there. At those banquets, she was to flirt with the English courtiers when they were in their cups, draw secrets from them they were not even aware they were sharing. To watch the queen and the Spanish ambassador. To watch King Henry, and make sure the notoriously changeable monarch did not waver. To watch this Anne Boleyn, see if she had real influence, if she could be turned to the French cause.

And, if anyone stood in France's path, she was to remove them. Quickly and neatly.

It was surely the most important task she had ever received, a test of all her skills. The culmination of all she had learned. If she did well, if the treaty was safely signed and the betrothal of Princess Mary and the Duc d'Orléans sealed, she would be handsomely rewarded. Perhaps she would even be given leave to travel, to seek out the one man who had ever defeated her and thus finally have her revenge.

The Russian. Nicolai Ostrovsky.

The soft crackle of a footstep on the pathway behind her startled her, and she spun around, her knees bending and hands forward in a defensive position.

It was Pierre LeBeque, a young priest in the employ of Bishop Grammont. His eyes narrowed when she turned on him, and he fell back a step, watching her warily.

Marguerite dropped her hands to her sides, but still stood poised to dash away if need be. She did not often see Father Pierre, for he was usually scurrying about the Court on errands for the bishop, but when she did encounter him she didn't care for the sensations he evoked. That prickling feeling at the back of her neck that so often warned her of "danger."

What danger a solemn young priest, tall but as thin as a blade of grass, could hold she was not sure. He seemed to bear nothing but dutiful piety on his bony shoulders. Yet he always watched her so closely, and not as others did, in admiration and awe of her beauty—it was as if he was trying to see all her secrets.

And she well knew how often appearances were deceiving.

"Father Pierre," she said calmly, drawing her borrowed cloak closer around her. "What brings you out on such a chilly day?"

He did not smile, just stared solemnly. His face, white as the frost, was set in stony lines too old for his youthful years. "I am carrying a message to the king from Bishop Grammont, *mademoiselle.*"

"Indeed? Such industrious loyalty you possess, coming out on such a day, when everyone else is tucked up by their fires."

"You are not," he pointed out.

"I felt the need for some fresh air. But I am returning to my warm apartment now."

"Allow me to escort you back to the palace, then."

Marguerite could think of no graceful way to decline his company, so she merely nodded and turned on the pathway. Pierre fell into step beside her, the hem of his black robes whispering over the swept gravel.

"I understand from the bishop that you are to join our voyage to England," he said tonelessly.

Alors, but news did travel fast! Marguerite herself had only just learned of her assignment, and here this glorified clerk already knew.

What else did he know?

"Indeed I am. The Comtesse de Calonne requires a companion, and I am honoured that my services have been requested."

"You are very brave then, *mademoiselle.* They say the English Court is coarse and dirty."

"I have certainly heard of worse."

"Have you?"

"*Oui.* The Turks, for one. And the Russians. I have heard that the Muscovites grow their beards so very long, and so tangled and matted, that rats live in the hair with their human owners none the wiser."

Father Pierre frowned doubtfully. "Truly?"

Marguerite shrugged. "So I have heard. I have seldom met a Russian myself, except for the ambassadors who sometimes visit Paris. Their fur robes are antique, but their grooming is fine." And there was one, who had no beard at all, but hair as golden and soft as a summer's day. One who always popped into her mind at the most inconvenient moments. "Surely the English cannot be as crude as rats in beards. I am certain our weeks there will be most pleasant."

"Nevertheless, we will be in a foreign Court, with ways we may not always understand. I hope that you will feel free to come to me for any—counsel you might require, Mademoiselle Dumas."

Counsel? As if she would ever need advice from him! Marguerite curtsied politely and said, "It is a comfort to know there is always a French priest ready to hear my confession if needs be. Good day, Father Pierre."

"Good day, *mademoiselle.*"

She left him at the foot of the grand staircase, now a bare expanse of marble waiting to be refurbished, reborn. As she made her way up, dodging workmen and stone dust, she could feel the priest's cold stare on her back.

Tiens! Marguerite rolled her eyes in exasperation. Would she have to avoid that strange man the whole time they were in England, in addition to all her other duties? It was sure to be a most challenging few weeks indeed.

Chapter Two

The sea was calm at last, after cold storms that had lengthened what should have been a short voyage into one that
seemed endless. Today, though, the sun struggled to break
through the thick banks of grey clouds, casting a strange
amber glow over the sky, over the choppy, pearly waves. The
air was chilly, humid, smelling of rain, but blessedly none yet
fell. Hopefully it would hold off until they made landfall.

Nicolai Ostrovsky leaned his elbows on the ship's railing,
staring out over the vast water. Soon they would land at Dover,
and have to make good time if they were to arrive at Greenwich before the French. It would be a hard push, with women
and servants and baggage, yet it had to be done.

Nicolai laughed at his own foolishness for setting out on
this task in the first place. It was folly indeed to travel across
the continent, when wise people were tucked up by their fire-
sides to wait for spring! Friendship got him into trouble
wherever he went.

He reached inside his quilted russet doublet and drew out
the letter from his friend Marc Velazquez, which had arrived
most inopportunely when Nicolai had just settled down for a

peaceful winter of wine and beautiful women in a small town in the Italian Alps. He had just finished an onerous task, one that nearly cost him his life—again. Surely he deserved a few months of ease and pleasure!

Then the messenger knocked on his door, that door he thought so well hidden from the outside world.

"I cannot trust anyone but you, my friend, with such a task," the letter read, the black ink words now stained and mottled with salt sea spray. "My mother has recently left her retirement at the Convent of St Theresa and remarried. Her husband, the Duke de Bernaldez, has been sent to join a mission to England with the new ambassador Diego de Mendoza, who is his kinsman. Their errand is very delicate, as the French are trying to negotiate a new treaty with King Henry, and they must be defeated at all costs—according to my new stepfather.

"My mother insists on joining him in England, and I worry greatly about how she will fare there. She is so very gentle, and her years in the convent since my father died have not prepared her for a royal Court. I must beg that you accompany her, and look to her welfare, as I must stay close to Venice at this time. Julietta will give birth to our first child any day now.

"My friend, I know this is a great deal to ask, but I trust no one as I do you. I will be deeply in your debt, even more so than I already am."

Nicolai refolded the letter, staring again at the cold, grey expanse of sea. How could he refuse? The claims of friendship *and* the protection of a gentle lady were his two greatest weaknesses. So, he had written back to Marc, stating that he expected this new baby to be named Nicholas if a boy, Nicola if a girl, and set out to meet Dona Elena Maria Velazquez, the new Duchess de Bernaldez.

And he found that his friend quite underestimated his mother. Yes, she was sweet and lovely, but the convent had not softened her core of iron. Her current mission was to see Nicolai wed to one of her ladies by the end of their time in England, and she was most determined. His protests that he led an aimless, mercenary life, most unsuited to fine ladies, made not a whit of difference.

"A good wife would settle you, Nicolai, make a home for you, as Julietta has for my son," she said. "Do you not desire a family?"

Fortunately, he was saved from her matchmaking by a round of seasickness that overcame Dona Elena and many of her ladies. He did not have time to fend her off *and* plan for their troubled mission in England!

Ostensibly, he was meant to be a sort of Master of the Revels to the Spanish party, devising entertainments to impress the English Court and the French, to show off Spanish wealth, piety and strength in the face of all their challenges. His years as a travelling player and acrobat would stand him in good stead in such a task, and in his less obvious assignments as well. Not only was he to protect Dona Elena and her new husband, he was to keep an eye out for the interests of the Tsar of Russia. Tsar Vasily III had seen much success in his new trading schemes with the East, and now thought to expand westward as well.

Tricky, indeed, to balance France, Spain, England, Venice, Russia on an acrobat's tightrope. And a far cry from the pleasurable winter he had once envisioned! But it was blood-stirring, as well. Masqueing was his life's work, and there was none better at it than he was. This English meeting was a challenge greater than any he had faced in a long time, and he was ready for it. And, if he had his way, it would be his last dangerous mission, as well.

Nicolai reached for the sheath at his waist and drew out a dagger, balancing it on his gloved palm. The emerald in the hilt gleamed in the pale light, glinting with a silent threat— a promise—that had yet to be answered.

He tossed it lightly into the air, catching it so he could see the tiny lily etched into the finely honed steel. He carried the dagger everywhere, a reminder that once he had met the notorious Emerald Lily, the shadowy French assassin feared throughout Europe. Met her—and bested her, though more by luck than any great skill on his part.

He never spoke of that strange night in a Venetian brothel to anyone, not even Marc and Julietta. For one thing, except for this dagger, he could not be sure it was not a dream. For another, he could never convey the power those eyes, as green as this emerald, held over him, from the first moment he glimpsed them through the smoke and haze of that whorehouse's common room.

She was beautiful, truly, like an angel or a fairy with that silvery hair, yet her allure that night was far more than mere loveliness. A thousand women possessed that. It was those eyes. So hard, so cold, yet with a spark underneath that could not be extinguished.

It was foolish of him to leave her alive, to show a mercy that was so unlike him, and that she would never have shown him. The Emerald Lily was rumoured to be ruthless, and she would not take well to being made a fool of. She would come after him again one day, probably when he least expected it.

Perhaps that was what made him leave her there, trussed up on the rumpled bed. The knowledge—or was it hope?— that they would one day meet again. She would want her dagger back, after all.

The trouble was, another meeting would surely leave one or both of them mouldering in the grave.

Nicolai tossed the blade in the air again, catching it with a light twirl of his fingertips. Until that fateful day, he had more to worry about than beautiful, green-eyed killers.

And his chief worry was coming toward him right now.

Dona Elena appeared on deck, followed by two of her ladies who had recovered from their *mal de mer.* She certainly seemed the pious Spanish matron, her coffee-brown hair, only lightly streaked with silver, smoothed back beneath a pearl-edged, veiled cap, garnet-crusted cross clasped around her throat. A black cloak covered her dark red gown, shielding her from the salty wind, and her gloved hands held a gilt-edged prayer book. But her soft brown eyes were full of determination.

Her son, Marc, surely got that from her. The Velazquez family *always* got their own way.

"Ah, Nicolai, there you are!" she said, joining him at the rail. "The captain says we will without doubt make land today."

Nicolai gestured toward the horizon, where towering, stark white cliffs were just peeking through the mist. "At any moment, Dona Elena."

"Thanks be to God." She quickly crossed herself. "This voyage has not been enjoyable."

"It is seldom a good idea to set out in the middle of winter."

Elena sighed. "Especially for someone as accustomed to the comforts of land as me! I know Marc would have preferred I stay at home in Madrid and wait for Carlos to return, yet he does not understand. He and his wife are always together now, but it has been a long time since I enjoyed the pleasures of marriage." She frowned, and Nicolai knew all too well what was coming. "The comforts of a home, Nicolai, are inestimable. If you only knew the great benefits…"

* * *

By the time he had fended her off, and sent her and her ladies below decks to finish their packing, the ship had drawn closer to the rocky shore, those cliffs looming like a stark white welcome.

The rough sea voyage was ending at last, yet Nicolai feared his travails were only just beginning.

Chapter Three

Marguerite sat bundled in her cloak at the back of the barge
as they made their way along the Thames, her sable-edged
hood eased back so she could observe the scenery as it glided
past. The English were so proud of their little river, lined with
the estates of their nobles! Their escorts, a brace of Henry's
courtiers sent to guide them to Greenwich, gestured toward
stone towers and brick halls, declaring them the abodes of the
Carews, the Howards, the Poles.

Marguerite sniffed. If they could only see the vast, fairy-
tale spires of the châteaux along the Loire! They would not be
so quick with their boasts then, these swaggering English
boys.

She had to admit, though, they were handsome enough.
Rumour said that Henry enjoyed being surrounded by young
people, full of energy and fun and high spirits, and their
escorts seemed to confirm that. Tall, strong men, bright-eyed,
lavishly dressed—if not as stylish as Frenchmen, of course.
Quick with a jest as well as a boast, and with a keen eye for
a pretty face. Each of them had already bowed before *her,* and
she was one of the least of the French party.

Still pretending to study the river, she actually watched *them* from the corner of her eye, those exuberant young men. If they were full of guile and trickery, as all men were, they hid it well. There was no hint of suspicion on their handsome faces, no flicker of deception in their laughing voices.

Her task here was either going to be easier than she expected, or far harder.

"Have you even been to England before, Mademoiselle Dumas?"

She turned to see that one of the English courtiers, the raven-haired Roger Tilney, had sat down beside her on the narrow bench.

She smiled at him. "Never. I have been to Italy, but not your England. It is fascinating."

"Wait until we arrive at Greenwich, *mademoiselle*. The king has prepared a great surprise there, and there will be many entertainments every day from dawn until midnight."

Marguerite laughed. "Many entertainments? And here I thought you men had most important business to see to!"

"One cannot work all the time, especially with such welcome distractions in sight."

He leaned closer, and she found Englishmen did not *smell* like the French, either. His cologne was spicy rather than flowery, overlaying the crisp cold of the day, the scent of wool and leather.

Hmm. Surely this Master Tilney was correct—one could not work all the time.

Yet that was exactly what she had to do. Work all the time. For it was in the instant she let her guard down that all went awry. The Russian had taught her that.

"I do love to dance," she said. "Will there be time for such frivolous pastimes?"

Tilney laughed, and she felt the swift, warm press of his hand on her arm through her thick cloak. "Dancing is one of King Henry's greatest delights."

"I am glad to hear it. A Court that does not dance or make merry music could be called…"

"Spanish, mayhap?"

They chuckled together at the naughty little dig. As Marguerite pressed her hand to her lips to hide her giggles, she noticed Father Pierre watching her, a frown on his pale, thin face.

She turned resolutely away from him, determined that his stares would not distract her today.

"I do hear that the Spanish care little for such worldly pursuits," she murmured. "But is your own queen not Spanish? What does she think of dancing?"

Tilney shrugged. "Queen Katherine is usually of good cheer. She is most indulgent, and famous for her serene smile and even temper. She may no longer dance herself, but she is a gracious hostess."

"Usually?"

He opened his mouth to reply, then seemed to think better of it. Instead he smiled, and gestured to the bank of the river. "See there, *mademoiselle*. Your first glimpse of the palace of Greenwich."

Marguerite leaned to the side, watching closely as the barge slowed on its approach. Greenwich was not pale and graceful, as François's plans for Fontainebleau were. It obviously did not intend to convey a deceptive delicacy. It was long and low, and pretended to nothing but what it was—a strong palace, a home yet also the receptacle of power.

The pitched roof was as grey as the sky above, blending with the wispy smoke that curled from its many chimneys, but the walls were faced in red brick in the old Burgundian style.

There was no moat or fortifications; that would have been too old-fashioned even for the English. Instead, narrow windows, glinting like a thousand watchful eyes, stared out over the river.

"It is very pretty," she said. "A fit setting for revels, I would say."

"It is built around three courtyards," Tilney said. "Perfect for games of bowls. And there are tennis courts and tiltyards."

Marguerite laughed. "It *does* sound a merry place. Dancing, bowls, tennis…"

"Ah, *mademoiselle,* I fear you will think us nothing but frivolous! Look you there, the Church of the Observant Friars of St Francis. The queen is their patron, and they are always there to remind us of a higher purpose."

"And to immediately take your confession when needed?"

"That, too." Tilney was summoned to join the English courtiers as the barge docked, and Marguerite went to see if Claudine, the Comtesse de Calonne, required her assistance. The young comtesse was *enceinte,* and the voyage was not a comfortable one for her. She bore it all well enough, her face so pale that her golden freckles stood out in stark relief, but she spent most of her time with eyes tightly shut, listening to one of her ladies read poetry aloud while another massaged her temples with lavender oil. She did not often need—or want—Marguerite's assistance.

The rumours of her handsome husband's many infidelities could not help her temper, either. The comte and comtesse were cousins, married very young, but it was said Claudine cared more for her husband than he did for her.

"We have arrived, madame la Comtesse," Marguerite said,

kneeling beside Claudine to help her gather her gloves and smooth her cloak and headdress. "Soon you will be tucked up in your own feather bed, with a warm fire and a cup of spiced wine."

Claudine smiled tightly. "Or more likely pressed into a cold room with ten other people and only ale to drink! These English—pah. They do not understand true hospitality."

"Then we must teach them, *madame!*" Marguerite nodded to one of Claudine's maids, and between them they helped her to her feet so she could join her husband in disembarking. "We will set a fine French example."

"At least they sent a cardinal to greet us," Claudine said, gesturing to the man in scarlet who awaited them, surrounded by so many attendants in black he seemed enmeshed in a flock of crows. "Not some mere clerk."

"I am sure King Henry has a better sense of protocol than all that," Marguerite replied, examining the man. It had to be Wolsey himself—the dangerous, all-powerful Wolsey—for he had the wide girth and long, bumpy nose of his portraits.

She had heard tell that the great Cardinal, Archbishop of York, the one man Henry relied on above all others, wore a hair shirt beneath his opulent scarlet velvets and satins. And Marguerite could well believe it, to judge by his pinched, grey face. He did not look like a well man. Still, *she* would not like to cross swords with him. It was fortunate he promoted the French treaty so assiduously.

Marguerite fell into step behind Claudine as they all left the barge and the play commenced at last.

Claudine's fears proved to be unfounded, for she was given an apartment to herself, albeit a rather small one almost beneath the eaves of the palace. Marguerite had an even tinier room tucked behind, a closet with scarcely space for a bed and clothes chest, and one tiny window set high in the wall. But the insignificant space was perfect for her needs—private, quiet, and, as the page told her, near a hidden staircase that led to the jakes and then out to the gardens.

Ideal for secret errands.

Left to her own devices while Claudine rested before the evening's festivities, Marguerite set about unpacking her travelling cases. All the velvet gowns and silk sleeves, the quilted satin petticoats and jewelled headdresses, were shaken, smoothed and tucked with lavender into the chest. The high-heeled brocade shoes and embroidered stockings, her small jewel case and fitted box of *toilette* items, were arrayed on top.

Once the case was emptied of its fine, feminine cargo, Marguerite lifted out the false bottom. There, carefully swathed in cotton batting, were her daggers and her sword.

The blades were made to her own specifications in the king's own forge, smaller and lighter to fit her size and strength, perfectly balanced, delicate as a dancer, strong as marble.

Holding her sword outstretched, she took up a fighting stance and thrust once, twice at the air. The steel sang in the cold breeze, a quick, fatal whine, then perfect silence. It was truly a thing of beauty.

Smiling, she tucked it safely away, where it could rest until needed. She took up one of the daggers, a thin blade that appeared almost as dainty, and useless, as a lady's eating knife. But it was designed to slip quickly, neatly, between a man's ribs, leaving only a fatal drop of blood behind.

The hilt was set with tiny rubies, winking in the hazy light like serpent's eyes. For a moment, she remembered her old blade, her favourite, with its rare emerald.

She remembered, too, how she had lost it. But one day she would get it back.

Marguerite lifted the hem of her skirt, tucking the blade into a sheath attached to her garter. She couldn't think about *him* now. He had no place here. She had her errand laid out before her, and it would begin with tonight's formal banquet to welcome their delegation. She needed to bathe and change her gown, to don her disguise of velvet and pearls.

Why, then, did it seem like the Russian followed her everywhere she went, and had for more than the last year? Those icy blue eyes…

Marguerite slammed the lid of her case and pushed it beneath the window, as if she could break his memory in two. The tiny pane of precious glass was so high she had to climb atop the case to see out. Her room looked down on one of the three courtyards Tilney had told her of, a carefully laid-out garden that slumbered in the winter chill. The square and diamond-shaped flowerbeds were brown and brittle, the trees bare, the fountains still. Yet she could clearly see that come summer it would be spectacular, a riot of roses, lilies, violets, gillyflowers, scented herbs, green vines twisting over the low railings and trellises.

The gardens were hardly dead now, for people strolled along the white gravel pathways, their Court raiment as bright as any flower could hope to be. Were they English, French, Spanish? She could not tell from her high perch. But she would know all soon enough.

Chapter Four

"And you see there, Master Ostrovsky, the king's newly built banquet house. And, over there, at the other end of the tiltyard, the theatre," Sir Henry Guildford, the king's Master of the Revels, said, waving toward a long, low wooden building as they strolled through the gardens. Even at this late moment, as the sun set on the first day of this vital meeting, workmen scurried about, hammering, sawing, putting the last details in place on these new structures.

"That space shall be for the planned pageants and masquerades," Guildford said, leading Nicolai toward the theatre. They ducked around a crowd of servants building two towering silk trees, a Tudor hawthorn and a Valois mulberry. "The king is also very fond of spontaneous disguisings, but one never knows when *those* will occur, no matter how organised my office strives to be."

The tightening of Guildford's mouth in his plump face was the only sign of the vexation such "spontaneous" displays engendered. The Master of the Revels was meant to oversee all the Court's entertainments, even to keeping account of all the costumes and properties, the casting of various roles. That could not be easy when the one person most meant to be impressed by these careful displays kept subverting them!

Nicolai had a hard enough time herding his own small troupe on their travels. He did not envy Sir Henry his task of shepherding an entire Court. "It must be a fine thing to have your own space for this great task, Sir Henry," Nicolai said, nodding toward the new theatre.

"'Tis not only *my* space, Master Ostrovsky. We must share it with the Master of the King's Minstrels and his musicians," Guildford answered. "But there is room for us to store our properties, which is a blessing. Usually they must be fetched from a great distance."

Nicolai's props were often stored in a painted wagon, with more dangerous items hidden among the masks and bells. Items for more—discreet tasks. But he merely nodded understandingly.

"We are very glad to welcome you here, Master Ostrovsky," Guildford went on. His smooth tone gave no hint of curiosity about what Nicolai, a player and a Russian to boot, might be doing among the Spanish party. "Assistance with our revels is always greatly to be desired, and Señor Mendoza tells us you have much experience with Italian pageants. All things Italian are very fashionable, you know."

"It is true I am recently come from Venice," Nicolai answered.

"Ah, yes, the Venetians. They do enjoy their masquerades and fêtes, do they not? Excellent, excellent! I have so very many tasks, and most of my idiotish assistants can do naught unless I watch them at every moment."

"I am happy to assist in any way I can, Sir Henry." In Nicolai's experience, it was often the actors at Court—both the professionals from the Office of the Revels and the courtiers who so often took on roles—who knew most of the secrets. The hidden plans and desires. If he could do what he did best, insinuate himself into a play, his task would be that much easier.

"The king has ordered a different entertainment for almost every evening. I will be happy of your assistance in directing some of our players." Sir Henry shook his head, muttering, "The ladies all want to take part, but they do not want to *work,* you see. Merely gossip and giggle together without learning their lines and postures."

Nicolai laughed. "I am told I work well with the ladies, Sir Henry."

"I would wager you do. They always seek to impress a handsome face. Well, here we are at the theatre, then. Just long enough for a quick glance round, I think, before the sun quite vanishes."

Sir Henry opened the tall double doors of the new theatre, the rich wood carved with vines and flowers, surmounted by the king's Tudor roses and portcullises, the queen's pomegranate of Granada and arrow-sheaf of Aragon.

How long, Nicolai wondered, would those badges remain, if the rumours were true? The tales of a certain Mistress Boleyn and the king's anguish over his lack of a son. And what vast trouble would their removal cause?

Today, though, the pomegranates were firmly in place, boasting of a long, solid marriage, a firm dynasty. Sir Henry led Nicolai into the interior of the theatre, so new it still smelled of paint and sawdust. It was beautiful, unlike any place Nicolai had ever performed in before. Long, soaring, lit with a profusion of flickering torches, the theatre gave the impression of a celestial realm. The ceiling was painted the pale blue of a summer sky, while below was hung a transparent cloth painted in gold with stars, moons and the signs of the zodiac.

Seats rose in tiers along the walls, while at the far end a large proscenium arch marked the performance space. Workmen were still putting in place terracotta busts and statues.

"'Tis a most glorious space, Sir Henry," Nicolai said truthfully. "And yet you say it is just temporary?"

"Oh, I am sure we will find a use for it once the French depart," Sir Henry said. "But it is all wood and gilt, meant to deceive."

He led Nicolai behind the arch, where several trunks were stacked. Scrolls, lengths of bright satin, cushions and spangles spilled forth in a confusing jumble. As Sir Henry dug through the glittering array, a chorus of angelic voices rose up somewhere in the shadows, a tangle of silvery sound that grew and expanded, soaring up to the ceiling-sky. Nicolai turned his head to listen, enchanted.

"The chorus of the Chapel Royal," Sir Henry said. "They are to give a recital after tonight's banquet. Fortunately, they are not *my* responsibility. Ah, here we are!"

He drew out a scroll, untidily bound with a scrap of ribbon, and handed it to Nicolai. "This is to be the pageant to follow the king's great tournament a few weeks hence. With your permission, Master Ostrovsky, I put *you* in charge of it."

Nicolai quickly read over the programme. *"The Castle Vert?"*

"The Green Castle, yes. An old piece, perhaps, but always a Court favourite. As you see, there are roles for all of sixteen ladies."

Sixteen? "Are the parts already cast?"

"Not at present. Lady Fitzwalter and Lady Elizabeth

Howard must have a turn, of course. And Mistress Anne Boleyn, who at least knows how to sing and dance already. Oh, and they say there is a lady among the French who is uncommonly lovely. A veritable angel, according to Master Tilney. Perhaps it would be a diplomatic gesture to cast her as Beauty. But, Master Ostrovsky, I leave it all up to you. I must work on *The Fortress Dangerous,* which fortunately only calls for six ladies."

Sir Henry clapped Nicolai affably on the arm, and turned to hurry off on some new task. "Good fortune, Master Ostrovsky, and my deepest thanks! I will send some of my staff to assist you on the morrow."

Nicolai grinned ruefully, slapping the scroll against his palm. Fifteen English Court ladies, and one French angel, all vying for their selected parts. All of them with the force of family and faction behind them.

Oh, Marc, Nicolai thought. *I hope you appreciate what I do for the sake of friendship!*

The French delegation was to gather in Queen Katherine's presence chamber before progressing to the great new banquet hall. Once Marguerite was bathed and dressed, in a gown of emerald green velvet over an embroidered petticoat of gold satin, her wide oversleeves turned back to reveal more gold and a sable trim, she joined the others in Claudine's apartment to wait for Bishop Grammont and his officers, including Claudine's husband, the Comte de Calonne.

A rest seemed to have done Claudine some good, Marguerite observed. She was not as pale, and even looked a bit rosy in her dark crimson silk gown, her stays loosely laced over her swelling belly. That was very good. If she was confined to her chamber, then Marguerite, her ostensible attendant, would be hard pressed to find excuses to go about in Court.

Claudine's maid was putting the finishing touches to her gingery red hair, lowering a stiffened gold headdress into place. Marguerite's own headdress was the newer, lighter nimbus shape, of green velvet trimmed with pearls, her silvery hair falling free down her back under the short, sheer gold veil.

Claudine's gaze narrowed when she saw Marguerite in her fine raiment. "How very youthful you look, Mademoiselle Dumas," she muttered.

"*Merci*," Marguerite answered lightly, smoothing down her sleeves. "I am sure we will all put the English and their rustic garments to shame!"

"And especially the Spanish," Claudine's husband, the Comte de Calonne, said, as he came into the room with his own richly clad attendants. "Michel tells me they are all in black, like a flock of crows!"

Everyone laughed, and fell into their places to be led into the English queen's presence. There could be no Spanish jests *there, naturellement!*

Marguerite did not know what she expected of this lady, who had been daughter to the legendary Ferdinand and Isabella of Spain, Queen of England for nearly twenty years. A lady renowned for her piety and great learning, beloved by her subjects. A woman who, as aunt to the Emperor Charles, stood in the way of France's interests on these shores.

Yet she did not look so formidable as she greeted them with a gracious smile, a few polite words in perfect French. She looked like a settled, contented matron of middle years, not very tall, stout from a plethora of pregnancies that had only produced one living child, Princess Mary. Her once fair hair was liberally streaked with grey, drawn back under a peaked pearl cap and gauze veil. She wore a fine gown of red-and-black figured brocade, flashing ruby jewels and a pearl-encrusted cross, yet all the finery did not conceal the deep lines of worry and care on her round face.

She took them all in with a sweeping glance of her dark eyes. "How very kind you are, Bishop Grammont, to relieve our winter doldrums with your presence!" she said, holding out a be-ringed hand for Grammont's salute. "We have a great deal of merriment planned for your stay."

"We thank your Majesty for such a gracious welcome," the bishop answered. "Our two nations are united, as ever, in the warmest bonds of friendship."

After a few more pleasantries, Grammont offered Katherine his arm, and they led the whole party along a gallery hung with tapestries of the story of David, lit on their way by green-and-white clad pages bearing torches.

"May I escort you, Mademoiselle Dumas?" a quiet voice asked, as Marguerite moved to take her place behind Claudine.

She turned sharply to find Father Pierre LeBeque standing close, his arm in its black woollen sleeve politely extended. His eyes glowed in the dim light, and he watched her with a tense expectation.

Marguerite glanced hastily around, but there was no one to come to her rescue. At any second it would be their turn to move forward, and she could not fall behind.

She nodded, and placed her hand lightly on his arm. It was coiled beneath her touch, stiff and bony. Was he frightened of something, then, to be so tense?

She had little time to ponder the oddities of Father Pierre. The long gallery opened to a vast banquet hall, where it seemed all the world waited in glittering array.

For a moment, her eyes were dazzled. This must be an enchanted kingdom, like in tales her father told her when she was a child! A land of gods and goddesses, powerful witches and princesses, not the stolid red-brick English world she saw outside. Roger Tilney had told her this space was newly built for this meeting, at vast dimensions of one hundred feet long and thirty feet wide, and she well believed it. The walls and floor were painted to look like marble, with gilded mouldings, the low, timbered ceiling covered with red buckram and embroidered with roses and pomegranates. Tiered buffets lined the walls, displaying a vast amount of gold plate. Bright banners hung from the ceiling.

And the people were clad in such sparkling raiment they added to the golden dazzlement. Many of the Spanish *were* in black, or wine red or burnt amber, but they served as an outline, a counterpoint to the English in their violet purple, silver tissue, sky blue, vivid rose, tawny and turquoise and sunny yellow.

And, at the end of the room, rose a triumphal arch painted with a large scene of—*non!* It could not be.

But it was. A painting of Henry's long-ago victory over the French armies at the Battle of Therouanne.

Alors! That was not so very diplomatic of the English king. Marguerite's dazzlement faded into cold clarity. That audacious scene was just the reminder she needed of why she was really here. Why they were all here. To protect France from just such another defeat.

"Welcome, welcome!" a stentorious voice boomed, soaring above the hum of laughter and conversation. All other voices echoed away, and the crowd parted. "Bishop Grammont, for the great love we bear our brother King François, welcome to our Court."

And the king himself appeared, for it could be none but the legendary Henry. He leaped down from a dais set up beneath the arch, a tall, broad-shouldered, barrel-chested figure swathed in cloth of gold trimmed with ermine and diamonds. He, unlike the queen, was just what Marguerite imagined. His red-gold hair cut short in the French style, covered by a crimson velvet cap, his square face framed by a short beard.

He was all bluff heartiness, tremendous good cheer as he greeted the French. All lighthearted welcome. Yet Marguerite saw that his small, shining eyes missed nothing at all. They moved over her—and widened.

She gave him a deep curtsy, and he grinned at her. So, his rumoured regard for the ladies was true! But was it also true he now had attention only for Mistress Boleyn?

Which one was she? Marguerite wondered, studying the array of ladies behind the queen. She saw none there whose beauty could rival her own, but there would be time to look for Anne Boleyn later. They were shown to their seats, at a long table to the right of the hall. The Spanish were to the left, and Henry escorted Katherine back to the dais where they were seated with Grammont and Ambassador Mendoza.

The tables were spread with white damask cloths, embroidered with roses, crowns, and fleurs-de-lis; the benches where they sat were lined with soft gold velvet cushions. In the centre of the table was a golden salt cellar engraved with the initials *H* and *K,* and each place boasted a small loaf of manchet bread wrapped in a cover of embroidered linen and a tall silver goblet filled with fine Osney wine from Alsace. Servants soon appeared with great golden platters of venison, capons, partridge, lark and eels, game pie with oranges and King Henry's favourite baked lampreys. A peacock, redressed in its own feathers, was ceremoniously presented to the king amid copious applause.

A lively song of recorders, lutes and pipes struck up from a gallery hidden behind one of the tapestries, and the conversation grew in vast waves around Marguerite. She nibbled at a piece of gingerbread painted with gold leaf, listening with half an ear as Father Pierre talked to her. All around her were the people she would have to get to know, would have to guard against and fend off, and perhaps even destroy in the end. Her first glimpse of the opposing army.

She knew she was not likely to learn much of use tonight. Everyone was on their best, most guarded behaviour, despite the flowing wine. They, too, were unsure of their surroundings. Unsure of the enemies' real strength. In a few days, when everyone had settled into long days of delicate negotiations and longer evenings of revelry, when enmities and flirtations had both sprung to full flower, she would be better able to gauge the atmosphere. Better able to take full advantage of rivalries and passions.

Tonight she could only observe, perhaps begin to collect precious droplets of gossip.

An acrobat in motley livery and bright bells performed a series of backward flips along the aisle between the tables, followed by a gambolling troupe of dwarves and trained dogs. Pages poured more wine, carried in yet more platters of fine delicacies. Marguerite laughed at the antics, nibbled at what was put before her, yet always she watched. Watched and listened, as the voices grew louder and the laughter heartier as the night went on.

King Henry, she saw, betrayed no hint of ill will toward the queen. Indeed, he was all solicitude, making sure her goblet was full, that she had the choicest morsels of venison and capon. He laughed heartily at his fools' jests, and listened intently when Wolsey murmured in his ear.

Princess Mary, the proposed bride of the Duc d'Orléans, sat by her mother, pale-faced and bright-haired, small for her age in her fine white brocade gown. She seemed shy and serene, speaking only to her mother, or to the Spanish ambassador in perfect Castilian Spanish.

The Spanish party across the aisle were not as raucous as the English, but neither were they so dour. They talked and jested just as everyone else did, led in conversation by a pretty woman of near Queen Katherine's age, a lady with a ready smile and soft brown eyes. As Marguerite watched, the lady laughed gently, holding out her goblet for a man seated next to her to refill.

He leaned forward, illuminated by the rich amber glow of the candelabra. His loose, long hair, golden as the summer sun, fell forward like a curtain, and he swept it back over his shoulder in one smooth movement. His profile, sharply etched as an ancient cameo, was limned in the light.

Marguerite gasped, and shook her head hard, certain she was dreaming! That she had imbibed too much of the fine Alsatian wine and was imagining things. She squeezed her eyes tightly shut.

Yet when she opened them, he was still there. *The Russian.* Laughing boldly, and just as beautiful as that night in Venice. The fallen angel she had vowed to kill if ever their paths crossed again. There he was, mere steps away, in the last place she ever expected.

She banged her goblet down on the table so violently that vivid red wine splashed over its etched lip, spilling on to her fingers. Bright spots, like blood, bloomed on the white damask cloth.

"The bold *cochon*," she muttered roughly.

"Are you ill, Mademoiselle Dumas?" Father Pierre asked solicitously.

Marguerite shook her head. "I am quite well, thank you. Merely tired from the journey, I think."

"Perhaps a bit more wine will help," he said, gesturing to one of the pages.

As the boy refilled her goblet, Marguerite surreptitiously studied Nicolai Ostrovsky. He did not appear to have noticed her yet. He sat there laughing and jesting with his companions, making sure the lady had the finest sweetmeats on her plate.

He was certainly far better dressed than in Venice! Or at least more elaborately so. Nor was the motley he wore to walk the tightrope in the Piazza San Marco in evidence. He was clad in a fine silk doublet of dark red trimmed with dull gold braid, his only jewel a single pearl in one ear, half-hidden by that shining golden hair.

What game did he play now?

She would just have to find out. Very soon, before he found her out first.

Chapter Five

The palace was quiet as Marguerite slipped out of her chamber, muffled in a hooded cloak. It was surely somewhere near morning, for the banquet and recital had gone on for long hours. And it was no easy thing to persuade hundreds of courtiers to retire! But all was silent now, almost eerily so in the purple-blackness of deepest night. The only sounds, so soft they were almost imperceptible, were the shuffles of the pages who slept on pallets outside doors, the whispers of Claudine's maids in their truckle beds.

Marguerite crept down the narrow back stairs, lit on her way by the smoking torches set high in their sconces. She had changed her heeled brocade shoes for soft-soled leather boots and left off her cumbersome petticoats, tucking her skirts into a kirtle to keep them out of her way. Her progress was swift as she dashed down the stairs and out into the gardens.

She had bribed one of the pages into telling her where the Russian was lodged, but it was in a section of the palace off one of the other courtyards, behind the Spanish apartments. She hurried along the twisting pathways, so crowded only that afternoon but now completely deserted. Only the stars and the moon, like tiny crystals in the violet velvet of the sky, watched her progress. The darkened windows of the buildings were blank, turning away from her actions as they had so many others in the past. The doings of humans were swiftly gone, those windows seemed to say, and of no interest at all. Only bricks and mortar, and the river beyond, were eternal.

Or perhaps it was all her own fancy, Marguerite thought, her own imagination taking strange flight. Well, she had no time for fancy now. This was the moment for action.

She had not expected to see Nicolai Ostrovsky again so soon in her life, to have him dropped before her like a ripe prize plum. She had watched him throughout the banquet and during the recital in Henry's fine new theatre, observing him closely while staying out of his sight.

How very careless he seemed, how caught up in laughter and jokes, the doings of his own companions! How had he ever survived his life of travel and intrigue? She had heard tell of how deftly he moved through the treacherous Courts of Venice, Mantua, Naples, Madrid. Yet he seemed to take no notice of the danger swirling around him.

He could not be so careless and still live, Marguerite knew that well. He and she were two of a kind in many ways, making their way in a cold world with only their wits, their blades, their good looks—their ability to pretend, to be all things to all people. But in his eyes she saw no flicker of awareness, no tense watchfulness like she always felt in herself. And she had watched him very closely all evening.

She finally had to conclude he had indeed taken no notice of her, and that was all to her advantage. Seldom had she found a task so easy. And now it was near to completion. She saw the wing housing the Spanish party just ahead, its silent brick hulk slumbering peacefully.

She slowed her steps, automatically rising on to the balls of her feet as she rounded a marble fountain. The faun poised at its summit stared down at her knowingly, her only witness as she slid the dagger from its sheath beneath her skirt. The hilt was cold and solid in her grasp, a stray beam of moonlight dancing down the polished blade. She was so close now…

Suddenly, a hand shot from behind the fountain, closing like a steel vise on her arm. Startled, Marguerite opened her mouth instinctively to scream, but another hand clamped tight over her lips. She was jerked off her feet in one quick movement, dragged back against a hard chest covered in a soft silk doublet.

Marguerite twisted in that steel trap of an embrace, kicking back with her heels. She managed to work her hand free, and stabbed out with her blade. The sound of tearing fabric echoed loudly in the cold, silent night, but she felt no solid thud of dagger meeting flesh.

"*Chert poberi!*" her captor cursed roughly. His grasp slid down to her wrist, squeezing until her fingers opened and the knife fell to the pathway.

Of course. She should have known. The Russian. Had she not been sure no one could be as careless as he appeared? Now it seemed she was the careless one.

Her anger at herself, at him, flared up like a white-hot shooting star, and she lashed out madly, kicking and squirming like a wild animal caught in a steel trap.

"*Couilles!*" she cried out behind his hand.

"Parisian hellcat," Nicolai growled, his arms tightening around her in a vise. She remembered, in a great fireworks flash, that night in Venice. The coiled, lean strength of his chest and abdomen, the way his long, lazy body, so lithe from years of backflips and somersaults, concealed a core of steel. Her only weapon against such hidden strength was speed and surprise, and she had squandered those with her own carelessness.

She had underestimated him twice now. She could not do so again.

If, that is, she ever had another chance. He could very well slit her throat now, and leave her for the English crows.

The thought was like a cold, nauseating blow to her stomach, and she bent forward in one last struggle to break free. He was too lithe to let her go, though, his body moving with hers.

"We meet again, Emerald Lily," he said in her ear, his voice full of infuriating amusement. "Or should I say Mademoiselle Dumas?"

"Call me whatever you like," she said, as his fingers at last loosened over her mouth. "I shall always think of *you* as *cochon*. A filthy, barbaric Russian!"

He clicked his tongue chidingly. "How you wound me, *mademoiselle*. And one always hears of the great charm of the French ladies. How sad to be so disillusioned."

"I would not waste my charm on you. Muscovite pigs have no appreciation of such delicacies."

"How you wound me, *petite*." He spun her around, backing her up until she felt the solid brick wall at her back, chilly through her velvet. He was outlined by the moonlight, his hair a shimmering curtain, falling in a golden tumble over one shoulder. His face was in shadow so she could not read his expression, but his breath was cool on her cheek, his clean, summery scent surrounding all her senses. He wore no wrap against the cold, and his body in the thin silk was hot where it pressed against her.

She shivered, suddenly frightened beneath her anger.

"I should be the one hurling angry names about," he said chattily, as if engaged in light conversation in the banquet hall. "After all, *mademoiselle,* you are the one who tried to kill me. Twice now, if I am not mistaken."

"You have something that belongs to me."

"Your pretty dagger, you mean? Ah, but I believe it belongs to *me* now. I claimed it as a forfeit that memorable night in Venice."

Marguerite twisted again, overcome by the nearness of him, his heat and strength. She hated this sensation of losing herself, of falling into him, of drowning! "You should have died then."

"Perhaps I should have, but it seems I have one or two lives yet to go. Fate, *mademoiselle,* has other plans for me. For us both, it would seem, for here we meet again. What are the odds of that?"

"Fate? Do you believe in it?"

"Of course. Do you not?"

"I believe in skill. In hard work. We all make our own fate, monsieur."

"Ah, *'monsieur'* rather than *cochon!* I must advance in your estimation."

Marguerite tilted her head back against the hard wall, staring at him in the moonlight. He was certainly still handsome, the sharp, symmetrical angles of his face softened by that mocking half-smile, his pale blue eyes glowing. His hair, his lean acrobat's body—all perfection. But beauty, as Marguerite well knew, was only a tool, a weapon like any other that a person could learn to wield with skill. She was usually unmoved by that weapon, both in herself and in others. Unmoved by a handsome man's touch.

Why, then, did his clasp make her tremble so? Make her thoughts tilt drunkenly in her mind? She had to get away from him, to regroup.

She pressed back tight against the wall, but he followed, his hair trailing like silk over her throat, her bare *décolletage* above the velvet bodice. "I have esteem for any worthy enemy."

"Am I a worthy enemy?"

"You have defeated me twice now, which no one else has ever done. You are obviously strong and clever, *monsieur.* Yet you will not defeat me three times."

His smile widened. "I see I shall have to watch my back while I am in England."

"At every moment."

"I shall consider myself fairly warned, *mademoiselle.*"

They stood in silence for a long moment, studying each other warily. Marguerite glanced away first, her gaze shifting over his shoulder to the stone faun, who seemed to laugh at her predicament.

"What are you doing here?" she asked tightly. "Do you work for the Spanish now? Was your task in Venice complete?"

He laughed, a low, rough sound that seemed to echo through her very core. "*Mademoiselle,* you must know I work for no one but myself. As do you. And as for what I am doing here at Greenwich—well, I must keep *some* secrets, yes?"

Secrets. That was all life was. Yet Marguerite had spent her own life keeping her own secrets, and discovering those of other people. Even ones they thought so well hidden. She would find his, too.

He seemed to have read her very thoughts, for he leaned closer, so close his breath stirred the fine, loose curls at her temple, and his lips softly brushed her cheek. "Some things, *petite,* are buried so deeply even you cannot dig them out again."

"Secrets are my speciality," she whispered back. "I have not met a man yet who could withhold them from me. One way or another, I always fulfil my task."

"Ah, but I am not as other men, Mademoiselle Dumas." He pressed one light, fleeting kiss to her jaw, so swift she was not even sure it happened. "I shall look forward with great anticipation to our next battle. *Do svidaniya.*"

Then he let her go, his hands and body sliding away from her as one long caress. He melted away, vanishing into the night as if he had never been there at all. Except for the spot of fire that marked his kiss.

Marguerite spun around, but she could find no glimpse of him, no trace of his bright hair or red silk doublet. She was completely alone in the cold garden.

"*Abruti,*" she muttered. Her whole body felt boneless, exhausted. She longed to fall to the walkway in a heap, to sob out her frustration, to beat her fists against the jagged gravel until they bled!

But there was no time to give into such childish, useless tantrums. Womanish tears would never gain her the revenge she sought, would never achieve her goals for her. So, she scooped up her dagger where it had fallen and hurried back toward the palace, running up the stairs to her quiet little room.

Soon, very soon, a new day would dawn. A new chance to at last best the Russian and get back her emerald dagger.

This time, she would not fail.

Nicolai closed the door to his small chamber, sliding a heavy clothes chest in front of it. He was wary enough to take the Emerald Lily at her word. She would be coming sooner or later for her dagger. At least this way she would have to make a great deal of noise forcing the door open. Unless she could somehow transform herself into a column of mist and come down the chimney, which would not surprise him in the least.

She was not like any woman he had ever met, this French fairy-sprite. She looked so very delicate, so angelic, and yet she was a veritable hellcat. A powerful, shrieking *vodyanoi,* a sea witch, just like the terrifying tales his nurse told him when he was child.

Perhaps her claws only came out in the moonlight, though, for at the banquet she was all smiles and light charm, even with the dour young priest who sat beside her. None of the men in the vast hall could turn his eyes from her, and that included him, though he carefully did not let her see that. He pretended not to notice her at all, to let her think herself safe, yet in truth he had seen her as soon as she walked in at the end of the French procession.

How could he help it? It was as if she was surrounded by a silvery pool of light. His Emerald Lily. The woman who incited his lusts and then tried to murder him.

He knew she would come for him. She was rumoured to be ruthless to the enemies of France. Such as what had happened to a certain Monsieur Etampes, who dared attempt to be a double agent for Spain! A grotesque end indeed. And Nicolai had slighted her by daring to live.

But over the long months since Venice, he had forgotten how very potent her presence was. Her exotic perfume, the cold light in her eyes—they were like a strong wine, lulling and lovely. He would have to be more cautious in the future, and find a way to fight her from a safe distance. Or he would end up like poor Etampes, or Signor Farcinelli in Milan. Another bad end.

Nicolai laughed, suddenly exhilarated. He was always buoyed by a good fight, and the Emerald Lily—or Marguerite Dumas, as he had learned she was called—certainly gave as good as she got. Despite her small size, it took a great deal of strength for him to hold her still, to keep her from kicking and clawing. It also took all his strength to ignore the feel of her in his arms, the press of her soft body against his.

He unfastened his doublet, and tossed it along with his shirt over the narrow bed, letting the cold breeze from the open window wash over his face, his naked chest. The sun was just peeking over the horizon, a thin line of pinkish-gold light that promised bright hours ahead.

He would have to write Marc and thank him for sending him on this fool's errand. This English meeting seemed suddenly full of colour and interest. Surely anything at all could happen in the days ahead.

Chapter Six

Marguerite bent her head over her embroidery, pretending to be absorbed by the tiny flowers in blue-and-yellow silk as she listened to the soft murmur of voices around her. Queen Katherine had invited Claudine and her ladies to sit with her in her privy chamber for the afternoon, while her husband and the other men were occupied with their "dull" business in the council chamber.

In truth, Marguerite was sure that far more of interest was happening here than in the king's group. The men, with their bluff deceptions, their great egos that convinced them of their imminent victory, could learn a great deal about prevarication from their ladies, whose gentle smiles and soft, flattering words were veritable poniards.

Queen Katherine sat by the fire in her carved, cushioned chair, stitching on one of the king's fine batiste shirts. She had sewn his shirts and embroidered the blackwork trim on them since the early days of their marriage, and she would never surrender the task now. At her feet, her pet monkey, clad in a tiny blue doublet, frolicked, while lovebirds chattered away in a cage by the windows. The animals' high-pitched exclamations blended with the giggles of the ladies, their whispers and the crackle of the flames, the sound of a lute being played by the queen's chief lady, Maria de Salinas.

Thus far the talk had all been of fashion, of household matters, of Claudine's forthcoming baby and Princess Mary's education. Little enough to glean there, but Marguerite was patient. She had to be.

She drew her needle through the fine, white cloth, embellishing a petal on a cornflower. One stitch, then another and another, and the scene would soon be whole. It was the same with listening. One seemingly insignificant detail built on another until the greater vision was apparent.

"That is quite lovely, Mademoiselle Dumas," one of Queen Katherine's younger ladies, Lady Penelope Percy, said. She held out her own work, a hopelessly crooked pattern of Tudor roses and diamond shapes. "It is meant to be a cushion cover, but I fear I lack the skill you possess. No one will ever want to sit on it!"

Marguerite laughed ruefully. "In truth, Lady Penelope, needlework is not a favourite pastime for me. I find it rather dull."

"You do it so well, though."

"In my position at Court, serving Princess Madeleine, there is little else to do all day. I had no choice but to become proficient. See, Lady Penelope, if you pull the thread thus, it keeps the tension in your needle and makes a neater stitch."

"So it does! How very clever." They sewed in silence for a moment, then Lady Penelope leaned closer to whisper, "Your normal place is not in the household of the comtesse, then?"

"No. She needed extra assistance to travel such a distance in her condition, and I was the most easily spared of the princess's household. I confess I was glad of the opportunity to travel, to see England."

"As I wish I could see Paris! Alas, I fear I will be here in the queen's service until my father finds some whey-faced squire for me to marry. I shall never have much merriment in life at all," Lady Percy said, her lower lip protruding in a distinct pout.

Ah-ha, Marguerite thought. A dissatisfied lady was always the best confidant of all, *if* she could persuade them to confide in her. Some were simply too jealous. But Lady Penelope Percy was quite pretty herself, and obviously lonely. "How very sad for you. Everyone should enjoy themselves when they are young, yes?"

"Exactly so! Time enough for dullness later, when one is as old and fat as…" Her voice trailed away, but she glanced at the stout, complacent queen.

"We all must dance while we can," Marguerite said. "Yet I have seen few signs of dullness here at your English Court. The banquet last night was most delightful."

"That is because we must entertain you French!" Lady Penelope said with a laugh. "When we are alone it is much quieter, aside from a bit of hunting and dancing."

"No flirtations? In a Court so full of handsome gentlemen? Come now, Lady Penelope, I cannot believe it of a pretty young lady like yourself! You must have a favourite among all these charming courtiers."

Lady Penelope giggled, ducking her head over her untidy sewing. "I think the most handsome men are among your own party, Mademoiselle Dumas. The comte de Calonne, for instance."

The comte? Marguerite had scarcely noticed Claudine's husband, but she supposed he was handsome. Certainly nowhere as attractive as Nicolai Ostrovsky…

Marguerite closed her eyes against the sudden lurch of her stomach that the thought of the Russian inspired. That sick, nervous, excited feeling she hated so much. She remembered last night, the hot feeling of his body pressed against hers in the dark, his breath, his kiss on her skin. The vivid *aliveness* of him.

Why did he haunt her so?

"You admire the comte, then?" she said, opening her eyes and going back to her embroidery. Her stitches were now distinctly less even.

Lady Penelope shrugged. "He has such fine, broad shoulders! I would wager he is a very good dancer. Yet his wife seems so sour."

Marguerite glanced at Claudine, who did seem pale and out-of-sorts in her ill-chosen tawny silk gown. "Many women are out of humour when they are in such a condition."

"Perhaps so." Lady Penelope giggled, as carefree as only a girl who had never been pregnant could be. Or a lady who could *not* become pregnant, such as Marguerite herself. "But it leaves their husbands in such great need of consolation!"

Marguerite laughed. That was certainly all too true. In her experience, men needed "consolation" for too many things far too often. That did not mean *she* had to be their consoler.

"Who do you think the handsomest man is, Mademoiselle Dumas?" Lady Penelope asked.

"I fear I have not been here long enough to judge."

"Well, just guess, then. From the ones you have met."

Marguerite thought again of Nicolai, of his golden hair against that red doublet. He looked like a flame, one that threatened to consume her if she got too close. "Perhaps your own King Henry."

Lady Penelope shook her head. "He still looks well

enough, I suppose, for his years. But you would have to battle for him with Mistress Boleyn, and that *I* would not care to try. Her tongue is as sharp as her claws."

"I have not yet had a glimpse of this famous Mistress Boleyn. She must be quite beautiful."

"I would not say *beautiful.* Not like yourself, Mademoiselle Dumas! She is—interesting, rather. She was in France, you know, when the king's sister was Queen of France, and is much more fashionable than the rest of us."

"I wonder when I shall see her."

"Tonight, no doubt. They say there is to be dancing after supper, and she never misses the chance to show off her dancing skills." Lady Penelope lowered her voice even further to whisper, "She is meant to attend on the queen, but she is usually far too busy with her own pursuits."

"Indeed?"

Lady Penelope nodded. One of the other ladies, a pale young woman named Jane Seymour, began to read aloud from *The Romance of the Rose,* and everyone else fell silent. There was no chance for Marguerite to ask Lady Penelope what those "other pursuits" might be, yet she was sure she could guess. Most interesting.

She also ruminated on the comment about how Mistress Boleyn had been in France and was thus "fashionable." Had not the Russian himself said she, Marguerite, lacked the famed French charm? It was hard to be charming in a knife fight, but she knew she had charm a-plenty when she needed it. Maybe it was time to employ it…

Nicolai reached up to test the tensile strength of the tight-rope, to make sure it was taut and firmly anchored. From outside his small, hidden nook in the theatre, he could hear

Sir Henry Guildford directing his assistants. Their voices, the sounds of hammering and sawing, seemed far away, as if he hid in a cave where the real world could not touch him.

If only there was such a place, a single, hidden spot of peace. Yet if there was, he had never found it in all his travels. Everywhere—Moscow, Venice, England, Holland, Spain—people were the same. Noisy and striving, beautiful and cruel, strutting about in all their vanity and longing until everything was extinguished in only a moment.

Only in friendship had he found a true haven, a reminder of grace and kindness that *could* be found, if one searched hard enough. Cherished it when it was discovered, like rubies and gold. Nicolai had lost his family so long ago, had wandered the world alone until he discovered a new family— Marc and Julietta, Marc's long-lost brother Balthazar, Nicolai's own acting troupe.

Only these bonds, so precious and fragile, could have brought him to this nest of French, Spanish and English vipers, all spitting and hissing. Yet, now that he was here, he felt some of the old excitement coming back to him. The soaring exhilaration only danger could create.

He felt restless today, filled with a crackling energy. A good fight would take that edge off, yet thus far at Greenwich everyone was behaving with disappointing civility. Except for Marguerite Dumas, of course, but she was nowhere to be seen. Probably she was safely ensconced with the other French ladies in Queen Katherine's chamber, where she could hopefully cause very little trouble.

And she was part of this restlessness, if not its entire cause.

So, that left acrobatic tricks. Nicolai shed his fine velvet doublet, his Spanish leather boots, and, clad only in shirt and hose, swung himself up on to the rope. He balanced there on his bare feet, tall and straight, carefully centred, and took a few steps.

He was stiff from the long, idle days aboard ship and on horseback, out of shape after too much rich food and fine wine. It was fortunate the Emerald Lily was not able to overpower him last night, when he was foolish enough to ambush her in his poor condition!

But as he traversed the length of the rope, balancing on one foot and then the other, he felt his muscles warm, felt them grow pliant and supple again. His mind, too, was centred, leaving England and Marguerite Dumas and Marc's mother behind, until there was only his body and the thin rope.

Nicolai tucked and rolled into a forward somersault, springing up to do a backflip. One, two, then he was still again, his arms outstretched.

A flurry of applause burst the shimmering, delicate bubble of his concentration. He glanced up to find Marguerite standing in the curtained doorway, clapping her jewelled hands.

He would have expected to see sarcasm written on her face as she watched him, cold calculation. Yet there was none of that. Her cheeks glowed pink, and her eyes were bright, clear of their usual opaque green ice. Her lips parted in a delighted smile.

How very young she looked in that moment, young and free and alive. If he had thought her beautiful before, he saw now he never knew what real beauty was.

"Oh, Monsieur Ostrovsky, how very extraordinary that was," she exclaimed. "How can a human being perform such feats?"

Nicolai swung down from the rope, landing lightly on his feet. He stayed a wary distance from her, not trusting that she did not conceal a blade up her fine brown velvet sleeve. Not trusting himself to be near her, to step into the circle of that silvery glow she seemed to carry everywhere.

"'Tis merely practice, *mademoiselle*," he answered. "Many years of it."

"You must have a great gift," she said. "Anyone else would have cracked their skulls open!"

"And so I did, a dozen times."

"Yet you lived to tell about it."

"I have a very hard skull."

"And so you do. Thick-headed, indeed." She stepped closer to the rope, reaching up tentatively to test its strength. "Why, it's as thin as my embroidery silks."

"It's harder to find your balance if the rope is too wide."

"Truly?"

"Would you like to try it? It would not be easy in those heavy skirts, but you could surely stand."

She looked toward him, her eyes wide. That impression of youth, of wonderment, still clung about her, and Nicolai was surprised to notice she could not be more than two and twenty. What could have happened to such a girl, so lovely and graceful, so full of a wonder she hid even from herself, to run her to such a hard life, to the shadowy, sinful existence of a spy and assassin?

He suddenly had the overpowering desire to take her in his arms, to hold her close until whatever those hardships were faded away and she was only that young girl again. His cursed protectiveness. It always got him into trouble.

"Come," he said, holding out his hand. "I can help you."

But she stepped back from the rope, tucking her hands into her wide sleeves. She laughed cynically, and he could see the veil fall again over her eyes. "Nay, Monsieur Ostrovsky! I am sure you would let me drop at the first opportunity. I am too fond of my neck to see it broken on these paving stones."

He let his own hand drop, and turned away to fetch his doublet and boots. "How very suspicious you are, *mademoiselle.*"

"One has to be, to survive."

Nicolai shrugged into his doublet, fastening the tiny pearl closures. The room had suddenly grown very cold. "What do you do here, Mademoiselle Dumas? Are not all the ladies attending on the queen today?"

"I was, but they have joined the Spanish ladies for a stroll in the garden. And I received a note from the Master of the Revels summoning me here. Lady Penelope Percy says he wants to cast me in one of the pageants."

Ah, yes, the pageant. Nicolai had forgotten about it for a blessed five minutes. "I should have known you were the French angel."

"The French angel?"

"It seems one of Henry's attendants suggested that a lady of the French party, one who was 'beautiful as an angel,' should be given a role as a diplomatic gesture."

Marguerite laughed. "I know little of acting."

"Oh, *mademoiselle,* I beg to differ. You played the Venetian whore to perfection."

Her lips tightened, but other than that she betrayed no emotion. "I suppose I could always come to you for advice, Monsieur Ostrovsky. I've seldom met such a consummate player as you."

"I am at *mademoiselle's* disposal if you ever need advice, as always." Nicolai reached back for his hair, tied with a narrow black ribbon to keep it out of his face while he worked, and started to plait it. It was such a bother, the thick fall of it halfway down his back.

Marguerite's eyes widened and she took a step closer to him. "It does seem such a shame to confine it," she murmured.

"It is tangled, and I haven't the time now to see to it properly."

"Here, I will help you. If there is one thing I am good at, it's a proper *toilette*."

"I would wager you are good at many things, the least of which is wielding a comb."

A smile twitched at her lips. "I was told only this morning that my embroidery is rather fine. Now, sit here, and I will see to your hair before you hurry on your way."

She gestured toward a stool, which Nicolai eyed warily. "You will just take the chance to slit my throat, I fear."

Marguerite laughed, a clear, sweet sound. "Indeed I will not! I will appear as avenging angel when you least expect it, Monsieur Ostrovsky. At this moment I am only a woman who appreciates masculine beauty." She turned back the edges of her fur-trimmed brown velvet sleeves. "See, I have no daggers today."

"Except for what might be hidden in your garters," Nicolai said, quite beguiled against his will. Beguiled by her smile, the glow in her eyes.

"You shall not be allowed to search *there,* sirrah! Come, I give you my word, no sneak attacks today."

Nicolai slowly sat down, holding himself tense, ready to spring up if she made any lethal movements. She merely stepped behind him, her hands gentle as she untied the ribbon and spread his hair over his shoulders.

"Any lady would envy such hair," she murmured, running her fingers through the strands, untangling them slowly, massaging his scalp as she went. "You do not use a lemon juice solution on it? Or saffron?"

Nicolai laughed. "Why would I squeeze lemons on my hair? I am not a baked salmon."

"To brighten it, of course. Many ladies do, you know."

"Do you use such things?"

"Not usually."

"Nay. You would use your dark arts to capture moonbeams to colour your hair, and sunsets for your cheeks."

"Shh, Monsieur Ostrovsky! You give away my secrets." She hummed softly as she worked, a low, gentle lullaby that emphasised the quick, light movements of her fingers.

Nicolai slowly relaxed, lulled by her voice, her touch, the scent of her exotic lily perfume that seemed to curl around him in a silken net. He would hardly have guessed, after Venice, after their encounter in the garden last night, that she possessed such softness. What endless facets she had, like the fine emerald set in her dagger.

How very easy she must find it to winnow secrets out of men, who were so vulnerable to gentleness and sweetness. And he was a man like any other. His body stirred at her touch, becoming hard and hot, and he longed to fall into her arms, bury himself in her complex beauty and never emerge again.

Was this truly what she wanted, then, what she worked for? His complete eradication? If so, in that moment he would have happily given it to her.

Her fingertips lightly skimmed over his temples, his cheekbones, down his throat to rest on his shoulders. "There, Monsieur Ostrovsky, you are quite tidy now."

"You are indeed most gifted at the *toilette, mademoiselle*," Nicolai muttered, slowly coming back to the hard ground, to himself. It was a bit like emerging from the spell that overtook him on the tightrope.

"And a woman of my word, too, yes?"

"My throat does seem to be intact."

Marguerite laughed. "For now, *monsieur.*"

Nicolai stood and gave her a bow, his hair falling forward like a shining length of silk, all knots removed. "I am most obliged to you, *mademoiselle,* for sparing my poor life one more day."

"I do not have time to deal with you properly," she said, sounding quite surprised as she seemed to recall her original errand. "I must find Sir Henry…"

"No need, Mademoiselle Dumas, for he is here," Sir Henry's voice called from the doorway, where he had thrown back the curtain. Nicolai turned to find the Master of the Revels standing there, the crook of his arm filled with scrolls, a page behind him laden with russet satin costumes. "I am very glad to see that the two of you have already met."

"Already met?" Marguerite said.

"Ah, yes, for Master Ostrovsky has generously offered to supervise the great pageant of *The Castle Vert,*" Sir Henry said, obviously eager to be on his way. "And you, Mistress Dumas, must take the most important role, that of Beauty, for I see now that you are perfect for it. I am sure the two of you will work together marvellously well! Master Ostrovsky will tell you all about it, as I fear I must now take my leave. The play for tonight, you know."

As Sir Henry hurried away, Nicolai smiled at Marguerite, who watched him with narrowed eyes. "Well, *mademoiselle,*" he said. "It seems we are to be colleagues…"

Chapter Seven

That did not go at all as she planned.

Marguerite stalked along the garden pathway, her hands balled into tight fists against her skirts. She didn't even feel the chilly breeze, for her cheeks burned hot! She hurried around the corner of one of the buildings, away from the better-travelled thoroughfares. No doubt her face was as red as it felt, and she did not want anyone commenting on her agitation.

Here, close to the kitchen herb gardens, there were only a few servants, maids and pages too intent on their own errands to question hers.

She sat down on a stone bench, drawing out a book and pretending to read as she drew in deep, steadying breaths. What a fool she was! She had sought Nicolai out to use her "charm," her femininity, to beguile him, lull him into trusting her. Into telling her what his true errand was in England.

Instead, she came away far more *beguiled* than he could ever be.

When she went to that doorway in the theatre, she was determined to coldly draw him in. But she was brought up short by the vision of him balanced on that rope, so graceful and strong. He took feats that should have been impossible for any human body and made them appear effortless. He seemed to fly lightly through the air, as naturally as any bird.

Any bird of prey.

She stared, hardly daring even to breathe, as he leaped backwards, landing perfectly straight and unwavering on that flimsy rope every time. It was surely magic!

And she was swept away, her errand completely forgotten in the flurry of his movements, the musical flexibility of his body. She watched, completely mesmerised, out of all time, until he landed on the ground. He scarcely seemed even out of breath, and only when she drew near did she see the faint, glistening sheen of sweat on his bronzed skin, the tangle of his tumbled hair. He appeared golden all over, an ancient god flown down to earth.

Marguerite had met many men in her life, men with high opinions of themselves—some even deserved, by force of their great intellect, their fine looks or their artistry. Many who were fools, but never knew it. But never had she met a man who had her so entranced as Nicolai Ostrovsky. What was behind his lightness and ease, his lazy, graceful sensuality? What did he hide in those pale blue eyes?

She found she *wanted* his secrets, not to use as weapons, not to gain the power that secrets always bestowed, but just to *know*.

She lost her careful concealment in that little room, giving in to the force of her wonder and awe, her attraction for his glittering goldeness. Only for a moment, yet long enough to show her the graceful danger he posed.

When he offered to help her walk the tightrope herself, when he held his hand out to her, she was seized by such longing. Longing to feel the freedom he must know when he flew high above the sordid world. Longing for things she knew could never be hers.

She did avoid *that* temptation, the desire to feel the rope under her feet, his hand in hers. But she gave in to a darker desire—she actually touched his hair.

Marguerite groaned, burying her face in her book as she remembered that compulsion which would not be denied. That rush of need to feel the cool silk of his hair against her skin. Pressed close to him in that dim, dusty space, inhaling the scent of him, the green, herbal freshness of his soap overlaid by the salty tang of honest sweat, she had wanted nothing more than to wrap her arms around him, throw herself into his lap and kiss him, until they drowned in the hot tide of passion.

She remembered too well the taste of his mouth in Venice, the feeling of his lips on her body, those graceful fingers on her stomach, her breasts. He was surely as skillful in the arts of lovemaking as he was on that rope.

Yes, she lost herself for a moment, drowned in the force of that cursed Russian's allure and charisma. Only Sir Henry's arrival saved her, and she had to flee when she heard she was actually to be working with Nicolai!

"Idiot," she muttered. She could not succumb to weakness now. There were yet long days ahead here in England, and she needed her wits and skills to see her through. She would not give in to the allure of a lithe body and golden hair.

Remember, he stole your dagger, she told herself sternly. She had to get it back, and find out what his business was among the Spanish.

She closed her eyes, envisioning a sheet of pure, white ice

encasing her whole body, her mind and heart, erasing the heat and light of Nicolai Ostrovsky. When she opened them again, she felt calmer, more rational.

She lowered her book to her lap, hands steady. Passion, agitation, achieved nothing. Her feelings for Nicolai were a mere physical manifestation, her weak, womanly body clamouring for pleasure. Focusing on her work would soon overcome such foolishness.

Marguerite heard a burst of laughter, a flurry of chatter in Spanish, and she turned to see a group of ladies strolling toward her. At their head was the woman Nicolai sat next to at the banquet, the one with the sweet smile. That smile was in evidence now as she drew near Marguerite's bench.

"Ah, *señorita,* are you alone this afternoon?" she asked. As she stopped before Marguerite, her dark red velvet skirts swaying in a cloud of violet scent, Marguerite saw she was older than she first appeared. Tiny lines fanned out from her brown eyes and her lips, and grey threaded her brown hair at the temples. She was obviously quite wealthy, too, with a heavy garnet-and-pearl cross around her neck, hanging low over her fur-trimmed surcoat, and pearl drops in her ears. An important member of the Spanish party, then, Marguerite decided. But her eyes were kind.

Marguerite stood up to make a curtsy. "I am reading, *señora…*"

"This is the Duchess of Bernaldez," one of her attendants said sternly.

The lady waved these words away. "Dona Elena when we are outdoors, if you please, Esperanza." She whispered to Marguerite, "I have spent many years at a quiet convent, you see, and have yet to become accustomed to the strict etiquette my husband seems sadly to enjoy so much."

Marguerite laughed in surprise. "I, too, prefer informality. I am Marguerite Dumas, Dona Elena."

"I know. You are quite famous, Señorita Dumas."

"Famous?" Oh, no. That would surely make things so much more difficult! It was hard enough to engage in subterfuge in a crowded Court without being well known.

"Of course. The men can talk of nothing but your rare beauty. I see now why that is so."

"You are very kind."

"I just speak as I find, and I must say I enjoy having beauty around me as much as anyone. It brightens these grey English days. Would you care to walk with us? We were going to take a turn by the river."

Ah, an opportunity! They so rarely just fell into her lap like that. Hoping to compensate for her silly behaviour with Nicolai, Marguerite nodded and said, "I would be honoured, Dona Elena."

She fell into step next to the duchess as they strolled around the palace to the long walkway that ran beside the Thames. The river was placid today, grey and flat as a length of sombre silk, broken only by a few boats and barges floating past on their way to London and the sea. Dona Elena's attendants gradually went back to their conversations, their whispers like those waves that broke and ebbed along the banks.

"You have not long been married, then, Dona Elena?" Marguerite asked.

"A few months only. My first husband, a sea captain, died many years ago, *señorita*. I loved him a great deal, and when he was gone I sought the refuge of a convent. I thought to stay there for the rest of my life."

"Until the duke swept you off your feet?" Marguerite teased.

Dona Elena laughed. "You certainly have it aright! His sister, you see, is abbess of the convent, and we met when he came to visit her. We spent a great many hours walking in the garden together, and before he left he asked me to marry him."

"Such a romantic story!"

Dona Elena gave her a wink. "And an unlikely one, you are thinking. An old lady like myself—why would an exalted duke choose such a wife?"

"Not at all, Dona Elena. You can hardly be so 'old' and still be so beautiful."

"You *do* possess the art of flattery, Señorita Dumas. I had heard that of the French."

"Like you, I must speak as I find."

"Are you married yourself?"

Marguerite shook her head. "I fear not."

"I was first married when I was fifteen. My new husband was also wed when he was quite young, and his wife gave him many children before she died. We did our duty in our youth, you see; we have our families. Now we are blessed to find companionship and affection in our old age."

"It sounds a marvellous thing indeed, Dona Elena. I can only pray to find such contentment myself one day."

"You must surely have received many offers!" Dona Elena examined her closely, until Marguerite felt her blush returning. "I wonder you are yet unwed."

"My duties at Court keep me very busy. And, too, I am an orphan, with no one to see to such matters."

"Oh, *pobrecito!* How very, very sad." Dona Elena took Marguerite's hand in her plump, be-ringed fingers, patting it consolingly. "Have you been alone in the world very long?"

"My mother died when I was born, and my father died above seven years ago."

"And you were their only child?"

"I fear so."

Dona Elena sighed. "I have but one child myself, my son Marc. He has been the greatest blessing of my life, but I would have wished to give him brothers and sisters." She drew a gold locket on a chain from inside her surcoat, opening the engraved oval to show Marguerite the miniature portrait inside.

Marguerite peered down at the painted image of a dark-haired young man. "He is certainly very handsome."

"That he is. And he is soon to make me a grandmother!"

"How very gratifying. You must wish to hurry back to Spain to see the new baby."

Dona Elena pursed her lips as she snapped the locket shut. "Alas, he makes his home near Venice now. But I hope to see him again soon after we leave England."

Whenever that would be. Marguerite feared they would all be at Greenwich, strolling round and round the gardens for weeks to come, with nothing at all resolved. And she could not even devise how to discover what this lady knew of Nicolai.

"You must wish for children of your own one day, Señorita Dumas," Dona Elena said.

For one flashing instant, Marguerite remembered the kicks of the horse's hooves, the burning, searing pain in her belly. Her twelve-year-old body, barely budding into womanhood, bleeding on to the ground. "If God wills, Dona Elena," she said, knowing full well His will for her had already been revealed. He turned from her long ago.

"If you were one of *my* ladies, I would have you settled with a fine husband in a trice," Dona Elena said confidently. "Even from the convent, I arranged seven happy marriages among the children of my friends! I am known for my eye for a good match."

Marguerite laughed. "That must be a useful gift indeed, Dona Elena."

"It gives me great satisfaction. *Some* people, though, do not trust my skills. They resist what is best for them."

"Do they? I vow *I* am convinced, Dona Elena! I would be happy to put my fate in your hands, if I was fortunate enough to be one of your ladies."

Dona Elena shook her head ruefully. "If only you could help me convince poor Nicolai."

"Nicolai?" Marguerite asked innocently, a bubble of excitement rising up in her at the mere mention of his name. She was a fool in truth.

"Nicolai Ostrovsky, who is a friend of my son. He leads such a disorganised life, *señorita!* Travelling up and down, no home of his own, though his fortune could surely afford one. Such a lovely gentleman."

"Is he the handsome one, with the golden hair?" Marguerite whispered.

"Ah, you see, Señorita Dumas, even *you* have taken notice of him! All the ladies do. I have told him many times that any of my young attendants would be most happy to marry him, but he refuses."

Marguerite glanced back over her shoulder at Dona Elena's chattering ladies. They were pretty enough, she supposed, with their smooth, youthful complexions and shining dark hair. Surely too young and pious and—and *Spanish* for Nicolai! How could any of them possibly understand a man like him, when not even Marguerite herself could?

"Does he give a reason for his refusal?" she asked casually.

"Only that his life has no room for a wife. But I say he

grows no younger! If his life has no room for a family, he must change his life. Make a home before it is too late."

A home. Marguerite feared she did not even know what the word meant, as wondrous as it sounded. "He must be a great friend to your son, Dona Elena, for you to take such concern."

"He is indeed! He saved Marc's life."

Very interesting. "How so?"

"I do not know the particulars. It happened in Venice. Or was it Vienna? No matter. He saved my son, and I shall always be grateful to him. And now he comes all this way to watch over *me!* Such a good man, *señorita.* If only he would let me repay him by finding him a fine wife."

They walked on, the conversation turning to lighter matters of fashion, but Marguerite's thoughts whirled. Could it really be that Nicolai was *not* here at Greenwich on matters of state and politics, but merely—friendship?

It scarcely seemed possible. Marguerite had never heard of such a thing. There must be something else, something Nicolai hid from the sweet Dona Elena, that brought him to this meeting. He had to be in the pay of someone else. But what was it he really sought?

Marguerite was more determined than ever to find out.

Chapter Eight

"What will you wear tonight, mistress?" asked Marguerite's borrowed English maid, sorting through the clothes chest.

"Hmm?" Marguerite asked, distracted. She was sitting before her small looking glass, restlessly moving combs and jars about though she was meant to be dressing her hair. She would never be ready for the banquet in time if she carried on like this! Then she would have to go down in her chemise and stays. "What do you think?"

The maid examined the jumble of garments, at last holding up a skirt and bodice of silver-and-white satin. "This one, mistress! And the gold tissue sleeves."

It was one of Marguerite's best outfits, with the trim worked in a flower pattern of tiny crystals and silver-gilt embroidery, and she had meant to save it for the end of their English stay. But she remembered Dona Elena's pretty attendants, her vow to see Nicolai married to one of them. It aroused in Marguerite a fierce, irrational yearning to out-pretty them all, to capture Nicolai's gaze and hold it only to herself. To never surrender it to some Spanish ninny, who might indeed make a fine, sweet wife, but who could never keep his interest for long.

"*Abruti!*" she cursed, throwing down a comb so hard one of the delicate teeth snapped. What was wrong with her tonight? She didn't *want* Nicolai's attention. Indeed, those unearthly blue eyes watching her just made her task that much harder. And it was nothing to her if he married fifty featherbrained Spanish girls. A hundred, a thousand!

Marguerite pressed her hands to her temples, feeling the throbbing veins just under her skin. She had sometimes heard of François's spies going mad under the unceasing pressure of their work, turning into raving lunatics who had to be locked away because they no longer knew friend from foe. Was that what was happening to her?

"*Non*," she whispered.

"Mistress? Is aught amiss?" the maid asked, her voice full of concern. Perhaps she did not often see ladies throw small tantrums, as the placid, polite English queen kept everyone under such control.

"Nay, I think I am just tired," Marguerite answered steadily. "The white will do very well. You have a good eye."

As the maid laid out the garments, Marguerite reached for her bottle of perfume. It was a special scent, blended for her by the royal perfumer. Her father used to tell her how her mother wore the fragrance of springtime lilies all the time, so Marguerite wore it, too. Its fresh sweetness seemed to revive her now, quiet the rush of her blood.

She *was* tired, that was all. The long journey, and now this unceasing round of activity. She could scarcely draw breath, let alone think. And Nicolai was just an unexpected complication.

She had to confess she did not understand him, could not

decipher him at all. She, who prided herself on her knowledge of people, her ability to discover what motivated them, what they craved, and then using that for her own ends. She had no idea of what Nicolai desired, what brought him here to Greenwich. For all his lightness, his seeming good humour, he had depths she could not read.

Unless he was just here for the Spanish ladies…

The maid held up the white satin skirt, and Marguerite left the looking glass and the mess she had made of her toiletries to let her fasten it over the petticoats, the quilted silver underskirt. Marguerite stood still as the maid adjusted the bodice, the stiff silver stomacher, and tied on the delicate gold sleeves.

Every person had weaknesses, desires. Every person had a price. Nicolai Ostrovsky's was just harder to find—and surely far more expensive—than most. He had to be up to something—no one would come all this way for the sake of mere friendship. To leap into the fray of Henry, François and Emperor Charles just because a friend asked? Absurd!

Non, he had some agenda, and the Spanish were surely part of it. She just had to be patient and steady, and she would find what his motives were. What price he asked.

To do that, she would have to be very careful. No more temper tantrums. And no more touching his hair! It was clear she could not trust herself in that direction.

She fastened her silver brocade shoes, and let the maid settle the nimbus-shaped headdress over her smooth hair. It was made of stiffened silver satin, embroidered with crystals and pearls that sparkled in the candlelight. The effect was of an angel's halo, shimmering atop her pale hair.

It was a good fashion choice the maid had made, Marguerite thought, examining herself in the looking glass. Who would suspect an innocent, shining angel of any subterfuge?

Except perhaps Nicolai himself. For had she not compared *him* to an angel? And he was full of prevarication, of feints and dodges.

Marguerite opened her jewel case and took out a piece she rarely wore but always treasured, a large, square-cut diamond on a thin silver chain. Like the essence of the perfume, it had been her mother's. Tonight it would give her courage.

When the doors opened on the banquet hall, a gasp went up. Marguerite stood on tiptoe, peering around Claudine's shoulder to see that the arrangement of the tables was changed. Rather than two long, straight tables, French and Spanish, on either side of an aisle, they were arranged as a large horseshoe, facing the king's dais.

"My beloved guests!" King Henry boomed, striding toward them like a purple velvet-clad bull, all hearty enthusiasm and good fun. He held Princess Mary by the hand, clad in a matching purple gown. Her large eyes were wary in her pale face.

"Welcome to our feast," Henry went on. "It is much deserved after all our hard work this day. As we are united in the great cause of peace, so must we be united at the banquet table. My servants will show you each to your seats. We can no longer be divided!"

A murmur of speculation rose up, mutters of excitement and protest. "How can one know one's proper place, in such an arrangement?" Claudine said, gesturing angrily toward the rounded table.

"Just play along with the English king's whims, *chère,*" her husband answered through gritted teeth. "It will be over soon enough."

Marguerite watched with interest as they were each led

away to their assigned seats, men and women, French, Spanish, and English alternating. This could serve her purposes very well indeed! An easy way to chat with the enemy, much like her stroll with Dona Elena. Simple, informal, completely unsuspicious.

Plus, it would get her away from Father Pierre, who appeared to have assigned himself as her official escort, or perhaps guard, while they were at Greenwich. His silent presence at her side, the rustle of his black robes, his strange watchfulness, was becoming an irritant.

She waved to him as he was led away, protesting, to a place at the far end of the horseshoe. A page took Marguerite to a seat at the middle curve, where she was between Roger Tilney and Dona Elena's husband, the Duke of Bernaldez. Dona Elena, across from them, greeted her happily, telling her husband of their afternoon walk by the river.

"And she listened to me prattling on about Marc, and about how you and I met, *mi corazon,* with nary a complaint!" Dona Elena said. "Such great patience."

"Not at all, Dona Elena," Marguerite answered. "I enjoyed our meeting very much. It can get lonely, being in a strange country, and your wife, Don Carlos, is so very amiable."

He gave her a cordial smile, and Marguerite saw that he matched his wife for fine looks and kind eyes. Despite the stark formality of his black velvet clothes and thick white hair and beard, his glance was most gentle when he looked at Dona Elena. "She is indeed amiable, Señorita Dumas, and I am grateful she has found a new friend here. It is not easy for her to be so far from her son at this time. I'm happy for any distraction you can provide for her. Perhaps you would do us the honour of joining us for a small card party in our apartment after the banquet?"

"Oh, yes, do say you will come, Señorita Dumas," Dona Elena urged. "It is only a few friends for a hand of primero, and will be much quieter than these great feasts. I would enjoy knowing you better."

"*Merci,* Dona Elena. I happily accept your invitation."

That was even easier than she expected. Marguerite sat back, satisfied with her progress. Then she felt a sharp, stabbing prickle on the back of her neck, like a sewing needle jabbing at her skin. She laid her fingers over the spot, under her hair, and glanced down the table to find Nicolai watching her.

For an instant, she caught him unaware, and his mask of merriment was down. His face was hard and serious as he looked at her, his eyes hooded. Even thus she could feel the force of them, like celestial blue daggers. She felt caught, pinned in place, unable to move or think. The entire vast, crowded hall vanished, narrowed to that one point—just him.

He grinned at her, breaking the spell, and lifted his goblet to her in mocking salute. As the room widened out again, she saw that he sat next to one of Dona Elena's ladies, a young woman who stared up at him with shining adoration writ large on her pretty, heart-shaped face.

Marguerite turned away, taking a large gulp of her wine. It was fine stuff, a golden sack from Provence, that even her father, who firmly believed only his home in Champagne could produce truly fine wine, would not have scorned. Yet she hardly even tasted it.

Across the table, Dona Elena caught her eye and gave her a wink. "My plan is working!" she mouthed.

She could say nothing else, though, for a procession arrived bearing an enormous subtlety for the courtiers' applause. It was a rendition of Greenwich Palace itself all in sugar and almond paste, its turrets and courtyards and windows, even a river of blue marzipan dotted with tiny boats and barges. Yet, like the wine, Marguerite did not fully appreciate the fine artistry. Her skin still prickled, and it took all her strength not to turn back to Nicolai. Not to stare at him like a dull-witted peasant girl.

The subtlety was presented to King Henry and Queen Katherine, and followed by more practical fare of meats, fish and stewed vegetables.

Roger Tilney laid a tender morsel of duck with orange sauce on her plate. "How are you enjoying your time in England thus far, Mademoiselle Dumas?" he asked.

Marguerite smiled at him, and speared the duck with her eating knife. She imagined the blade entering Nicolai's golden flesh, and it gave her a childish flash of satisfaction. "Very well, Master Tilney. You were right, Greenwich is endlessly fascinating."

"I am glad you find it so. I hear of nothing else but 'the beautiful Mademoiselle Dumas' everywhere I go!"

Marguerite laughed, reaching for a bite of the soft white manchet bread. "I doubt that. Perhaps *two* people have said that, including yourself. But I do hear that I have you to thank for one thing. Thank—or curse."

"I am most intrigued. Ladies have surely cursed me before, but rarely on such short acquaintance. What must I beg pardon for?"

"For recommending me to the Master of Revels for his pageants."

Tilney laughed. "I merely suggested that it would be a fine gesture to include some of the French ladies. Your beauty and sweetness recommended themselves."

"I am scarcely *sweet*, Master Tilney! In fact, I have often been told quite the opposite."

"Mademoiselle Dumas, methinks you protest too much."
He reached for a sugar wafer from one of the silver platters,
offering it to her with a flourish. "These rare delicacies could
not be more agreeable than you."

Marguerite accepted it with a smile, but the delicate flavor
turned dry in her mouth as she saw that Nicolai still laughed
with his pretty Spanish companion. *Her* sweetness no doubt
far surpassed any honey or sugar.

The banquet went on for what seemed like hours, a suc-
cession of artichokes in cream sauce, whole pigs stuffed with
spiced apples, swan and peacock, lamb dressed with mint, and
sweetmeats coloured pink and pale green and dusted with
more sparkling sugar.

As the wine flowed, the shrill laughter grew, until Marguerite could scarcely hear above the hum in her head. She
ate little and drank less, her smile growing more pained as the
revelry went on. Would her face simply crack, like one of the
statues in the garden? The marble of her skin corroding under
the bombardment of rain and laughter, flaking away until she
was nothing at all, just a handful of white dust.

At last, the platters and cloths were carried away, the
curved table pushed forward so there could be dancing in its
hollowed space. The musicians, who had been playing sweet
madrigals practically unnoticed during the feasting, struck up
a stately pavane. King Henry led the dance with his daughter,
her tiny hand in his giant paw.

Princess Mary was a graceful little thing, Marguerite
observed, pointing her toe, turning with a flourish of her
wrist. Her thin face was solemn with concentration, but her
father beamed down at her. Queen Katherine watched it all
with a serene smile. Would the princess truly marry the Duc
d'Orleans one day, and be a credit to the French royal family?

Marguerite could not yet say. It was early days yet in the treaty negotiations, and Princess Mary seemed so solemn, so— Spanish. But it could be an important, and long-lasting, alliance for François and Henry both.

As the music ended, Henry lifted Mary high, twirling her around as he laughed. "You behold here, gentles, my pearl of the world!" he announced. Amid applause, the princess bowed prettily.

"Pearl or not, girls need their rest," Queen Katherine said placidly. She took her daughter's hand as Henry lowered Mary to her feet. "I will take the princess to her apartment."

With the queen and her ladies gone from the hall, the music changed. From the slow, traditional pavane, the tempo increased to a lively saltarello, the newest dance to arrive from Italy. Marguerite watched closely as King Henry led a new lady on to the floor, and the other couples edged to the sides of the pattern to make room for them.

This, then, must be the famous Anne Boleyn, Marguerite thought. Lady Penelope Percy had been right, Mistress Boleyn was not beautiful. She was small and very thin, her complexion too sallow to ever aspire to the fashionable roses-and-lilies. Her hair was almost as black as the night sky outside, thick and straight, glossy, held back from her pointed face by a jewelled band. Her dark eyes flashed with a bright, naughty wit as she smiled up at the king.

But Marguerite saw that she possessed something deeper, more valuable than mere prettiness. She had style, and a light, lithe grace. She had self-possession and confidence. She looked at the gathering as if she owned it, as if they were all— Henry especially—hers to command. And the king in turn stared at her as if he would be commanded in an instant by anything she said.

Non, Anne Boleyn was not someone Marguerite would care to tangle with. She would just have to take care to steer clear of her. If such a thing was possible.

"That must be the English king's new harlot," Marguerite heard a low, hard voice murmur. She glanced up to see that the Duke de Bernaldez had moved to sit beside his wife, and Father Pierre had taken his place. The priest watched the dance with burning, disapproving eyes.

"I would not let King Henry hear you say such things," Marguerite warned. "You could find yourself sent back to Paris in a trice." Which might not be such a bad thing, Marguerite reflected, except for the bad light it would cast on the whole French party.

"And why is that? She will surely be gone soon enough, just like Elizabeth Blount and Mistress Shelton."

Marguerite reached for her goblet, sipping at the wine left in its gilded depths. "What do you know of *them?*"

"I know they are not at Court, even though Mistress Blount gave the king a son. They have no place here once the king tires of them. They were sent away, an embarrassment, and Mistress Boleyn will be, too. Just as her sister was before her." Father Pierre's voice was filled with low, bitter spite.

Marguerite watched the dancing. Mistress Boleyn was very deft; she leaped and ran, snapped her fingers, twirled in a graceful snap of her sky-blue silk skirts. And Henry stared, enraptured, his hands reaching for her as a praying supplicant would touch the Virgin's robe. "I am not so sure of that."

"Why, these English dances are only trotting and running," Don Carlos said, laughing. "Not at all graceful. We should show them what *true* dancing looks like, *querida.*"

Marguerite looked back to see Dona Elena hide her own

laughter behind her fan. "My dancing days are long done, I fear."

Her husband smiled ruefully. "As are mine." He pressed his hand to his wife's arm, a couple obviously united in deepest contentment.

Marguerite's heart gave a sour pang, and she longed to turn away from the whole room. All these damnably loving couples. Dona Elena stopped her with a word. "I am sure Señorita Dumas's dancing days are in their prime!"

"Oh, no, Dona Elena," she protested. "I do not care to dance tonight, and my skills in the saltarello are nothing to Mistress Boleyn's." Beside her, she felt Father Pierre's stare burning on her skin.

Dona Elena would not hear it, though. "Nonsense! They say you French ladies are the finest of all dancers, that you begin to learn as soon as you can walk." She waved her hand, calling, "Nicolai! Come here a moment, I need you."

The duke laughed, giving Marguerite a complicit shrug. "My wife, you see, will not be turned when she gets a thought into her head. If she wants to see you dance, *mademoiselle,* you will surely dance."

Marguerite had to laugh. Was that not what she always did? Dance when commanded? First for her father, then King François. Why not for Dona Elena?

But did it have to be with Nicolai? She watched warily as he drew nearer, the abandoned Spanish girl taking his departure with a pretty little pout. He went down on one knee next to Dona Elena, smiling up at her. Marguerite saw, though, that he was also cautious, his blue eyes shadowed.

"I am at your command, as ever, Dona Elena," he said gallantly. "What is your desire? Shall I fetch oranges from Madrid? Cinnamon from the Indies? Pearls from the depths of the seas?"

Dona Elena laughed merrily, patting his cheek with her soft hand. "Perhaps later! For now, I have a far simpler task, one I think you will enjoy."

"Merely name it, my duchess, and it is yours."

"You must partner Señorita Dumas in the next dance. I want to see her dance, and there is no more skilled a partner than you."

Marguerite remembered Nicolai on his tightrope, the light, effortless movements of his bare feet, the powerful contraction of his lean body as he leaped in a backwards arc. *Oui,* he would be a skilled dancer indeed. She shivered as she imagined his steps guiding hers, his touch on her body. The friction and caress as he lifted her. Could she trust him?

Could she trust *herself?*

Nicolai glanced at her from the corner of his eye, as unreadable as a cat. "It would be my pleasure to dance with Mademoiselle Dumas, if she will have me as a partner," he said.

Dona Elena smiled with obvious satisfaction, like a soft, devious kitten who had just filched a dish of cream. That was what the entire Spanish contingent was like, then—a pack of cats, sly, changeable, beautiful, untrustworthy.

As Nicolai came around the long table, Father Pierre suddenly seized her arm in a hard grasp. Marguerite stared at him, startled. He was so silent she had almost forgotten he was there, lurking beside her.

"You should not be so involved with these people, *mademoiselle,*" he hissed. "They are not what they seem!"

Marguerite tried to laugh lightly, tried to extract her arm from his dry, fevered touch. What had possessed him? True, she did not care at all for his intent stares, but he had never *grabbed* her before. "La, Father Pierre, I am only dancing with the man! I am not running away to Madrid with him."

Though, at that moment, fleeing this place, all these people with their hidden agendas, for the sunny dustiness of faraway Spain was tempting. She wrenched her arm away just as Nicolai reached her side, and gratefully accepted his hand. He led her to the edge of the floor, where they waited for the saltarello to end. The king and Anne Boleyn were lost to sight now amid a press of dancers, a shifting constellation of bright silks and flashing feet. The thunder of stamping and clapping.

"Who is that skeletal young man?" Nicolai asked.

Marguerite glanced back at Father Pierre, who still watched her, and shivered. He *did* look rather skeletal, like a figure in an old *memento mori* painting, death come to the banquet. Pale and solemn, an ever-present reminder of duty and fate.

As if she needed *him* to remind her she was damned! She knew it every moment.

"Father Pierre LeBeque," she answered. "He is one of Bishop Grammont's attendants."

"He seemed most reluctant to let you go, though I can scarcely blame him."

"I do not know what he wants," she said impatiently. She turned resolutely away from the priest, fiddling with a ribbon at her sleeve. She had to keep her fingers busy, to prevent them from reaching instinctively for the beckoning golden flame of Nicolai's hair. It rippled down his back like a smooth, bright banner, warm as the summer sun after a long winter.

But his eyes were so, so cool.

"I am sorry Dona Elena importuned you," she said. "I told her I did not care to dance tonight."

Nicolai shrugged. "As the duke said, once she has a thought in her head you will never get it out again. Besides, it is no great hardship to dance with the most beautiful lady at the banquet."

Marguerite laughed, ridiculously pleased at the gallant, empty compliment. "More beautiful than your Spanish companion? She seemed so very fascinated by all you had to say."

"You noticed that, did you? How very observant you are, *mademoiselle*."

"I like to know all things about all people."

"An ambitious goal indeed. And yes, Señorita Alva is quite pretty."

"Dona Elena told me how convinced she is that a fine wife and home would surely add greatly to your happiness, Monsieur Ostrovsky."

Nicolai gave a startled laugh. "She confides in you already, does she? You do have a gift for drawing people in."

"We took a stroll by the river this afternoon. I think that Dona Elena would not be a difficult person to 'draw in' by anyone. She seems a very sweet-natured lady, so open and artless. Perhaps it was the convent that made her so?"

"Ah, Mademoiselle Dumas, and here I thought you knew better. The people who appear the most artless are usually the most dangerous of all."

The music ended and the floor cleared, sets forming for the next dance. Once again, King Henry and Mistress Boleyn were at the head. Nicolai led Marguerite to their places at the end of the line.

But she had to ask one more thing before the steps of the dance parted them. "Will you marry your Señorita Alva, then?"

Nicolai laughed. "Mademoiselle Dumas, marriage is not for such people as you and me. Another lesson I thought you had learned."

The music began, and he blew her a kiss from his fingertips. Marguerite could vow she felt it land softly on her cheek, where he had kissed her earlier.

The dance was a passamezzo, a livelier version of the pavane and much less dignified. Henry and Anne clasped hands and twirled down the line, all the other couples peeling off after them. Marguerite's hand reached out for Nicolai's, and they, too, spun away.

The steps were quick—as the duke said, prancing and trotting. Marguerite hopped and swirled around Nicolai, until his hands caught her about the waist and lifted her from the floor, spinning her around and around. The crowd shifted and blurred, a humid, wild tangle, like a dream. Marguerite laughed helplessly, leaning her hands on his strong shoulders as he lifted her higher and ever higher. Surely, with his touch she could fly!

It was even better than running away to Madrid. This was leaving the ugly, deceptive earth altogether, free of everything but his touch, which kept her safe.

At last he lowered her back to the floor, grounding her, yet she still felt as light as the earth itself.

Yes, he *was* a fine dancer, just as she suspected he would be. He turned and moved her so easily, she was hardly aware she moved at all. The banquet hall, the other dancers, even all that awaited her when the music ended, disappeared.

The music built and built, faster and faster, the lines growing tighter and closer until at last the great finale arrived. Nicolai lifted her again, spinning her until she gasped dizzily, laughing in sheer delight. She stared down at him, at his smile, his glowing face. Had she thought his eyes cool? Nay, they burned with the light of a dozen suns, and she basked in their heat.

The song ended in a crash, and Nicolai lowered her for the

last time, slowly, slowly, their bodies in a delicious friction of satin on velvet, flesh on flesh. In the rush of the crowd, Marguerite pressed her forehead to Nicolai's shoulder, inhaling the heated scent of him, her breath tight in her throat.

She had the fearful sense that, if she let go of him, she would fall.

His hands held on to her arms, strong and solid, warm through the thin silk of her sleeves. She felt the rise of his chest as he breathed, and her own breath moved in unison with his. For this one, ephemeral moment, she sensed what it was to have something to cling to when the cold winds of the world howled.

But then the moment was gone. Nicolai stepped back, and the winds swept around her again. Marguerite threw her shoulders back, held her head high, resisting the urge to wrap her arms tightly around herself against that icy hollow in her belly.

Nicolai did not smile, did not even really look at her, gazing somewhere above her head. "Shall I take you back to your seat, *mademoiselle?*" he asked tightly.

Marguerite shook her head. She couldn't face Father Pierre just yet, nor even Dona Elena with her sweet smiles. "I cannot breathe in here," she murmured. "I think I shall walk outside for a moment."

"Let me go with you."

She shook her head again. He was part of her confusion, the very worst part! When he was near she could not think clearly. She could not be the Emerald Lily, cold, merciless. "You should return to Señorita Alva."

Nicolai laughed. "In truth, Mademoiselle Dumas, I cannot catch my breath in here, either. There are far too many people, too many wine fumes. And I would not like to encourage

Dona Elena where any of her ladies are concerned. Please, at least let me see you safely to your lodgings."

Marguerite longed to protest, to run away, but she feared her legs would not carry her. She felt lightheaded, and so very sad. She nodded, and he took her hand in his and led her through the milling, laughing crowds. The press of people, the roil of their drunken chatter, King Henry's loud bellow—it was all too much. It was her world, the one she had fought so hard to belong to, make a place in, but tonight she couldn't bear it.

What was wrong with her? Surely she just needed fresh air. Needed to clear her muddled head and regain her sense of purpose.

Maybe the only way to do that was by pushing Nicolai Ostrovsky into the Thames!

As they emerged from the banquet hall into the chilly night, Marguerite chuckled at the image of Nicolai cartwheeling into the river. Vanishing under the waves, leaving her to be as she was before, whole and cold and untouchable. The only trouble was, he might very well drag her in with him.

"And what makes you laugh so, *mademoiselle?*" he asked, as they turned down one of the pathways, shining white in the starlight. They ducked behind a concealing hedge, away from curious eyes.

Marguerite shook her head. "Merely a jest of my own."

"I am glad to see you catch your breath enough to make jests."

She drew in a deep breath of the cold, smoke-tinged air. She was surprised to find that she *had* caught her breath, that her lungs were expanding, opening up so she could smell everything. The clear breeze, the chimney smoke, the frosty river, the flowers slumbering under the ground. The stones and grass and wine. Nicolai's scent, his hair and wrist and neck.

Her world tonight kept expanding and retracting in ways she could never have imagined. She remembered what it was to fly free in the dance, and now she twirled in a circle, her head tipped back to take in the night sky. The endless expanse of stars. She imagined herself soaring up into the endless blackness, free.

What had got into her tonight? The wine, the music? She could not fathom it. She could only twirl faster, her arms outstretched to take it all in.

The world would retract again soon enough, pull back inside to that one pinpoint that was her life—to deceive and defeat.

Nicolai laughed, catching her hands in his as she twirled. He tried to still her, but she would not let him. Instead, she pulled him into her circle, and they whirled and whirled until the sky and the palace and England itself were nothing but a buttery blur.

"Who is this mad creature?" he cried. Just like in the dance, he caught her around her waist, lifting her up and up until she flew into the sky. She lifted her hands as if she could grasp the very stars and pull them down to put into his beautiful hair.

"What has possessed you, Marguerite?" he said. "My wild *rusalka*."

"I *am* possessed," she gasped. She buried her fingers in his hair, the warm strands slipping silkily from her grasp. "Come, Nicolai, be mad with me. We shall have to be sane again soon enough."

"I fear one of us will have to be sane right now," he said, lowering her to her feet. "Or trouble such as we have never known in our very troublesome lives will descend on us."

"*Non, non,*" she said, still caught deep in the moon's spell. "Kiss me, Nicolai."

"Marguerite…"

She grasped his hair again, and drew him toward her. Their lips met, and there was no practice to it, no artifice. Just a hot, blurry melding of their mouths, their passionate needs, so long denied.

She remembered Venice, how for one fateful moment she lost herself in him there. Just as then, she fell into him, into that bright essence of him, drowning, overwhelmed. She could not pull away, could not reach for her dagger. She threw herself heedlessly into him, deeply, madly. She held onto him as if she would never, ever let him go. She was his captive, but he would be hers, too.

He tried to draw away, to resist her. She could feel it in the tension of his shoulders, the supple arc of his back. She refused to let go, though, and he surrendered with a groan, falling into her as she did him. His arms closed around her, drawing her close against him, so close she could feel every inch of his body, every lean muscle and sharp curve, the heavy press of his penis through her skirts.

His lips dragged from hers, tracing fiery kisses to her jaw, her throat, the tiny fluttering pulse where her blood burned so hot just above her diamond. The plump curve of her heartbeat, concealed by her bodice.

How she wanted him! Every bit of him, his beautiful acrobat's body, his laughter, his strength, his sex and, yes, his kindness, too. All that tenderness he showed Dona Elena and her son, she wanted it for herself. The terrible, desperate sense that it could never be hers, that it—he—was too good for her made her all the more desperate on this strange night.

She buried her fingers in his hair, pressing him closer to

her heartbeat, the very life of her. *"Mon ange, mon beau ange,"* she whispered. And she meant it. Only an angel, or the worst sort of demon, could make her forget everything as he did.

He went still, perfectly still, his lips to her breast, and just like that she felt his soul fly away from her. It was as if her voice broke their spell. She clung to him, as he did her, his arms around her waist, his lips moving to the curve of her neck, their breath mingling. They were nearly as close as a man and woman could be, yet he was gone from her.

"Will you kill me now, Emerald Lily?" he said roughly. He slid his clasp to her hand, drawing her arm straight as he peeled back her sleeve to reveal the small blade strapped to her forearm. She had forgotten it was there, forgotten all but his kiss.

Now, as she stared down at the polished steel, she felt everything again. The cold night, the hollowness at her centre. She heard the distant thunder of revelry from the banquet house, and remembered where she was.

She pulled her arm away, shaking the sleeve into place. "If I had wanted to kill you tonight, you would have been dead long ago."

"So, why am I not? What is it you want?" His Slavic accent, usually so faint, so lightly musical, was hoarser, rougher. He stepped back from her, wiping his lips with the back of his hand as if to erase the very taste of her.

Marguerite turned away, wrapping her arms tightly around herself. Her madness leached away, leaving her feeling brittle, angry. But angry at who, what? Nicolai—or herself?

She forced herself to laugh mockingly. "La, *monsieur,* I only desired a kiss! A kiss from a handsome man—is it so much to ask? So odd to you that it must be madness?"

He stood there in silence, just watching her as if to say he knew her too well now to believe that. To believe that her only motive could be a stolen kiss in the moonlight.

How *infuriating* he was, with those knowing eyes! How she wanted to kill him—or to weep.

But she would never give in to tears, especially not here and now. "I am sorry, *monsieur,* if I offended your modesty," she said teasingly. "I assure you it won't happen again. Now, shall we go back inside? I have an invitation to join Dona Elena for cards later."

He gave her a low bow, his hand flourishing in a gallant, theatrical gesture toward the palace. "By all means, *mademoiselle,* let us go play games—of cards." His voice lowered to a rough whisper, just loud enough for her to hear as she brushed past him, "But you know well this is not over."

Ah, yes, she knew that all too well. This, whatever it was, would not be over until one of them was dead.

Chapter Nine

The scene in the Duke and Duchess de Bernaldez's apartment was very different from that of the grand banquet hall. Indeed, it could almost have been taking place in an entirely different palace, Nicolai thought.

He gazed around the room as he strummed lightly at his lute, taking in all the people. The players in this little pageant. It was mostly the Spanish party, friends of the duke, the lilt of their Castilian accents soft above the music, the flicker of gilt-edged cards, the clink of golden goblets. Their laughter was gentle and muted, unlike the raucous banquet, the colours of their rich clothes subdued, glowing like ancient jewels. The whole room was dim, full of shifting shadows, hidden nooks that melted into the dark linenfold panelling.

Except for one spot of bright silver, where all the light in the room gathered. Marguerite Dumas. She sat at a table with Dona Elena and two of the Spanish gentlemen, her eyes demurely cast on to her cards, an untouched goblet of wine at her elbow. She never glanced toward Nicolai, not even the merest flicker. Yet that thin, shimmering, unbreakable cord that seemed to bind them since the moment they met tightened between them.

"How do you find England thus far, Señorita Dumas?" one of the men asked.

Marguerite smiled. "Very cold, *señor.*"

The others at the table laughed. "And not just the weather, *si?* The people are so strange, so rough."

"Queen Katherine is very charming," Dona Elena protested. "She has been most welcoming to my ladies and me, and her hospitality cannot be faulted."

"Ah, but she is Spanish, is she not, my love?" her husband said from the next table. "The daughter of our own sainted Queen Isabella. Of course she will be charming and gracious! It is in her blood."

"If not for her," one of Dona Elena's ladies said, "this place would be quite unbearable. They do not correctly observe etiquette. They do not even dance properly!"

"Poor Princess Mary," another lady said. "Her mother does her best to raise her properly, I am sure, but to be trapped in such a barbaric place…"

"With women like that Boleyn creature, flaunting about," a man added. "In Spain, such a thing would never be."

"A virtuous and faithful queen would never be so disregarded," Dona Elena agreed sadly. Then she brightened, laying down her cards. "Ah! A double six. I am in good fortune tonight."

"And you, Señorita Dumas?" one of the men asked.

Marguerite shook her head. "Alas, I have not Dona Elena's luck! The cards are against me." She fanned her losing hand out on the table, studying their configuration wistfully. Her gaze lifted, meeting Nicolai's across the room for only a moment. A quick flash, but long enough for him to see the hollow ache deep in those sea-green pools.

It seemed she found fortune against her tonight, in more

than just cards. He remembered the mad fairy creature in the garden, twirling under the moon, arms outstretched to take in all the world had to offer. He remembered her lips on his, her hands grasping at his body, hungry, passionate, desperate.

It awakened an answering desperation in him, too, a feeling like a drunken craving deep inside. He wanted her, *needed* her, and not just her beautiful body, the fragile, fleeting allure of a lovely face. Her secrets, too. Her true soul, hidden so deep beneath deception and double-cross. He did not understand her, but he wanted to, so very much. And, for one moment in that winter garden, he felt he came so close.

Now, her gaze dropped back to the cards, and she laughed merrily. The gossamer cord slackened, and she was an opaque mystery again.

Surely he would never know what madness came upon her, upon them both, in the garden. She would kill him if she could, yet that cold fact never lessened the flame of pure need that seemed to flare up whenever they were near each other.

He would just have to take care *not* to come near her.

She was obscured from his sight by a line of pages bearing platters laden with more wine and fresh sweetmeats. Suckets of fruit in syrup, marchpane, jellies, "kissing comfits" made of sugar fondament, all to fortify the hungry gamblers.

"Nicolai!" Dona Elena called. "Would you sing for us?" She turned to Marguerite. "Señorita Dumas, Señor Ostrovsky has the loveliest voice, a veritable Orpheus. Yet he has rarely favoured us with it on this journey."

Marguerite smiled at her, not looking at Nicolai. "I hope that this will be an occasion for a song, then. I adore music, and have missed it sorely since I left Fontainebleau."

"I knew it," Don Carlos said. "You French could never be as cultured as the Spanish, *señorita,* but you do share our love of fine music."

Marguerite laughed. "Unlike our English hosts?"

"Do the English compose any good songs at all?" Señorita Alva asked, wrinkling her pretty nose. "Surely the queen must listen to some in her own apartments, but I have heard little but *noise.*"

"Do you know of any fine English songs, Monsieur Ostrovsky?" Marguerite said, looking to him at last. Her eyes were no longer sad and hollow, just flat and icy. Unreadable as a deep green forest. "You have travelled so much, I hear, you must know much of other lands and their music."

Nicolai shrugged. "Perhaps I know *one* fine English song, yet I could not say if it would please you, Mademoiselle Dumas."

"Oh, la, I am not so difficult to please as all that! A goblet of wine, some sweets…" She held up her bowl of suckets, skewered with a long, forked sucket spoon. "A melodic song from a handsome man, and I am most content."

"You see, Nicolai, you cannot disappoint our fair guest," Dona Elena said. "She is a homesick stranger in this cold land, just as we are."

"And music is the universal language to warm any chilly night," said Marguerite.

"I would never wish to disoblige *two* lovely ladies," Nicolai answered. "If it is an English song you desire, 'tis an English song you will have."

Nicolai tuned his lute again, strummed a few chords, standing as he began his song. The words were only half-remembered, a poem by Sir Thomas Wyatt, who, like Nicolai, had led something of a nomadic life. They had caught Nicolai's fancy and he set them to music, only for his own amusement. He had never sung them for an audience until now.

And truly it seemed only an audience of one. Marguerite's steady gaze followed him as he strolled around the room, stopping beside this lady and that while really he sang only to *her.*

"'And wilt thou leave me thus, that hath loved thee so long in wealth and woe among? And is thy heart so strong as for to leave me thus? Say nay, say nay!'"

Marguerite propped her chin in her cupped hand, wine and sweetmeats seemingly forgotten as she watched him. Her face was bland, serene, she gave naught away, yet she did not turn from him. And, deep in her eyes, there was spark like a ray of light in that ancient forest.

"'And wilt thou leave me thus, that hath given thee my heart never for to depart, neither for pain nor smart? And wilt thou leave me thus? Say nay, say nay!'"

He smiled at Señorita Alva as he rounded her table and she giggled back, but he ended his song next to Marguerite. Her shoulders tensed warily beneath the white satin of her gown, yet she did not turn away.

"'And wilt thou leave me thus, and have no more pity on him that loveth thee? Alas thy cruelty! And wilt thou leave me thus? Say nay, say nay!'"

Nicolai strummed out the last of his tune, a soft flurry that echoed the "say nay, say nay," and the song died away. He bowed amid applause, his watchful gaze never leaving Marguerite.

"Well, *mademoiselle,* what say you to my song?" he asked. "Did it please you?"

She paused for a long moment. "Perhaps there is *one* fine English song. When it is sung by a Muscovite."

There was a wave of laughter, a round of more wine. "Perhaps you would favour us with a French song, Señorita Dumas?" Dona Elena asked. "I am sure you must have a pretty voice."

"Not as pretty as Monsieur Ostrovsky, I fear," Marguerite said. "I would make a poor showing after him, especially as I am rather weary. I would be most happy to sing for you on another occasion, though, if I am given a Spanish song in return."

"Another time, then, Señorita Dumas. We will look forward to it," Dona Elena said kindly. "Nicolai, will you escort Señorita Dumas to her chamber? We have kept her too long tonight."

"Oh, no, Dona Elena, one of the pages will light my way back," Marguerite said. "It is not far, and I would not wish to deprive you of Monsieur Ostrovsky's interesting company. Thank you for your kind hospitality tonight, I have greatly enjoyed it."

With a graceful curtsy, a swirl of white-and-silver skirts, she was gone, led by one of the eager young pages. The chamber went back to its low hum of conversation, the soft flicker of new hands of cards being dealt. But to Nicolai it seemed that all the light had vanished, leaving only smoky, smudged shadows.

Dona Elena beckoned him closer. "She is very beautiful, is she not?" she whispered.

Nicolai smiled. "I think that can hardly be denied."

"Yet she seems so sad. She is an orphan, you know, with no one to look after her interests in this world."

Nicolai thought Marguerite more than capable of seeing after her own "interests." But Dona Elena was right about the sadness. Sometimes it seemed to cling to Marguerite like a winter mist, blurring and obscuring her real self, hidden behind that beauty, which was all anyone seemed to see. "It was kind of you to befriend her."

"And you, too, Nicolai? Your song tonight seemed to cheer her. Truly, *amado,* you are the most merry person I know!"

"Dona Elena, are you trying to matchmaker again?" Nicolai teased.

She laughed. "You could not marry a *French* woman! But everyone needs music, diverting company. Especially lonely young ladies—as long as it does not go too far."

Nicolai remembered Venice, his hand on Marguerite's naked thigh, his mouth on her breast, the smell and taste of her wrapping around his senses, driving him to lunacy. They had already gone past "too far"!

"I fear Mademoiselle Dumas could hardly escape my company," he said. "We are to work on a pageant together."

"Very good! I am sure it will be the finest ever seen in this dull place. Now, will you sing us another song? Señorita Alva seemed to enjoy the last one as well…"

Chapter Ten

Marguerite slipped the thin wire into the lock and, with a quick flick of her wrist, popped it upward. She felt the give of the mechanism as it parted, and the lock fell from the box's clasp.

Really, she thought. *These Spanish are surprisingly lax.* That lock was far too easy to pick. Could it be some kind of trap, a test? She glanced back over her shoulder, but the room was empty. Silent.

She had noticed this box during the card party, a plain, unadorned wooden chest of the sort often used to transport or store documents. It sat amid a welter of empty diplomatic pouches and blank sheets of parchment on a table near the window, too tempting to resist. It could not contain anything too secret; Don Carlos did not strike her as a fool. But any information at all could prove useful.

And Marguerite sorely needed a distraction from thoughts of Nicolai. When she went to lie down in her bed she could not sleep, for she kept hearing his song in her mind. *And have no more pity on him that loveth thee.*

Marguerite frowned as she slid the lock free and raised the

lid of the box. He was a talented actor indeed, for his words, his countenance, his entire being reflected the words as he sang, as if he truly knew what love was, what it could be. As if he alone possessed the secrets to all hearts.

She could never share that knowledge, for love was only a mystery, a puzzlement, to her. She had seen it only as a lie, a game, a flirtatious song with no meaning behind it. A hollow, shining little bubble.

And that was all Nicolai's poetry was, too. Yet his eyes imbued the sweet words with more…

"*Couilles,*" she cursed. The wire she still held bit into her hand as her fingers tightened over it, leaving a thin line of blood. Nicolai Ostrovsky was a distraction, and she had to forget him. Work was all that mattered.

Hastily wrapping her hand in a handkerchief so she wouldn't leave telltale spots of blood, she began to sort through the box. The papers appeared to be personal letters to Don Carlos and his attendants, as well as an inventory of the rich gifts brought for King Henry. She had been right, there was not much here to be of help to King François. All the information she gleaned as she surveyed the missives told her only what she already knew, that the Spanish were to stop the French alliance in any way they could. That they were allied with Queen Katherine, as always.

She quickly memorised a few useful titbits, and started to put them back carefully in the order she found them. But in the bottom she found one more letter.

Marguerite unfolded the parchment, soft from its journey, from having been read many times, even though the date written on the back indicated it had only been delivered yesterday.

"For the most exalted Duchess de Bernaldez—or should

I say Mother? I trust your journey was safe and England all you expected. May you and Don Carlos achieve all your ends and return home to meet your new grandson, Antonio Velazquez. Julietta was safely delivered…"

Ah, a letter from her son. For the first time, Marguerite felt she was intruding by reading those words. She started to refold the letter, when Nicolai's name caught her eye and she glanced at it again.

"…as I cannot be there to guard you myself, you must always continue to put your faith in Nicolai and trust him as you would me. I know I told you this before, when I sent him to you, but I will rest easier knowing he watches over you. My dearest Mother, you go into the lion's den at Greenwich, yet Nicolai's sword arm is strong, his mind shrewd. He saved my life, and Julietta's, too, or there would be no Antonio crying in his cradle this morning. Listen to his counsel and stay close to him, and with God's blessing we will all be together this summer."

Strong and shrewd. Truly he was both, the most formidable obstacle she had found in England. The Englishmen, like Tilney and his ilk, were blinded by her good looks and fine clothes, her sweet smiles. They did not suspect she was anything more than a French featherhead. And King Henry was too occupied by his diplomatic meetings and Mistress Boleyn to even look about him. Her face, the face she inherited from her beautiful courtesan mother, was always the best mask to hide behind.

Yet when Nicolai looked at her with those sky-blue eyes, she sensed that he saw more than her pretty façade. That his own life of masks enabled him to peer right through hers, to all the tangled, black ugliness beneath.

Why could he not just go away, back to Venice or Russia or—or anywhere but here?

Marguerite put the missive back in the box and slammed the lid. In the next room, Dona Elena's bedchamber, she heard a burst of laughter and chatter as maids came in to clean. It reminded her that she had lingered too long over the papers. She clasped the lock and dashed out of the room, silent on her tiptoes, skirts held close to her sides. Once in the corridor, she smoothed her hair and glided slowly away, as if she hadn't a care in the world and no reason to hurry.

It was quiet in this wing of the palace, aside from the servants airing the rooms and setting fires in the grates. The men were all in conference with the English king, and Dona Elena and her ladies walked in the gardens again. Marguerite had seen them set out from her window, and excused herself from Claudine to check this box while she had the chance. Marguerite doubted Claudine, embroidering with her attendants and snappish from morning sickness, missed her at all.

She started to turn back toward the French apartments, but realised she had no desire to sit placidly and sew with a woman who did not like her, who thought she dallied with her husband. Marguerite had listened to the other ladies giggle over the *démodé* English fashions until she thought she would scream from it. Whatever had come over her in the gardens last night—that wild madness that made her long to fly away into the sky—had not left her. Not entirely.

Rather than go to her room, she turned instead down the staircase and followed it until she was out the palace doors and into the garden once more. She did not wear a cloak or surcoat, only her black-and-gold velvet gown, but she did not feel the bite of the wind as she hurried along a gravel pathway.

There were not so many courtiers out this morning, just a few people whispering together as they strolled along. They watched her curiously as she passed, yet no one stopped her.

She feared she could not make polite conversation right now anyway.

She hardly knew where she was going, she just walked and walked, hoping that the exercise would burn away that strange restlessness. She rounded a corner of one of the tall, sculpted hedges, and found that her steps had led her to the theatre.

The doors stood half-open to the winter breeze, and she drifted toward them, as if compelled to move forward by some dream or spell. She didn't *want* to go in there. What if Nicolai waited, luring her to him with his tightrope, with a freedom she knew was not hers? But her steps wouldn't turn, and she soon found herself inside.

The splendid theatre, with its elaborate painted sky, its shimmering hangings, was silent and darkened. The only sound was a faint, distant hammering as Sir Henry Guildford's servants built new scenery. The air was chilly, smelling of new paint, sawdust, sweat and stiff satin. Like all places of night-time merriment, in the day it had a forlorn, shabby air, a deep loneliness that suited her strange mood today.

Marguerite shut the doors quietly behind her and crept deeper inside. Soon, this space would be a castle or a meadow, Mount Olympus or a heavenly cloud. She preferred it like this, quiet and empty, all its possibilities still ahead, still intact.

She tiptoed into Nicolai's little room. The rope was coiled in the corner, a few travelling chests stacked against the walls. Had she not just determined to stay away from Nicolai, that he was a distraction she did not need? Yet here she was.

He was not there, but she could vow that the smell of him lingered in the air, that clean, fresh herbal scent. The very essence of him.

Marguerite opened one of the chests, peering inside to

find thin, shining rapiers wrapped in a length of brown velvet. They were stage blades, of course, not as sharp and lethal as her own hidden sword and daggers, but dangerous enough if wielded correctly.

She remembered one afternoon in the Piazza San Marco, when she watched Nicolai and his troupe performing for a raucous Carnival crowd. It was a scene where an adventurous wife and her lover were confronted by the buffoonish husband. Nicolai was the lover, of course, and even masked, clad in close-fitting, multi-coloured motley silk, he radiated sexuality, bawdy good humour. All the comic wiles of the wife and lover did not turn away the angry husband, and Nicolai at last had to fight him. Perhaps with these very blades, he had parried and feinted, pricked and prinked, tumbling and leaping out of the increasingly clumsy husband's way.

At last the husband was defeated, frustrated, his black robes in rags, as the Arlecchino ran off with his wife. By then, every woman around Marguerite would have gladly shared the wife's fate.

Marguerite, though, now sympathised with the husband. She, too, was most thoroughly befuddled by Nicolai.

She drew out one of the blades, balancing its gilded hilt on her hand. The thin cut still stung a bit, but the hilt was light on her palm, well balanced, shimmering in the dusty light. She lifted the blade in *prima,* the first guard position, with her arm high to the right, palm facing out. She moved smoothly into *seconda,* the second guard position, palm down, arm at shoulder height. *Terza,* arm at waist level, palm to left.

Then she raised her arm again, lunging forward on the right foot, sword thrusting ahead. She imagined it plunged into Nicolai's maddening, confusing heart. The blade was light, and whistled in the still air as she sliced it across and stepped into a reverse pass, her right foot moving back, kicking her skirts out of the way.

"*Brava, mademoiselle,*" she heard Nicolai's Slavic voice say. She whirled around to find him standing just inside the doorway, arms crossed over his chest as he watched her intently. "You are very deft."

"I was trained by Signor Lunelli, the famous sword master from Milan," she answered. Her heart still pounded, and she remembered pretending it was *him* she stabbed at, his muscled chest that met her slicing blade. "But I fear I am out of practice, with these easy days at Greenwich."

"You? Ah, no, *mademoiselle.* I am sure you could never be—out of practice."

"Perhaps not any longer." She reached down and slid the tip of her sword beneath the blade that still lay on the ground. She caught it up, flipping it in one neat movement toward Nicolai.

He caught the hilt in his hand, reflexes sharp despite his lazy appearance. He gave her an amused half-smile.

Marguerite adjusted her stance, lifting her blade invitingly while also carefully situating her guard. "*En guard, monsieur.*"

Nicolai's smile widened, and he took up his own stance. At first they circled each other warily, blades poised, trying to gauge weaknesses, techniques, strengths. Marguerite's senses shimmered with tense awareness; it was as if time slowed around her, and she was attuned to every tiny flicker of his muscles. Every shift and movement and breath of his body.

There was a small noise outside their hidden room, the distant fall of a hammer. Nicolai did not turn, but she saw his eyes widen slightly and she took the perceived advantage. She moved in with a lunge and a low, straight thrust.

But he was *not* distracted. His blade came up in a smooth stop-thrust. Marguerite fell back, bringing her sword up to attack again.

She heard the echo of Signor Lunelli's voice in her head. *Remember, signorina, your male opponents will have two advantages over you—reach and strength. But you, you have speed and agility. Use them! And never lose your calm centre. That is fatal.*

She rose up on the balls of her feet as if dancing, her blade flashing in delicate, swift feints, faking her line of attack. Speed and agility—he would think she was one place, as she delivered quick, small blows until she moved into compound attack.

Yet Nicolai did not fight as she expected. He parried her blows, his blade shifting as hers did, almost imperceptibly. He had a lean, easy strength she could not match, and that infuriating half-smile never left his lips.

Marguerite felt her calm centre, so essential to Signor Lunelli's instructions, melt away under a hot flare of anger. She rushed in close to his strong side, wrapping her weaker arm about his sword arm and twirling her body around to slide her blade into place. She had to do it quickly, before he realised her impulsive plan and dropped his sword to grapple with her. Then all her agility could never stand up to that strength.

The tip of her blunted blade just touched him when he *did* drop his sword, his fingers closing tightly over her wrist, like an iron vise.

"*Chert poberi!*" he growled. "You *do* fight dirty."

"*Oui.* But I always win."

"Almost always."

His grip tightened on her wrist, not painful but numbing, until the blade fell from her nerveless grasp to clatter on to the floor. Marguerite cursed herself for forgetting all her training, for getting too close to him, allowing him to gain the advantage. That speed and agility had availed her naught in the end, it was too bound up in that boiling anger.

He didn't let go of her wrist, and she stared up at him, her breath quick. His breath, too, was hard and uneven, his pulse thrumming through his veins and into hers, their heartbeats mingling. She still stared up at him into the glow of his eyes. His face was expressionless, yet she saw the faint flush of his cheeks, beneath the sun-bronzed colour of his Italian life. A muscle ticked along his jaw. So, he was not unaffected by their nearness, by whatever this was that flowed between them so inexorably.

Marguerite stretched up on tiptoe and pressed her lips to his, unable to resist for an instant longer. She had to taste him, feel him. Maybe then she could decipher this mysterious force that turned her cold, careful life tip over tail. Exorcise his spell. But she made another mistake, for his kiss only bound her tighter in the silken noose of anger, lust and painful need.

His lips opened beneath hers, and he let go of her wrist, freeing her to wrap his arms around her, to draw her closer and closer. If she was to be his prisoner, he would be hers, too, the two of them bound together as they tumbled down into the abyss. He groaned, a low, hoarse sound she felt deep inside of her. Their tongues met and clashed as their swords had, a humid blur that erased everything else. There was only Nicolai, the dark taste of him, the heavy press of his hard arousal against her skirts.

Not breaking their kiss, Marguerite snatched at his clothes, tearing the fastenings of his doublet, the thin linen of his shirt until her touch met naked, smooth, hot skin.

Nicolai dragged his lips from hers, pressing a kiss to her temple, her cheek. "Marguerite," he groaned. "*Dorogaya.* What are we doing?"

"I don't know," she whispered, her fingers playing lightly over his bare chest, the uneven pounding of his heart. She traced a circle over the flat disc of his nipple, and felt his breath suck in. "I tried to fight it, deny it. But you have some strange spell, you beautiful demon, some magic…"

He gave a harsh laugh, and took her hand to drag it down over his hard penis, sheathed in the rough cloth of his hose. "Is *this* magic?"

She laughed, too, running her touch over his throbbing erection, feeling it strain for her caress. "Do you not think so?"

"You are the one with the spell, *vedma!*"

"What does that word mean?"

"It means you are a witch. A sorceress, come from the dark fairy realms to torment us poor mortals. You tried to kill me once in the midst of passion."

Marguerite swallowed hard, remembering Venice, her dagger arcing toward that heartbeat. The thought of his life-blood spilling out, of the warm flesh she now caressed turning ice-cold, made her shiver.

She stepped back from him, reaching up to unlace her sleeves and draw them off, dropping them at her feet in a black velvet puddle. "I have no hidden daggers today," she said, loosening the thin sleeves of her chemise. "Not there—not here."

She clasped the hem of her overskirt and petticoat, drawing the heavy fabric up, up, until his narrowed gaze could take in the length of her legs, clad in silk stockings and jewelled garters. She drew it up farther until he could see the shadow of her womanhood, damp with desire.

Still holding her skirts with one hand, she reached up with the other to free her hair from its gilded veil, shaking the silvery length free over her shoulders.

"I will not try to kill you this day, Nicolai," she said. "I give you my word. Now, will you kiss me again?"

In answer, Nicolai gave a low growl, and lunged forward to catch her around her waist. As their lips met again, he lifted her high, twirling her around to press her up against the wall. Marguerite wrapped her legs tightly about his hips, drawing him into the curve of her body. His hose abraded the soft skin of her thighs, but she didn't care or even notice. She just wanted him closer, closer.

He trailed a ribbon of kisses to her throat, biting and licking at the curve where her neck met her shoulder, the hollow where her pulse pounded. She let her head fall back against the wall, offering him all she had, all she was.

He tugged her low-cut French bodice down to bare her breasts. Her nipples strained for his kiss, aching.

"You are so beautiful," he murmured. "So very beautiful."

She had heard those words so often, but never, not until this moment, had she believed them to be true. Perhaps she *was* beautiful—in his eyes.

He could not see her black-spotted soul. "Not as lovely as you, *mon ange,*" she whispered.

He captured her nipple between his lips, rolling it, biting gently, teasingly, before he at last gave her what she craved, longed for, and drew it deep into his mouth.

Marguerite found she could stand the intense need, the fire, no longer. She pushed him back until her breast was free of his kiss, until she could touch her feet to the earth. Then she clasped him by the shoulders, moving his unresisting body to the floor.

He watched her closely in the dim light as she straddled him, reaching out with desperate hands to strip him of his doublet and shirt, to tug at the lacings of his hose.

"Marguerite…" he said roughly.

"*Non!*" she answered. "Don't say anything, Nicolai, not now." Words would just break the witch's spell, and she did not want to awaken. Not yet.

He lay back, his hair pooling around him like the golden allure of the sun. His eyes glowed as he stared up at her, wary and lustful in equal measure.

Marguerite wanted to erase that wariness, to find only passion, a deep need to match her own. She swooped down on him, like a little, lethal kestrel after her prey, trailing her mouth over his throat and naked chest, tasting the clean salt of his skin. Breathing in all his heat and life until she found her own soul stir.

As she kissed him, his fingers moved through her hair, wrapping the strands over his chest, binding them together. Marguerite smiled against his shoulder, and reached down to free the heavy, throbbing length of his erect penis into her hand. It was weighty under her gentle touch, and he shuddered as she ran her fingers up and down its iron-satin, veined shaft. She carefully balanced his balls on her palm, her embrace tightening with a threat—or promise.

In answer, Nicolai grasped her waist, rolling her beneath him in one quick, smooth movement. He pulled her skirts out of his way, parting her legs as his thumb slipped inside her wet, welcoming folds.

"*Oui, oui,*" she groaned. She would surely burst into flame at his touch! She spread her legs farther, urging him over her, into her, urging him to make her his. Her eyes closed as her head fell back, her body tense as a bowstring as he eased himself into the very core of her.

Their joining was not slow or gentle. They came together with the force of a summer storm, fast, violent, desperate. He thrust into her, and Marguerite wrapped her legs about his back, keeping him inside her as the delicious friction, the heat, built and built. The world turned red and bright orange around her, and a high-pitched sound grew in her ears. Greater and greater, higher and higher.

She exploded in climax, a shower of bits of the sun and stars, too bright. Too much.

Above her, around her, Nicolai shouted out, "*Moya doro-gaya!*" Marguerite grasped his hair, clutching at the tangled strands as his back arched. At the very last instant, he drew out of her body, spilling his seed on the floor. Then he collapsed beside her, their limbs entwined.

Marguerite still held on to him, running her trembling fingers through the bright strands of his hair, smoothing them, spreading them over her breasts and throat. How heavy she felt, as if she could sink down into the earth itself and never be seen again. She was weighted, replete.

And not at all sorry. Remorse would surely come later. At this moment, she felt something she had never known before.

Contentment.

Chapter Eleven

Nicolai slammed the leather ball against the curved wall of the tennis court, his racket arcing through the air with a sharp, swift whine. Again and again he swung, practising his serve, his arm twisting back and overhand, until his shoulder muscles shrieked with the ache and sweat poured down his back. His shirt clung to his damp skin, yet still he swung, beating at the helpless ball in the empty, echoing court.

When he came here, he was sure this would be the one place at Greenwich he could be alone, could sweat out his anger and frustration. Everyone else was in the banquet hall, feasting and drinking yet again. Including Marguerite.

At the thought of her, the mere breath of her name, Nicolai swung the racket harder, the "crack" as loud as a cannon. Yet still she would not be banished. That image of her, sprawled out on the theatre floor with her breasts bare, her hair spread around her, her legs open to him, smiling up at him as she welcomed him into her body—it was all still there. Burned into his memory, his senses. The way she smelled, of lilies and clean water. The smooth feel of her skin, satiny and warm.

The way her green eyes glittered, like the emerald she was named for, as she whispered his name.

Chert poberi! He did not trust her. What was the woman about? Did she try to kill him with sex now, as she could not with her dagger? If so, she was doing wondrously well.

He still hardly knew what had come over them there in the theatre. He had lusted for women before, of course, desired them with what he thought was overwhelming passion. He loved women, loved their laughter, their soft voices, the clean sweetness of them, the complex, mysterious ways their minds worked. And often they loved him back.

But never in his life had he felt anything like what happened with Marguerite Dumas. One moment he sparred with her, his muscles moving in the practised way he employed in so many fights before. To give in to anger was the kiss of death in swordplay, especially with an icy, untrust-worthy opponent like the Emerald Lily.

But then the next minute it was as if his body was consumed by a great sun flare, his mind drugged, full of only her. Desperate need. Fully dressed, they copulated on the floor, their bodies bound together in a lust gone unfulfilled since Venice.

Yet why, then, did he still feel so very *frustrated?* So tied up in anger, tension?

He swooped up another hard leather ball from the bucket and slammed it against the wall. He imagined it was Marc Velazquez's head, cursing his friend for sending him into this snakepit of a palace. A snakepit ruled by an emerald-eyed viper, as alluring as she was dangerous.

"I am too old for this," he muttered.

"Oh, on the contrary," Marguerite's voice said from behind him, "only a man in the very prime of his life could wield a racket like that."

He spun around to see her standing in the doorway, outlined by the torchlight. The dishevelled, flushed woman who had fled the theatre after their lovemaking was no longer to be seen. She was again an elegant lady of the French Court in her rosy-red silk gown, her silvery hair parted in the middle and swept back beneath a jewelled band.

But her eyes shimmered with the dark light of memory. Her hand was tense where she braced it against the doorframe. That thin, delicate cord grew tense in the air between them, taut and quivering.

Nicolai tossed aside the racket, swiping his sleeve over his damp brow. His hair clung to his neck. "How did you find me?"

"Dona Elena asked me to discover what had become of you, and one of the pages told me of the 'mad Spaniard' in the empty tennis court," she said. "I did not take the time to explain the difference between Spain and Russia."

He gave a rough laugh. "It would seem a pointless exercise. What did Dona Elena want?"

"She was worried about you, and did not believe your excuses to avoid the banquet."

"She is surrounded by her attendants. I'm sure she can do without me for an hour. I will join her for the pageant after."

"'Tis true that King Henry's banquets seem to last far past the point where they are amusing," Marguerite said, taking a step closer. Her hands clasped at the fine fabric of her skirts, and she seemed uncharacteristically hesitant. "But I think she was concerned you might be ill."

He grinned at her. "I have never felt better, thanks to you, *mademoiselle.*"

She laughed, ducking her chin so her face was cast half in shadows. "I was glad of the excuse to escape the feast. All that noise, the stares…"

"The stares of your companion, the priest?" Nicolai said, remembering the thin, pale cleric who seemed to be her Court shadow.

"Father Pierre, yes. He is always warning me to beware of spending too much time with the Spanish. He says you are all not as you seem."

"That seems a pointless warning to someone like you."

Her head tilted quizzically. "Someone like me?"

"Someone who lives at Court."

"Hmm, yes. Surely your own life as a travelling player has prepared you well to be a courtier."

"The ability to pretend to be someone we are not is useful anywhere. To be able to shift and change whenever we desire."

"To deceive," she murmured.

Nicolai moved closer to her, reaching out to gently take her chin in his hand, lifting her face toward him, into the light. The shadows played over her fair skin, the slant of her cheekbones. She stared up at him solemnly, giving nothing away.

Yet she trembled under his touch, like a tiny captive bird trying to escape.

"Who are you, really?" he said softly. "I called you a fairy enchantress, a witch, and so you seem to be."

"I could not tell you."

"Because you do not trust me?"

She reached up to take his fingers in hers, bending her head to press a kiss to them. It was a soft, gentle salute, strangely sad. "Because I do not know."

She let him go, stepping back, easing away from him, from their situation. "I have to go back. I will tell Dona Elena you are well, and will see her at the pageant."

Then she spun around and dashed away, leaving her lily

scent, and her cryptic words, heavy in the air. Nicolai followed to the doorway, watching after her as she hurried into the night, a shimmering, silken figure, like the fairy he called her. She vanished not into some enchanted, misty realm, but into the well-lit, noisy banquet hall. Into her courtiers' life.

As Nicolai stared after her, a tall, thin shadow detached itself from the night and trailed behind her. An ominous crow flocking after the bright, trembling bird. Father Pierre.

So, Marguerite was far from the only French person with secrets tonight.

Marguerite sat on her clothes chest, her body erect, tense, as she listened to the palace around her. It was deep into the darkest part of the night, the sky outside her little window a purplish indigo. Almost everyone tucked inside Greenwich's stout walls slept. Claudine's chamber next door was silent.

But Marguerite could not sleep, could not even lie down on her turned-back bed. She was too restless, every sense humming with acute awareness of the world around her.

What had she meant when she told Nicolai she could not tell him who she was, because she did not know? Of course she knew who she was! She was Marguerite Dumas, the Emerald Lily. Faithful servant of France. Dependent on no one as she made her way through the world. It was all she had worked for, all she had wanted since she was fifteen years old.

Yet when she was near Nicolai, all that vanished. Her world shifted, cracked, reformed into something new and strange, something she did not recognise. When she was near him, these restless longings for she knew not what overwhelmed her.

And she did not know who she was.

Marguerite rose from the chest, drifting toward the looking glass. She wore only a sleeveless sleeping chemise, as thin and light as cobwebs, her hair loose over her shoulders. The glow from the one candle shone through the fine fabric, revealing the slender lines of her body, the high, erect, pink circles of her nipples. She was all white and silver, like a ghost in the night.

She hardly recognised herself. Surely she would just vanish like a wisp of mist, and no one would remember she was there at all.

Marguerite shrugged one long strand of hair back from her shoulder, staring at the tiny red mark just at the upper curve of her breast. Nicolai had left it there, his kiss on her skin a reminder of their wild sex on the theatre floor. A reminder of his touch, of the exploding need that overcame her.

It couldn't go on. He was a distraction from her work, and any misstep now could prove fatal. She was given this chance after her failure in Venice, this one last chance. She balanced on that acrobat's tightrope, wobbling, wavering, unable to move forward or back.

She had to decide which way to jump.

Marguerite spun away from the glass, reaching for her cloak before she could let caution overtake her. She swung the black velvet over her chemise, and left her chamber on silent, bare feet.

The corridors were silent, filled only with the soft snores of the pages on their pallets, the sputter of torches in their sconces. From behind some of the closed doors could be heard the cries and sighs of passion. No one stopped her as she crept down the stairs and through the labyrinthine halls, her hood up to cover her pale hair and conceal her face. Surely she was turning to mist already.

The wing housing the Spanish was just as deserted as the rest of the palace, though there were signs of an abandoned gathering in empty goblets and scattered cards, a lute in the corner. Marguerite tiptoed up to a door, half-hidden behind a tapestry, and reached down to test the latch. It was not locked, and clicked open at her touch. She slid inside, hardly able to breathe, and closed the door behind her.

Nicolai was not asleep. He lay propped up in his bed, a book open beside him, candlelight flickering over the tumble of the bedclothes. She could see that he was naked under the sheet, his skin glistening gold against the white linen, the thin fabric skimming lightly over the lines of his body. She shivered as she recalled the slide of that body against hers.

He frowned as he glanced up, one hand edging toward a bolster where she was sure a dagger was hidden. But he went still when she folded back her hood, his eyes widening as the light fell over her face.

There was surely a price for what she did tonight, Marguerite knew that well. She was willing to pay it.

Would he?

Nicolai sat straight up, watching her in the tense silence. The sheet fell back, revealing the lean, muscled contours of his body. The light glimmered on the fine blond hairs of his legs and arms, making him seem gilded, like an ancient idol.

She shrugged the cloak away, leaving it in a pool on the floor as she moved slowly toward the bed. She didn't know what he would do. Kill her? Kiss her? Laugh at her, and send her away? She would rather he plunged his dagger into her heart than do *that!*

He said nothing, just studied her with his unearthly eyes as she slowly climbed on to the mattress beside him. She reached out and gently pushed him back on to the tangle of sheets and velvet blankets.

"Marguerite…" he said tightly.

"I am not Marguerite tonight," she whispered. "I am your fairy enchantress."

She leaned over his taut body, her hair falling around them in a pale curtain, closing off the world. She touched the hollow of his throat with the tip of her tongue, feeling the pulse of his life, tasting the salt of the tiny bead of sweat that pooled there. He was so tense under her, like a drawn bow, but he leaned back, gave her her own way.

As she trailed kisses across his shoulder, she reached her fingers down to lightly trace the circle of his flat, brown nipple, which pebbled under her caress. Her tongue followed, darting out to lick before blowing on it gently. Ever so softly.

"An enchantress indeed," he groaned.

Marguerite laughed, revelling in the sudden wave of power that rushed through her. The heady, giddy pleasure. Her lips trailed along his chest, over his taut abdomen, soft, quick, teasing kisses.

At last her mouth closed over the throbbing length of his manhood. His fingers clasped in her hair, as if to push her away—or hold her closer. In that one, perfect moment, he was hers. And it was everything she wanted.

Chapter Twelve

Marguerite drowsed in Nicolai's loose embrace, lying on her side in his bed, curled back against him as she ran her fingertips lightly along his arm. From his wrist to his elbow and back again, until she twined her fingers with his and pressed his hand to her stomach.

There were old scars there from the horse's kicks, the cuts of the iron shoes, a tracery of rough red lines she had never let anyone see before. But now she let Nicolai touch them, his fingertips playing over them gently.

"What will you do when you leave England?" she asked quietly.

Nicolai chuckled, his warm breath stirring her hair. He drew her even closer into the heat of his body. "Why? So you can chase me when I go? Run after me across the continent until you kill me at last?"

"If I wanted to kill you, you would be dead tonight, Muscovite!" she said, kicking back at him. "Remember, I had your most precious organ balanced right in my hand."

He laughed, spinning her in his arms until her head rested on his shoulder. "How could I forget?"

Marguerite propped herself on her elbow, gazing down at his face in the sputtering candlelight. He was relaxed, laughing, so young. "I will not kill you in bed. I will face you fairly on a dueling field."

"Would you indeed, *dorogaya?*" He took her hand, kissing each fingertip in turn. He sucked her littlest finger into his mouth, laving it lightly until she shivered. "Well, you will not have to search for me very hard for our duel. I intend to stay in one place for a good long while once this errand is done, and Dona Elena safely on her way back to Spain."

"But you are a travelling player!"

"And so I've been nearly all my life, since I was nine years old, and I am twenty-seven now. I grow weary now, too old for this life. Too old to don motley and walk the tightrope."

Too old to spy? Surely she did know how he felt. She was barely twenty-one years of age herself, and yet there were times she felt so very ancient. "What will you do instead?"

"I fear you would laugh at me, my sophisticated *mademoiselle.* My worldly fairy queen."

"I could never laugh at you. Unless you play the Arlecchino. Then you are diverting beyond measure!"

"Ah, so you have seen my Arlecchino, then?"

"Once, in the Piazza San Marco, when you and your pretty young lover outwitted her sour old husband."

"Then you know what I mean. I would soon be more likely to play the husband."

"Au contraire, monsieur!" She traced a light, teasing caress along his chest, his taut abdomen. "There can be no player in all Europe who would look finer in those tight silks."

"Lecherous lady! Now I know why you came to me—your lust for Arlecchino."

"Can you blame me?" She rested her head on his shoulder,

listening to the steady thrum of his heartbeat, the pulse of his very life. "So, if you will be a player no more, what will you do?"

"I will turn farmer."

"Farmer? You? In Russia?"

"Nay. I have lost my taste for bitter winters. I bought some land from my friend Marc's wife Julietta, on the mainland near Venice. It is an overgrown tangle right now, and the villa burned. I will build a new house, though, one that is entirely mine. And I will tend my grapevines and fields of barley, will learn to make wine and press olive oil. I'll grow old in peace there, under the warm sun."

Marguerite closed her eyes, picturing it all in her mind. The house, glistening white stucco crowned with a rust-red tiled roof, shimmering under that bright light. White curtains fluttering at the open windows; tables spread with bread, cheese, olives, and the vineyard's own wines on the warm terrace, shaded by cypress trees. The twisting, beautiful vines, spread out as far as the eye could see, plump grapes ripening happily, full of sugar, until they could be gathered and turned carefully, painstakingly, into that magical elixir—wine.

"My father, he had one passion in life besides the memory of my mother, and that was wine," she said dreamily, looping one satin strand of his hair around her finger.

His finger traced a lazy pattern on her shoulder. "Do you mean to say you had *parents,* Marguerite?" he teased. "Human beings? That you were not left on their doorstep as a changeling?"

She laughed. "Of course I had real, human parents! I do not remember my mother, but my father used to carry me through his vineyard when I was a child, talking about his hopes for the grapes, his plans to improve the harvests. New methods for producing the wine, which he read about in agricultural treatises from Spain or Italy."

"Your father's vineyards did well under his care?"

She shook her head. "Not at all, yet he never ceased to try. We lived in Champagne, you see, in the north of France where the winters are cold and come early. But the soil was good for grapes, or should have been—chalky, so it drains well and doesn't dry out quickly. Loose, so the vines could penetrate deep and retain the precious heat of the day. My father, he was working on pressing the red grapes without much skin contact, producing a white wine with only a faint colour, a *vin gris,* much desired at Court."

"Was he successful?"

"Nay, there was a blight on the fields. It nearly ruined harvest after harvest when I was a child. But he never ceased to study, to try to find which vines would best flourish, how to best handle and mature the grapes."

Nicolai's fingertips moved lightly up and down her spine, until she laughed at the soft, tickling feeling. "It sounds like he passed his knowledge on to his daughter."

"A bit. I don't have time now to study as I would like, to experiment. But one day…"

"One day what?"

She shook her head. She could not say it aloud, could not give voice to longings she only half-understood herself, and dared not hope for. She shouldn't have spoken about her father and the vineyards at all, but Nicolai's plans had brought them out. The white villa, the fields under a sky as blue and endless as his eyes…

She kissed him instead, a language she understood. His lips pressed to hers, warm and hungry, as she reached down to draw the rumpled sheet away from his naked body. "It is surely hours yet until dawn," she whispered against his skin.

"Hmm," he murmured, pulling her down across his chest until there was not even a breath between them. "However shall we spend all that time?"

Chapter Thirteen

Shouts of laughter bounced off the black-painted walls of the tennis court, fairly vibrating the screens at the windows, the net of fringed cord. A much louder place, Marguerite thought, than when she came upon Nicolai here alone, practising his serve. Yet he had filled the arched space with more energy than all these courtiers together. He was not there today, and all the merriment seemed hollow.

King Henry was playing against his friend Sir Nicholas Carew, his Master of the Horse, and there was a lull in the game as they consulted with the marker on a point of play. Marguerite sat with the other spectators in the dedans, behind Claudine, who conversed with Queen Katherine and her ladies. From her seat, placed high on a riser but half-hidden, Marguerite could observe everything around her.

None of the Spanish were there, not even Dona Elena, only the French, Claudine and her husband and their various attendants, mingling with the English. Everyone laughed together amiably as they placed wagers on the game.

"Will you not bet on the king, Mademoiselle Dumas?" Roger Tilney asked, slipping into the empty seat beside her.

Marguerite smiled at him. He *was* handsome, she thought, with his brown eyes and glossy dark hair. And he seemed to admire her a great deal. That was always very useful. Yet whenever she looked at him, whenever he smiled at her, she imagined blue eyes instead…

"I am not a gambler, Monsieur Tilney," she answered. "I fear I always seem to choose the wrong side."

"The king is an excellent player, you could not fail in placing your wager on him."

"Perhaps not. But I prefer to invest my coin in properties I understand." She leaned closer and whispered, "Ribbons and jewels and such."

Tilney laughed, lightly fingering the white satin ribbon trim of her green velvet sleeve. "You make very wise fashion decisions, I'm sure, Mademoiselle Dumas. No one looking at you could think anything else."

Marguerite playfully shooed his hand away with her feather fan. "I have watched King François play *jeu de paume* at home, yet this English game does not look quite the same to me."

"We English always have to put our own mark on our pastimes," he answered, moving away with a good-natured shrug.

"So, what is happening now?" Marguerite asked, watching as the marker returned to his box adjoining the net, and King Henry and Carew switched ends of the court.

"When the players change ends, the first point played is the chase."

"The chase?"

"Aye. The marker will call out the chase the receiver—in this case, Sir Nicholas—hopes to beat."

"Chase two and three," the marker announced.

"Thus two and a half yards from the back wall," Tilney said. "The players, you see, can win a point by hitting the ball into an opening in the dedans penthouse, above our heads. The server has to protect these openings, since the player on the receiving end of the court will often use powerful shots to score a point. Players can also employ a strategy of long shots and hits that rebound off the penthouse roof or side walls. King Henry is quite deft at these types of challenging shots."

"How very clever you are, Master Tilney," Marguerite said. "I wonder you do not play today yourself."

"Against the king?" He laughed. "No, I thank you. I prefer to show off my physical dexterity in ways less hazardous."

"I can imagine," Marguerite murmured.

She watched as the game progressed, the fine linen shirts of the players growing wet with sweat, the plays more inventive, more vicious. Tilney explained the various manoeuvres to her, and she listened with half an ear as she watched both the players and the audience.

Queen Katherine's face radiated nothing but serene good humour as she applauded her husband, and she leaned in to speak quietly with Claudine. Claudine, too, seemed in better humour today, as her husband was beside her. Whenever the comte spoke to her, no matter how offhand his comments, her eyes glowed. Poor Claudine.

Husbands—such a strange, pestilent breed. Marguerite had always been glad she was not plagued with one. Especially not one like the English king or the Comte de Calonne.

Marriage settles a man, she remembered Dona Elena saying, or something to that effect. That had never been *her* observation. But then, she had never met a man like Nicolai, either. A man whose entire existence was not bound up in advancing himself. Maybe marriage *could* settle someone like that, man or woman.

She was learning a great deal here in England, just not the lessons she had expected.

The game wound to an end, King Henry the victor, of course. As the two opponents donned velvet tennis coats to keep from catching a chill, and changed their soft shoes for boots, the spectators filed out of the gallery. Wagers were settled, appointments and assignations made for later.

"And did you win, Master Tilney?" Marguerite asked, as he tucked away his purse.

"Certainly. I am not fool enough to bet against the king. In anything."

"Does he always win, then? How very dull."

"Not always. King Henry does love to be the victor, no matter what the game. But equally he hates to feel he has been *allowed* to win due to his rank. Thus he must sometimes lose."

"And the key in wagering is to know when those losing times are upon us?"

"You are quite clever yourself, *mademoiselle!* I think you make a mistake in refusing to use your gaming skills."

Marguerite laughed. "I use them all the time, in surer games than tennis."

"Are there any sure games in life?"

Marguerite had a flashing vision of that white, sun-washed villa, twisting grapevines, fields of barley. Of Nicolai's golden body against pale sheets. "I begin to hope there might be."

"Then you must tell me what they are, for I fear I have never found one."

They followed the others out of the court into the grey, misty day. Claudine went off with Queen Katherine, her husband strolling away in the opposite direction as his wife's face grew pinched and closed again.

The cold air was bracing after the humid, stuffy warmth of the court, and Marguerite drew in a deep breath of it. Her mind, too, felt heavy, her thoughts reeling after the quick flash of revelation. She didn't *want* to think Nicolai was different! She didn't want to yearn for a sunny Italian farm.

She didn't want to care.

"Would you walk with me in the gardens, Mademoiselle Dumas?" Tilney asked, breaking into her thoughts.

"Thank you, Master Tilney," she said, taking his proffered arm. "A bit of exercise will be welcome after sitting so long in one place."

Others also had the same idea, as the gardens and low hedge mazes were filled with people walking and chattering, obviously glad to be freed of stuffy rooms and stuffier diplomatic meetings. They paused to watch a game of bowls on one of the grassy lawns, the wheel-shaped ball, or "piglet", rolling close to the jack.

"Have you always lived at Court, Master Tilney?" Marguerite asked, listening to the groans of defeat as the stubborn piglet failed to hit its mark.

"Since I was a child," he said. "My father died when I was very young, and my mother sent me here to serve as a page."

"And you never left?"

"Where else is there to go? Where the king is, that is the very centre of the world. Surely it is the same in France."

"Yes. Like you, I came to Court when I was very young. It is all I know."

"'Tis a marvellous game, is it not?"

"I have always found it so." And so she always had, truly. An exhilarating, dangerous game, one she played well. Yet surely one could not be a gamester for ever. It could not be all there was.

He shrugged. "I have nothing I would rather do. There is nothing *to* do, without royal favour."

They strolled on, edging around fountains and benches, a lively game of blindman's bluff in a clearing. The shrieks and giggles of the young players, pages and maids of honour, echoed joyfully.

Had she ever been that young? Marguerite feared not. And now, as Nicolai said of himself and his life as a travelling player, she felt she grew old. Older every day, until naught held joy for her any longer. Not even this cat-and-mouse game she played with the English and the Spanish.

What if the Duke and Duchess de Bernaldez proved to be an obstacle to the new alliance? Could she eliminate them, as she was instructed to do?

Marguerite shook her head, that hazy sense of confusion growing. She wanted to flee, yet she had nowhere to go. Tilney was right—there *was* no place but the Court. She had no skills but those of a spy and a killer, no family or friends. No choice but to go on with her task, come what may.

She tightened her clasp on Tilney's arm. "You have been attending the meetings between King Henry and Bishop Grammont, have you not?"

"Of course. They are very delicate negotiations, and the king requires a great deal of advice."

Advice—yes, and everyone's would be different. Wolsey for the French, Queen Katherine for the Spanish. Katherine was not so much in favour now, but that could change in an instant.

"The Comtesse de Calonne worries for her husband," Marguerite said carefully. "She is concerned that their long journey here, so perilous in the winter time, will prove to be for naught."

"I am sure the comtesse has many fears, as ladies in her condition are wont to do," he said indulgently. "But I am also sure the thought that her journey was in vain should not be one of them."

Marguerite slowed her steps, facing him. He had to know more than that, had to know exactly why the negotiations were going in the French favour or against it. Men never wanted to talk to women of politics; they imagined frail females could not understand the intricacies of it all. Marguerite knew how to use that to her advantage, to get them to tell her things they didn't even realise they had revealed.

She gave him a sweet smile, swaying closer so he could smell her perfume, see the glint of the pale light in her hair. "The king is a wise man to trust you, Monsieur Tilney," she murmured.

He gave her a smile in return, a confident grin, and reached out to touch a strand of her hair as if he could not help himself. As if he was mesmerised. "I have only a very small place at Court."

"I am sure that cannot be true. Someone so very wise, so handsome…"

He kissed her, and she leaned into him, resting her hands lightly on his shoulders. He was a fine kisser, practised, sensual, his lips moving over hers in a skilled, alluring way. Soft, soft, then deepening as his tongue sought hers and his arms came around her waist, drawing her close.

Yet she felt nothing. Nay, less than nothing, she felt trapped. Closed in, captured, and she could not escape. Her heart pounded in sudden fear, her body turned cold and clammy. She could not do this!

Marguerite pressed hard against his shoulders, breaking their kiss. She turned her face away, afraid he would see the hot tears lurking in her eyes.

"Forgive me, *mademoiselle*," he said hoarsely, his arm sliding away from her. "I did not mean to take advantage. You are just so very beautiful…"

Marguerite forced herself to laugh, waving her hand in a careless gesture, as if she could banish her tears and all the fear in one instant. "La, monsieur, what is a little kiss in the garden! You are as skilled with the ladies as you are a courtier. You must have many flirtations."

He laughed, flattered as she knew he would be, and not insulted when she made her excuses to return to the palace. She strolled slowly away from him, her skirts swaying lightly, until she turned out of sight. Then she ran, as fast as her heeled shoes and tight bodice would let her, running and running until she reached the edge of the river and could go no farther.

Marguerite leaned over the grey water, fearing she would be sick. Her stomach roiled with a cold nausea, and she crossed her arms tightly over her belly. Something had changed, something deep and fearful. It had shifted so swiftly she did not even notice until Roger Tilney kissed her.

Her careful, icy shell cracked. She felt the wall she had built around her heart and soul, brick by brick, coming apart. No matter how frantically she tried to repair it, remortar the fissures, it just kept crumbling around her.

She straightened, staring down at the water. It flowed on, unchanging, indifferent to any human panic or passion. What was happening? She did not understand. Was it Nicolai? Her strange attraction to him? The snare of his lovemaking, his words, his visions for a future of peace and warmth, living close to the earth?

For one instant, she saw herself slipping into the river, diving under the cold waves never to be seen again. Yet she knew that doing away with herself would only add to her troubles. Her sins were too great already.

But never, not even when her father died, had she felt so very alone.

She turned away from the water, walking slowly back toward the palace, toward the life that awaited her there. It was all she had, all she knew.

"Mademoiselle Dumas!" she heard someone call, and she turned to see the Comte de Calonne walking in her direction, Father Pierre trailing behind him. She quickly swiped away her tears, pasting a bright smile on her lips.

"What are you doing here all by yourself?" the comte said, raising her hand to his lips for a gallant salute.

"I was just seeking a breath of fresh air after watching the tennis," Marguerite answered. She smiled at the comte; unlike his wife, he always seemed light-hearted. Devoted to his duty to France, but also fond of a jest. His hazel eyes sparkled in his open, freckle-dotted face. "Your wife has gone back to the palace with Queen Katherine."

"*C'est bon!* I hope Claudine is adjusting to life here at last. It seems we may be here for several weeks more."

"Indeed? Are the negotiations not progressing as desired?" Marguerite said, trying to ignore Father Pierre's silent stare.

"It is progressing very well, yet it seems King Henry enjoys our company and is loath to let us go. He uses many excuses to keep us here," the comte answered. "And how could he not? We are French, *n'est-ce pas?* We have the wittiest conversation, the best dancing—the prettiest ladies."

Marguerite laughed. "I have seen many pretty ladies among the English. Lady Penelope Percy, for example, and…"

"And Mademoiselle Boleyn?" The comte glanced back to

nod at Father Pierre, then offered Marguerite his arm. "We must take the barge into London before the tide turns against us, Mademoiselle Dumas, for we have business there this evening. Will you walk with us to the steps?"

Marguerite nodded, grateful for any distraction from her own thoughts. "Mademoiselle Boleyn is indeed lovely."

"She grew up in France, so I hear," the comte said, leading her along the walkway. Father Pierre followed, silent as always, only the rustle of his robes the only sign he was there. "Is she friendly to us, then? To our cause?"

"I could not say," Marguerite said. "I have had no conversation with her. But surely she can be no friend to any ally of the queen."

"Very true. Perhaps I should ask Claudine to talk with her, invite her to dine or play cards."

Marguerite doubted Claudine's cold hospitality would endear the merry, wittily cutting Mistress Boleyn to the French alliance. "If she is made to feel important…"

"Treated like a queen?" the comte said. "That makes sense. I do hear that the Boleyns have always had ideas above their station. Father Pierre thinks it is merely an infatuation on the king's part. A passing fancy, like Mary Boleyn or Mademoiselle Blount. What say you, Mademoiselle Dumas?"

Marguerite thought of the way King Henry looked at Anne Boleyn as they danced in the banquet hall, the reverent, awed way he touched her hand. "I do not know the thoughts of the English king, of course."

"Yet surely you *do* know something of the ways of men in love."

Marguerite smiled bitterly. "Perhaps a bit. And I would say the king is in some sort of love with Anne Boleyn. She plays him very skilfully, and seems to wield a measure of influence."

The comte nodded as they reached the waiting barge. "When I return tomorrow, I will have Claudine invite Mademoiselle Boleyn to dine with us. If you will attend us then, Mademoiselle Dumas?"

"Certainly. God speed you on your journey, comte."

Marguerite stood on the dock, watching as the vessel slid out into the river and vanished over the horizon, the merest speck. She imagined herself floating away on that water, growing smaller and smaller until she, Marguerite, no longer existed, until she transformed into something else entirely. A bird, flying up and up into the sky, or a fish, vanishing into the watery depths.

The wind sharpened, washing over her in a cold sweep, and she shivered. She turned away from the river, from what couldn't be, and hurried back into the shelter of the palace walls. She didn't know where to go, what to do.

She felt lost.

Then she saw the theatre, its doors standing half-open. Nicolai had not been at the tennis game; perhaps he would be there, in his quiet room. That haven she always sought.

At the thought of him, her heart lightened in a strange, frightening way, a way she had never known before. If she was wise, she would turn from the theatre, would hurry back to her own chamber to sharpen her daggers, make new plans. But her steps moved toward the theatre, slowly at first, hesitant, then faster, faster, until she was almost running.

She slipped inside the door, pausing to catch her breath. The choir of the Chapel Royal was rehearsing, their young voices rising up like an angelic choir, sweet and jubilant. Celebratory and certain.

Marguerite wished *she* could be so sure of her path. But all she felt was a cold, sick anticipation in the pit of her stomach.

She walked along the edges of the floor until she found the entrance to Nicolai's room. She leaned close, listening carefully, but she heard nothing except the rush of her own blood in her ears.

She slipped inside quickly, before she could come to her senses and flee. He *was* there, painting one pasteboard wall of a half-constructed castle green. He wore an old, thin shirt, laces undone, spotted with the paint, his hair tied back.

He glanced around at the sound of the door, and a smile curved his lips as he saw her there. "Marguerite! What do you do here?"

She opened her mouth to answer, but no sound emerged. How could it, when she had no words at all? No idea of what she did there at all.

She dashed toward him, flinging her arms around his neck, kissing him with every ounce of passion she had, every uncertainty and fear. His lips parted in surprise, and she touched his tongue with hers, tangling, drawing him ever deeper into her.

Dimly, she heard the paintbrush fall to the floor, felt his embrace close around her, pulling her against him so tightly she did not know where she ended and he began. Unlike her awkward kiss with Roger Tilney, this felt *right*. Their arms, their mouths, their bodies—they fit together as if they were always meant to be so.

That crack she felt as she stood beside the river burst open at the touch of his lips, a great flood of long-withheld emotion that would not be called back. Not be suppressed. She poured it all into their kiss, clinging to him as if for the last time— as it well could be.

"Marguerite," Nicolai muttered roughly, easing away from her. "What is amiss? Are you well?"

She tilted back her head to stare up at him. A small frown etched a line between his brows. "Of course I am well. I merely craved a kiss. Is that so terrible?"

"Terrible—nay, never. My lips are always at your disposal. Merely surprising."

She rested her head at the curve of his neck and shoulder, inhaling deeply of his scent. At last her heartbeat slowed, the sick feeling subsided, leaving only warmth.

She felt his chin on the top of her head, the softness as he nuzzled her hair. She smiled, and pressed even closer. She saw now why his friends trusted him so. There was a heat in him, like a bonfire on a cold winter's night, that was so alluring. So needful.

"Marguerite, what are you up to? What game do you play?" he said gently, solemnly. Suspiciously.

And a tiny dagger of ice pierced her heart. She came to him with the first true emotion she had felt in long years, and he thought she played a game. She could not blame him, really. Was her life not truly one long game? Was that not all she had ever shown him?

But it pained her none the less.

She pulled away from him, turning her back to blink away the hot, salty rush of tears. Tears accomplished nothing; they only made one's face splotchy and red, made things worse. She laughed carelessly. "La, *monsieur,* but a kiss is a game all in itself!"

She moved to the castle, pretending to examine its turrets, its small drawbridge. "What do you build here?"

He came to her side, his gaze on her still so watchful and wary. "It is your Castle Vert, of course, for the pageant."

"*My* castle?"

"Are you not to play Beauty, ruler of all within sight? You

will sit here, with all your fair ladies around you." He tapped at a high platform, hidden behind one of the turrets and reached by a set of shallow steps.

In truth, Marguerite had almost forgotten the pageant in everything else that had been happening. "When shall we begin rehearsals?"

"In two or three days, I hope. Once the paint dries so the ladies will not ruin their fine gowns. The casting is mostly done."

"And will you take a part? Perhaps one of the knights who besieges the great fortress?"

"Nay, I am merely the stage manager."

"Such a pity. Though I suppose it would be no feat for *you* to conquer a castle full of ladies. They would lower the drawbridge the instant they saw you."

Nicolai laughed, and the rich sound melted some of the icy slivers lodged in her heart. "Nothing will be conquered at all if the castle isn't built."

"Here, I will help you finish." Marguerite unlaced her velvet sleeves, removing them to roll up the cuffs of her chemise before reaching for a paintbrush.

"Do you not have other duties you must attend to?"

She smiled at him, brandishing the brush like a sword. "There is truly no other place I would rather be."

Chapter Fourteen

The clear breeze felt bracing after the paint fume-filled theatre, Marguerite thought as she sat down on a marble bench, Nicolai standing behind her, watchful as ever. The Castle Vert was nearly finished, and they took a reprieve to breathe the fresh air and sip some wine.

Her hands and arms were spotted with green flecks, and her shoulders ached as if she had just been in a duel, but she had rarely felt such a quiet, deep satisfaction. A sense of a task well done. The artificial castle was entirely green now, all thanks to her honest labour!

She sat there with Nicolai in companionable silence, watching the parade of courtiers and servants as they hurried along on their errands. In the distance, Marguerite saw Princess Mary walking with her tutor and her ladies-in-waiting. A tiny, pale, slender figure, nearly overwhelmed by her heavy purple velvet gown and matching cloak. Isolated, though surrounded by so many solicitous attendants.

Marguerite almost felt sorry for her, the poor little princess. What could await her in France, if she became the Duchesse d'Orléans? Would it be at all better than her constricted life here?

"I imagine that you were something like the Princess Mary when you were a child," Nicolai said musingly.

Marguerite laughed. Surely he could not have read her thoughts, her pity for the princess's loneliness? "I had no emperors or princes vying for my hand, as she does."

"Then the more fool they. Nay, what I imagine is that you had something of her seriousness, her solemnity. Of that air she has of being far older than her years. Of knowing things—grave, ominous things—we poor, immature fools cannot hope to see."

Marguerite watched the princess as her tutor pointed out something in her book and she nodded, as a maid solicitously straightened her fur-edged cloak. "Perhaps I *was* overly serious as a child. I read a great deal, and lived mostly in my mind. My daydreams. But I certainly did not have so many people hovering about, concerned for my well-being!"

Nicolai propped his booted foot on the bench beside her, leaning his elbow on his knee as he surveyed the endless parade before them. "Not even your father?"

Marguerite shook her head. "My father cared for me, in his way, but he had other concerns. And our household was always rather haphazard, as it had no mistress and servants came and went so fast. My mother, you know, died when I was born."

"I am sorry, Marguerite," he said, and she felt his gaze on her, heavy, dark, and concerned.

She did not want his pity! Never that, not from him of all people. She could bear anything from him but *that*.

She shrugged. "'Tis not an uncommon thing. King Henry's own mother, Queen Elizabeth of York, died in childbirth, did she not? Even being royal could not save her."

"Do you know much of your mother?"

Marguerite closed her eyes, envisioning the flash of Champagne's summer light on her mother's diamond pendant as her father swung it before her child's eyes, dropping it at last into her eager little hand. "She was a courtesan, the most beautiful, most famous in all of Paris. Princes and dukes vied for her favours. But my father always said that her beauty was only exceeded by the great kindness of her heart."

"So, he won her over all the dukes and princes."

Marguerite smiled as she remembered the story. "He did. My father was from an ancient family, but a sadly poor one. Made even poorer by his love of cards, I fear. He loved my mother beyond *primero,* though, beyond all else. They went to live alone at his old, crumbling château in Champagne, and they were happy there for two perfect years, as my father's tales always went. He tended his blighted grapevines. My mother kept house, grew fine roses. Grew fat with me. And then she died."

"What happened to the baby princess then?" Nicolai asked quietly.

"I fear I was quite disgustingly healthy. I grew and thrived, as my father's grapes did not."

"And your father? Was he a good man, despite his—concerns?"

Marguerite pondered this, for truly it was not a question she had ever considered. Her father was who he was, that was all. And what made a *good* man? She had seen many an example of the opposite, but rarely good.

Until now. Until Nicolai, who would suspend his own life to help a friend.

"He was good enough," she said. "He had his weaknesses, as we all do, and they were his undoing in the end. Yet I am sure he cared about me, in his own way. Perhaps because I looked like my mother, which he often remarked on. When I grew a bit older, he hired tutors for me, like Princess Mary, I suppose. Languages, philosophy, dancing, music, fencing. He also taught me about the grapes, about wine. And, when I was twelve or thirteen, he took me to Court."

"To find a fine husband?"

Marguerite laughed. "How could he? He was a nobleman, true, but I was—am—a bastard. And a poor one at that, a blighted vineyard and leaking house my only dowry. Perhaps he thought I could follow my mother's path to fame."

She glanced up to find Nicolai still watching her solemnly. "You are wondering, perchance, why I did not?" she said.

He shrugged. "I cannot make a judgement on anyone's choices in life. I have made too many puzzling ones of my own."

"Your entire being, Nicolai Ostrovsky, is a puzzle! At least it is to me."

He grinned at her, and all his seriousness, his dreaded pity, vanished in the bright glow. "Then my plan to intrigue you is working."

Indeed it was—too well. "My mother, you see, never really belonged to herself, not even when she left her fame and riches behind to go with my father. She gave herself up to him, to his whims and fancies; she abandoned whatever she had built herself in Paris. I never wanted that. Yet I was ambitious, in my way—I wanted to move forward in the world. Be more than a poor bastard child, married off to some country farmer. I didn't know what I could do."

"Be a winemaker?"

"Perhaps. I did love the vineyard, that strange alchemy that turns prosaic grapes into good wine. But my father died when I was fifteen, and the château was sold for his debts. I went back to Court alone, with my mother's jewels. I sold them all, except one, and lived off that money for a time."

"And became the Emerald Lily."

"Not right away. I was still lost, uncertain. Then I killed my first man, when I was sixteen. He tried to rape me, you see, in the garden of the château at St Cloud. Luckily for me, he was a Dutchman, a pestering enemy of the king, and I received a bag of gold and royal thanks rather than a noose around my neck."

Even those words, so stark and simple, left the bitter taste of ashes in her mouth. Marguerite stood abruptly, turning away from Nicolai before she could see the disgust that was sure to be writ across his beautiful face.

"And that is the end of the tale for today," she called, as she hurried back into the theatre. "We should return to work. The time before our pageant grows short."

"'Love, that doth reign and live within my thought, and built his seat within my captive heart…'"

Nicolai half listened to the Chapel Royal's choir, to the words of their song by Henry Howard, adapted from Petrarch. He watched Marguerite from across the crowded theatre. She sat with the Comtesse de Calonne and the other French ladies on the risers, her hands folded serenely in the lap of her pale green damask gown, watching the singers with a soft smile on her face. She looked like a fairy of spring tonight, all leafy green and silver, her hair shining with pearls.

She had been sixteen when she first killed a man. Those words of hers, so quiet and sad, would not cease to haunt him. She had been alone, vulnerable, young, with no one to help her, no one to defend her, surrounded by people who sought only to take advantage of her. Her tone had been matter of fact as she told her tale, but Nicolai sensed the pain underneath, the raw hurt as she recalled the events that changed her life for ever. He surely understood that, understood the cold realisation that there was no choice. No way forward or back.

It explained much. Especially that sense he had of her, that she was a small, beautiful bird beating at the gilded bars holding her captive. The way she held a deep, secret part of her aside, apart from the world, even as she lay in his arms.

For the first time, he saw a crack in her cold, perfect façade, glimpsed what was inside, beneath the beauty. The vulnerable, dark, tangled essence of Marguerite Dumas.

"'But she that taught me love and suffer pain, my doubtful hope and eke my hot desire with shamefast look to shadow and refrain…'"

She gazed down at her hand, her fingers smoothing the pearl trim of her gown. What did *she* think, behind her pleasant smile? Did she regret giving him that little glimpse of her past? Sharing that bit of her heart? Or did she now decipher how to use their confidences for her own ends?

Shadow and refrain.

She glanced up suddenly to find him studying her. For an instant, her mask was down, and her eyes were full of sadness. Loneliness. They were surrounded by people, by the hot, insistent press of humanity, and yet they were the only two people in the world. Bound by a flare of understanding and need.

Then her gaze turned away, back to the choir, and he saw only the marble curve of her cheek, the luminous pearls around her throat. In the dim light, they almost looked like the noose she had so narrowly escaped as a girl.

Nicolai had the sudden urge to hurry to her side, to gather her close in his arms and hold her so tightly nothing evil or ugly could touch her again.

But that was foolish. She had chosen her path in life. He had chosen his—to leave the world of intrigue and politics and danger far behind. They had no place for each other. Yet that did not erase that compulsion, that need to protect a woman who had once tried to kill him.

Who might very well try to kill him again, for all he knew. He remembered the dagger hidden in his room, the emerald flashing in its hilt. Perhaps it was time to return it to its owner. To let the Emerald Lily go.

The concert ended in a burst of applause from the audience, and Nicolai stepped back against the wall to let the gathering throng file out of the theatre. He would see Dona Elena safely to her apartment, and then decide what to do about that dagger.

Marguerite glided past him behind the comtesse, so swiftly and lightly that he was barely aware of the breath of her lily perfume, the quick press of a square of parchment into his hand.

She did not even glance back as she left the room, her pale green skirts blending into the night. Nicolai unfolded the note, scanning it hastily. "When the palace is quiet, I will come to you tonight. M."

Chapter Fifteen

"What happened later? After you killed the lecherous Dutchman?"

"Hmm?" Marguerite had been drowsing, her head on Nicolai's shoulder, fingertips lazily tracing circles on his naked chest. Drifting in slow, dreamy lassitude after the hot rush of their lovemaking. But his words, so quiet and lethal, jerked her into tense wakefulness. Her caress stilled. "What do you mean, *after?* Nothing, for him—he was dead."

"Deservedly so. Only a villain would attack a girl like that. But how did you go from that act of self-defence to…"

"To being the Emerald Lily?" She sat up against the bolsters, drawing the rumpled sheet over her bare breasts. Nicolai rolled on to his side, propping his head on his palm as he gazed up at her. She felt pinned down by that stare, unable to turn away or to hide, even from herself.

"I found I was fearfully good at killing," she said. "All those fencing lessons, reading all those manuals on warfare in my father's library. I was good at covering up bad deeds, too. Of giving the appearance of feminine innocence and ignorance. And I did like the bag of gold the king awarded me.

I had been able to hide the true dire straits I was in until then, but I could not have gone on much longer. I thought it a wondrous thing to earn money for ridding France of her enemies."

"Do you still think that?"

She shrugged. "I know nothing else, no other way of life. It is all I have now."

"I think you could have, do, whatever you wanted." He took her hand, turning it to examine her palm, the smooth lines, the soft pink skin, lightly laced with pale sword calluses along the base of her fingers. "You know that I cannot let you hurt Dona Elena or her husband. I have vowed to protect them."

Marguerite curled her fingers around his. "And I have vowed to make certain this alliance is fulfilled. But I will not hurt Dona Elena. She has been kind to me, though I cannot fathom why."

They lay there for a long moment in silence, their hands entwined. Marguerite gazed down at Nicolai, enthralled by him as always.

"You know of my sordid past now," she said. "My shabby childhood. What of you, Nicolai?"

"Me?" He grinned at her, raising her hand to press kisses to her knuckles, the curve of her wrist. "I am an open book, *dorogaya*."

She shook her head. "You are the only person I have never been able to read at all. Your parents must have been actors, too, for they have taught you well."

He let her go, easing on to his back, hands laced behind his head. "My parents were merchants in Moscow," he said quietly. "My father dealt in furs from the north, spices and silks from the east. We lived comfortably, my parents, my baby sister Aleksandra, and me."

Marguerite had a difficult time seeing him in a "comfortable" merchant's house in Moscow, clad in the long robes of a wealthy Russian, bargaining over casks of pepper, lengths of cloth. "What happened to your comfortable life?"

"They died, when I was eight years old or so, of the plague. The entire city was afflicted. I nearly died myself, but I survived to bury them." He held his leg out for her to see the faint scar on his inner thigh, the red mark of the plague. "Even little Aleksandra, my beautiful baby sister."

His voice was soft, with no inflection, no emotion. Yet Marguerite knew what it was to be suddenly alone. To have no one left to love. She slid down on the bed, until she could press one soft, gentle kiss to the old mark. His muscles tensed under her touch. "What happened then?"

He buried his fingers in her hair, tugging her up until she rested again with her head on his chest.

"I had only one relative, my father's younger brother Alexei. Uncle Alexei had never had an interest in business and trade. He wanted to travel, to learn things, magical things. He was something of a rogue, you see, a vagabond soul. He ran off with a troupe of acrobats when he was young, and my father seldom spoke of him. He was Alexei the shameful, Alexei the prodigal."

Nicolai smiled as he said this, and Marguerite sensed the deep affection that lurked there. "He came for you when your parents died?"

"He did, once I found where he was to send a message. It took him a long while; he had a great length to travel. In the meantime, I was cared for at a monastery. Those months were quite enough to show me I had no vocation at all for the religious life. I much preferred Alexei's existence."

"He taught you to be an actor."

"To walk the tightrope, fight with swords…"

"Attract the ladies?"

Nicolai laughed. "He was certainly adept at *that*. He died several years ago, and left me his costumes and properties to start my own troupe. He also left me something else…"

Marguerite was intrigued. "What was it?"

"Oh, no, *mademoiselle*," he said, smiling. "That is a tale for another time. I am weary of talking tonight."

He rolled her to her back on the mattress, trailing soft, alluring kisses along her shoulder, the curve of her breast. She shivered, her head falling back as she lost herself in the sensations. "I, too, am weary of talk," she murmured. "I can think of better uses for that talented mouth of yours, Nicolai Ostrovsky."

"Yes? Pray tell what *uses* you prefer, *vodyanoi*," he whispered against her skin.

"I think—you are doing very well to use your ingenuity," she gasped.

"Like this?" Nicolai's hand slid slowly, enticingly down the length of her leg until he held the arch of her foot. He raised it to his lips, kissing the instep, the curve of her ankle, until he gently sucked the very tip of her toe.

Marguerite laughed and gasped at the same time. "That is—a start."

"What of this?" His tongue eased along her leg, trailing fiery kisses that teased, aroused, nipped. Marguerite almost sobbed as he licked the tiny, sensitive spot behind her knee. The dimple at the edge of her thigh.

"*Mon ange*," she whispered, her head falling back, eyes tightly closed as the pleasure washed over her in a drugging, heavy haze. Every inch of skin he kissed, touched, woke to tingling life, and she lost herself. There was only him; this one, perfect moment where they were the only people in the world.

Her legs spread farther, clasped over his shoulders as he pressed hot kisses to her inner thigh, higher and higher, inch by slow, torturous inch. Until at last he gave her what she longed for, his tongue touching the wet opening of her womanhood until she cried out, opening fully for him. Giving him everything she was. Everything she could ever be.

His tongue plunged inside her, and Marguerite cried out, clasping his hair to press him closer, ever closer. He was as deft with a woman's body as he was on the tightrope or the lute. She sobbed his name, over and over, every sense sparkling and alive. She fell back limply amid the sheets as the world broke apart around her. A shower of stars, golden and red and vivid blue.

"Mon beau," she whispered. *"Ma coeur."*

She felt the lean length of his body slide up the bed to her side, kissing her hip, her shoulder, the edge of her jaw, her flushed cheek, until at last his lips claimed hers. She smelled the green herbal scent of *him,* the salty essence of herself. Everything they were, mingled together to form something new and strange. Something—magical.

She wrapped her legs around his waist, drawing his body into hers until she could not tell where she ended and he began. They were one.

And, when she returned to France and he went off to his sunny vineyard, when their one became two again, she would be missing a vast part of herself. She would surely be missing her heart.

Chapter Sixteen

"A picnic?" Claudine said, dismay in her voice. "You mean we are to eat on the *ground?* Like *animals?*"

"Oh, come, ma *chère,*" her husband said heartily, obviously trying to jolly her into cooperating with King Henry's latest whim. "It will be amusing. We can pretend to be shepherds, *n'est-ce pas?*"

Marguerite ducked her head over her embroidery, trying to hide her smile. She doubted anything the comte said could persuade Claudine that eating outdoors was a fine idea. Marguerite thought that an outing on this rare sunny day would be delightful, but then she was in an uncharacteristically merry mood today. Everything made her want to sing or laugh, to spread her arms wide and twirl around in circles, faster and faster until all the world was dizzy around her.

She was—yes, she surely felt *happy!* It would not last long. Such bright, ephemeral bubbles of joy never did. But she intended to hold it close and tight until it burst.

It was all thanks to Nicolai. Her smile widened as she remembered his kiss, his touch—his talented tongue against her most secret place, conjuring up ecstasy such as she had never imagined existed. She also remembered things even more precious and intimate—his words. His story of the loss of his parents and sister. The way he coaxed out her secrets, too.

Fleeting, indeed. But so very lovely. And very, very frightening.

No one else shared this good mood, though. The other French ladies huddled quietly in the corners, sewing or reading in silence, exhausted after long days in Claudine's demanding company. The English king's new invitation, to ride in the park and picnic under the trees, had sparked a wary interest. But Claudine's mood threatened to damp that spark before it could even catch.

"King Henry can play *shepherd* all he likes, and his strumpet Mademoiselle Boleyn can be his little birdcatcher," Claudine snapped. "I do not care to sit on the damp ground and catch a chill!"

"It is not so damp outside," her husband said. "We will bring cushions for you to sit on, and there will be spiced wine to warm the blood."

Claudine merely pouted, so the comte tried another method, standing up straight and stern, his hands planted on his hips. Much like the English king himself, Marguerite thought.

"We are not here for our own amusement," he said. "We are here to finalise this alliance, which will greatly benefit France. The treaty cannot be jeopardised by a woman's temper! We must humour King Henry, give in to his whims, at least for now."

"A woman's temper!" Claudine cried. "I came all this way in the middle of the winter, pregnant with *your* child, just to be ill and watch you flirt with that Lady Penelope Percy, and you dare to say…"

Marguerite sighed. She could see the situation was spiralling quite beyond control. She laid aside her sewing and said softly, "Pardon me, comte."

Claudine and her husband both swung around to face her, as if startled to find other people there in the room.

"I fear the comtesse is right," Marguerite said gently. "It is too damp outside for a lady in her condition, and even travelling in a litter would be jolting. We must consider the health of your heir. But we must also consider the sensitivities of the king. We cannot refuse his invitation. May I suggest that the comtesse invite Queen Katherine to dine with her, and Mademoiselle DuParc, Mademoiselle Malreux and I will accompany you to the picnic, comte?"

He nodded, backing slowly away from his wife. "Very sensible of you, Mademoiselle Dumas. That is a very sound plan."

Marguerite nodded. Sound it might be. Yet now she was prevented from slipping away to look for Nicolai. The happy bubble of the day now seemed just a tiny bit less shimmering.

The afternoon was a fine one for being outdoors, the breeze clear and cool, the pale sun arching overhead. Struggling and dim, but shining none the less! Their party was a small one as they galloped through the park, so as not to overly disturb the winter game.

Marguerite glanced over her shoulder as she guided her borrowed mare along the tree-lined path. There had been no need for her to slip away to find Nicolai after all, for he was there. Riding at the back of the group with Señorita Alva and two other Spanish ladies.

The young women, so pretty and pink-cheeked from the

exercise, their hair shining black as a raven's wing in the sun, giggled at whatever Nicolai said to them. Their glances were shyly admiring, their smiles flirtatious. How sweet and young and *innocent* they seemed, and how Nicolai seemed to enjoy their company. He smiled and jested with them, holding his own horse back to the slower pace of theirs.

They were *not* as adept in the saddle as she was, Marguerite noted with some satisfaction. It had taken her a long time as a girl to get used to horses again, after the accident, but she had done it and grown more accomplished a rider than ever. The Spanish ladies were more cautious, less certain of their control. They had not even taken the jumps as they all galloped over the meadows. Still, he stayed with them.

Marguerite faced forward again, wondering where her happy little bubble of the morning had gone. Vanished somewhere in the stableyard, perhaps. Or left far behind, in Nicolai's bed.

At the head of their little procession rode King Henry and Mistress Boleyn. Marguerite did rather envy Anne Boleyn's fine white palfrey, with its French saddle of black velvet with gold fringing and matching reins and harnesses. Her little greyhounds running alongside wore tiny black velvet coats and gold collars, embroidered with the initials *AB* and a falcon badge.

After the king rode a few of his English friends, Nicholas Carew of the tennis game, Anne's brother the handsome George Boleyn, Roger Tilney and Lady Penelope Percy's brother. Then came the French ladies and the Comte de Calonne and, strangely, Father Pierre. The priest seemed most ill at ease on his mount, Marguerite reflected, though he did manage to keep up. Maintaining his seat luckily occupied all his attention, so he was not able to talk to her, to renew his dire warnings about her "friendship" with the Spanish.

The Spanish themselves brought up the rear of their little party, the Duke de Bernaldez, Nicolai, and the ladies. Dona Elena, like Claudine, had stayed behind.

Marguerite was heartily glad she was not also stuck inside the palace today. Even with Nicolai paying court only to the Spanish ladies, even with Father Pierre watching her as he jolted in his saddle, she liked the breeze against her face. The exercise after long days indoors. She just wished she could let the horse have her head and go galloping off, as fast and free as she liked! To race Nicolai across the fields, through the woods, until they left everyone—everything—else far behind.

King Henry led them around a bend in the road, and they found themselves in a small forest clearing, surrounded by the bare greyness of the winter trees.

"My friends," he called out, "I welcome you to our new banquet hall!"

Marguerite laughed in surprise. So, Claudine would not have had to sit on the ground like a shepherdess after all! Tables were set up in a U-shape, draped with fine white damask cloths, laid out with great platters of roasted meats and spiced vegetables, bowls of sugared fruits and cinnamon almonds. Goblets of wine and loaves of soft white manchet bread sat at each place.

If not for the carpet of brown leaves and twigs, Marguerite would have thought they were back at the palace.

Servants who had been laying out the feast hurried to help them all dismount, and led them to their places. Marguerite found herself across the *U* from Nicolai, France again at one table, Spain at the other, while Henry and Anne presided at the head table. Musicians and jesters appeared, seemingly from the trees themselves, and soon songs and laughter blended with the rush of the wind in the bare branches.

As the wine and ale flowed, the laughter grew even louder, more careless, the jests bawdier. Even Marguerite laughed helplessly at the jokes of King Henry's fool, the skeletally thin and lethally witty Will Somers. She let Roger Tilney refill her goblet more times than was surely wise, but she fended off his flirtations by popping sweetmeats into his mouth.

As she turned away from him, giggling, she found Nicolai watching her, that unreadable half-smile on his face.

He *was* good looking, she thought with a bittersweet pang. Usually handsome men grew less so the more she knew them, the more she saw of their greed and selfishness. But Nicolai— his beauty just seemed to grow every time she saw him. It was so alluring. And so infuriating!

She smiled at him, kicking aside the hem of her velvet riding skirt to hold up her foot in its soft leather boot. She pointed her toe, reminding him of the night before, when he had held and kissed that very foot.

He laughed aloud, and suddenly the day did seem bright and new all over again.

"We must have a dance," King Henry announced. He gestured to the musicians to strike up a lively country bransle, and led Mistress Boleyn on to the "dance floor" of leaves and branches. Soon many of the others joined them, clasping hands to turn in a wide circle, whirling and clapping.

Marguerite laughed, clapping along in time to the rhythm.

"You seem in a fine mood today, Mademoiselle Dumas," Roger Tilney said, seemingly recovered from having sweet-meats shoved into his mouth.

"And so I am," Marguerite answered. "I'm always happy to be outdoors on a fine day."

"Perhaps you would care to dance, then."

Marguerite hesitated for an instant, and he whispered, "I vow I will not try to kiss you again."

She laughed. "You scarcely could, Monsieur Tilney, with so many people about! We can leave the kissing to the king and Mistress Boleyn, but I would enjoy a dance."

They slipped into one of the spinning circles, moving seamlessly into the whirling, slightly tipsy pattern. The tempo grew faster and faster, couples stepping and turning in double, triple time. Soon, even Marguerite was gasping for breath, giggling helplessly as another dancer collided with her, knocking her off balance.

"Hold! Hold, I say!"

The sudden shout brought the entire dance to an abrupt halt, couples almost falling over as their feet could no longer keep time with their brains. The music trailed away.

Marguerite swiftly steadied herself, spinning around to find a most extraordinary sight. For a moment, she feared the wine was causing visions. But she rubbed hard at her eyes, and still it was there.

Their dance floor was surrounded by outlaws clad in moss-green hose and dull brown tunics, brown leather masks concealing their faces. They held bows and arrows poised on the merrymakers.

One of the Spanish ladies gave a little yelp and promptly fainted. Marguerite went suddenly still, the mists of wine and laughter clearing from her mind in an instant. She slowly reached down for her skirt, feeling the weight of the dagger strapped to her leg. If she could just get a good line of sight on the outlaws' leader, she could surely throw her blade right into his heart…

But then she noticed an odd thing. The arrows notched into the bows were all blunted. And King Henry seemed singularly unconcerned that his banquet was being invaded by thieves. Indeed, he was smiling broadly.

Marguerite slowly let go of her skirt. Was this an English idea of a *jest,* then? She quite failed to see the humour of it, but the Englishmen of the group seemed to take it all in stride. No doubt the king had set up these masquerades before.

"What is your price to leave us in peace?" the king asked the "outlaw". "For we are merely an unarmed party this day, as you see."

"We demand wine," the outlaw answered. "And a dance with the prettiest lady among you."

"You ask a great forfeit indeed," King Henry said gruffly. What a terrible actor he was, Marguerite thought. Such an unfortunate trait for a king, who must be ever deceptive. "But to preserve our lives, I present to you the hand of the fairest lady here."

Henry took Anne's hand, giving it over ceremoniously to the outlaw leader, who gave the king a deep bow in return. The other men in green fanned out to pick over the remains of the feast, and to claim the other ladies for a dance. The musicians launched into a new song, each playing a different tune as they obviously could not recall what they were playing before.

Marguerite took advantage of the confusion to slip away, creeping toward the concealment of the trees. Her head was whirling with the wine and the silly joke.

She glanced back to find that Nicolai, too, stood apart from the noisy fray, watching after her as she left. She lifted her hand in a quick "follow me" gesture, and then slid into the shadowy woods.

The farther she walked the quieter it was, the noise of revelry fading until there was only the crackle of her booted footsteps on the underbrush. It was all grey and cool, soothing and solitary.

She took off her narrow-brimmed velvet hat, shaking her hair free of its silk caul. It fell loose down her back, and she turned her face up to the faint rays of the sun.

"You don't care to dance with a forest outlaw?" she heard Nicolai say.

She laughed, not turning away from the precious light. She felt his arms come around her waist, dragging her back against his body. His lips nuzzled at the side of her neck, and she melted into him.

"I would rather dance with *you*," she murmured. "Yet you did not ask me."

"Tilney was there before me."

"And you were so busy with Señorita Alva. You have scarce left her side all day."

Nicolai chuckled against her shoulder, his breath stirring her loose hair. "Are you jealous, *dorogaya?*"

"Of course I am." She whirled around in his arms, winding her arms tightly about his neck. He gazed down at her, bemused. "She is very pretty, very—sweet."

"Marguerite. Don't you know that when you are near I can't see anyone else? You are like no other woman, no other *person*, I have ever known."

"Truly?" And here she had thought the same of him. He was like no one else.

"Truly. No other woman could sword fight like you, ride like you, dance like you…"

"Make love like me?"

He laughed. "Assuredly not that. You drive me to madness, yet I cannot stay away from you."

"Perhaps we are both caught in some enchanted spell. Some witch's curse."

"What is the antidote?"

Marguerite shrugged. "If I only knew."

"You mean you have no counterspell in your box of tricks, *vedma?* No magical potion we could drink to be rid of each other?"

"We will be rid of each other soon enough," Marguerite whispered. It always ached so to think of their parting. To think of never seeing Nicolai again. She resolutely pushed aside the pain, going up on her toes to press her mouth to his.

How sweet his kiss was! More addictive than wine. She held on to him tightly, her body melded to his. How well she knew every inch of him now! Yet still she wanted, needed, more. Every taste of him only whetted her appetite for more and more. She craved all of him—his body, his thoughts, his past and future. Even his love, a word she had not dared not even think before.

She could have so little of that. So little of *him.* But she would take whatever she could get for as long as she had it. These moments would have to last for a very long time indeed.

Marguerite trailed small, soft kisses from his jaw, rough with a light golden stubble, to the curve of his ear and his neck just above the high collar of his doublet. How delicious he smelled, of leather and sunshine and *Nicolai.* Finer than any priceless perfume.

"We should go back," she whispered.

"Soon," he answered. He nuzzled aside a strand of her hair to kiss her temple, her cheekbone. She heard the rush of his breath against her ear. "They won't miss us for a few more minutes."

"Are a 'few minutes' long enough?"

Nicolai laughed roughly. "It depends on what you mean by 'long enough', *dorogaya.*"

She backed up, slowly trailing her touch away from his body until she stood several feet away. She tossed back her hair, smiling flirtatiously. Slowly, ever so slowly, she raised the hem of her skirt, revealing her boots and stockings, the curve of her knee and thigh. "Perhaps if we tried it against that tree over there…"

He groaned. "I believe you *are* a witch, weaving your spells of temptation."

"Only for you, *ange*," she said. "If you think—"

But her words were drowned by a sudden high-pitched whine, a swift rush as of wind. In an instant, an arrow flew between the trees, deeply scoring Marguerite's bared leg before burying itself in a rotten fallen log.

For a moment, she was too stunned to feel anything at all. Then the stinging pain rushed up her leg like a quicksilver flame. Her torn white stocking turned crimson with blood, and she felt herself falling toward the ground. Nicolai lunged forward, catching her up in his arms.

"Marguerite!" he cried, and his voice seemed very far away, as if he called to her down a long tunnel. Everything was turning hazy at the edges, all grey and misty. But Nicolai's arms were strong around her, holding her up above the pain.

"I let my guard down," she whispered. "Don't tell anyone…"

And the world turned black.

Chapter Seventeen

"*Vykhadyila, pyesnyu zavodyila, pro stepnovo, sizovo orla…*"

Vaguely, Marguerite heard a voice singing above her, deep and sweet, strange, mysterious words. She could hardly make them out, could not decipher their meaning. She turned her head, feeling the softness of a feather pillow under her cheek, the warmth of a fire against her skin.

Slowly, as if awakening from a deep spell, a half-remembered dream, she became aware of other things. A blanket tucked around her shoulders. A cool cloth pressed to her brow. The sting of her leg…

And she remembered. The picnic, the woods. Nicolai's kiss. The arrow.

Her eyes flew open. She was in a small bedchamber, and it was darkest night outside the window. The bed curtains were drawn back to the warmth of the fire, the light of a branch of candles on the table.

She knew where she was—Nicolai's chamber.

Slowly, holding her leg very still, she turned to find him sitting by the bed. He pressed a cool, damp cloth to her forehead, gazing down at her solemnly. His eyes glowed in the darkness, like blue beacons to hold her up. Guide her home.

"So, the enchanted princess awakens," he said softly, his sudden smile full of relief.

"I thought I was a witch," she whispered, her throat scratchy.

"Not tonight. Tonight, you are a princess, to be waited on hand and foot."

"By you, Nicolai?"

"Of course. I am your servant, at least until morning." He rinsed the cloth in a basin of water, ringing it out before he replaced it on her brow. "You had a touch of fever, but it seems to be coming down now. Do you remember what happened?"

Marguerite frowned. "I remember the arrow. Did you catch the shooter?"

Nicolai's lips tightened. "I fear not. There were too many people around, too many masks. King Henry swears his band of outlaws carried only blunted arrows. He sent you some of his precious malmsey wine, if you would care for a sip. It is probably not up to your Dumas standards for wine, but should suffice for now."

She nodded, and he slid his arm under her head to help her drink. The wine was sweet and cool on her throat, soothing. As he lowered her back to the pillow, she asked, "How did I come to be here, then, and not in my own chamber?"

"That is Dona Elena's doing. The king's physician wanted to bleed you, but I feared you had lost enough blood already. Dona Elena said I had trained as a physician in Turin, and that I had cured many arrow and sword wounds. So, you were given into my care."

"Is that all true?"

"The medical training in Turin? Not at all. I've never even been to Turin. But the wounds, yes. The leader of a troupe of players has to be prepared for anything."

Marguerite lifted the blanket, peering down to find her leg neatly bandaged below the hem of her short chemise. "It seems a very competent job."

"I cleansed the wound with some of that wine, then bound it up with a poultice of feverfew. It will have to be changed in the morning."

She lowered the bedclothes with a sigh. "*Alors,* Nicolai, but you are endlessly surprising."

"I could say the same about you."

"But if it was not an accident of one of Henry's faux-outlaws," Marguerite mused, "who could it have been, shooting off arrows like that in the king's park?"

"A poacher, mayhap?"

"A foolish poacher indeed, to go after his prey with the royal party so near." Her head was a bit fuzzy, and as she lifted her hand to rub at her temple she found her fingers were numb. She felt so heavy, as if she was sinking back into the mattress. Her thoughts fractured and flew away as soon as they were formed, and yet she was sure there was something important she had to know. Had to decipher. "What did you put into the wine?"

"Merely some herbs, to help you sleep. Dona Elena gathered them in the garden and ground them into a powder. She considers herself quite the apothecary."

"No doubt she learned it at the convent. They are effective—I can't keep my eyes open."

"Good. Sleep is the best healer of all."

"But I cannot sleep!" Marguerite fought against the warm

weakness, as if she kicked at a strong tide that tried to suck her under. "There is much I need to discover. I have to find out who did this."

Nicolai gently pressed her back to the bed, tucking the blanket around her shoulders. "There is nothing that cannot wait until morning."

"What if they come back to finish the job?"

"No one can hurt you, Marguerite," he said gently, soothingly. He smoothed the damp strands of her hair back from her face. "I will watch over you, never fear."

A warm peace settled over her, a sudden and profound stillness. Perhaps she *could* sleep, could let go, just this once. She caught his hand in hers, pressing his cool fingers to her flushed cheek. "I have enemies, you know."

"I know. But I will never let them near you."

"Will you lay here beside me, until I fall asleep?"

"Of course." She felt him slide on to the bed next to her, his arms gently around her waist. She curled into him, and felt her body drift away on that tide. She couldn't fight any longer.

"What was that song you were singing?" she murmured. "I heard you when I woke up."

"It was just an old folksong. My nursemaid sang it to me when I was a child. It's called 'Katyusha'."

"What is it about?"

"'Tis a tale of a maiden whose lover is far away. She walks by the river, and sends him messages of love into the wind."

"Will you sing it to me again? It was lovely."

"'When she walked, she sang a song about a grey eagle of the steppe, about him whom she loved, about him whose letter she held in her hand…'"

Marguerite drifted in that warmth, feeling his touch, so

very gentle on her hair, the certainty and strength of his body against her back.

"'Oh, you song, follow the bright sun and fly to the warrior in the far foreign country, and bring him greetings from Katyusha…'"

His song was like a bright candle, leading her onwards. Lifting her up out of the darkness.

Nicolai felt the instant Marguerite fell into sleep. Her body went limp and soft in his arms, her breath rhythmic and gentle.

His brave warrior-witch. How she fought! Against sleep, against pain, against life itself. She threw herself against all barriers until she was bruised and bloodied, but not defeated. Never defeated.

He remembered the moment she collapsed in his arms, her leg turning scarlet with her own blood, her eyes wide and startled. How still she was as he lifted her against him, still and cold and white. Almost like one already dead.

I have enemies, she had whispered. Everyone, even someone as mild as Dona Elena, had enemies in life. The Emerald Lily's must be legion, and they seemed to be everywhere. Even in an English forest, with a bow leveled on her.

Thank God the arrow found her leg and not her heart. What would he have done if she had indeed died in his arms? What would he have felt?

Once, after Venice, he could have heard of the demise of the Emerald Lily with only a pang of regret at the destruction of something so beautiful. But now—now he had come to know Marguerite, and not just her pretty face, her beautiful body. He had come to know something of what had made her the Emerald Lily, and even of the wistful yearnings of her young heart. She was a seeker, just as he was, wandering the world in search of something that remained so elusive.

If she had died today, that *something* would have remained hidden for ever, undiscovered. And he could never then decipher his own feelings for her.

Someone, one of those enemies, had nearly stolen her from him.

Nicolai pressed a soft kiss to her cheek, and slipped out of the bed. Her brow wrinkled, and she burrowed deeper under the bedclothes. He went to the window, peering down at the dark garden below.

No one was about, but in the distance he could see the figures of King Henry's guards, tall and burly in their green tunics, trading watch shifts. It must be near to morning, then, and all was quiet and still. For the moment, anyway.

He would find whoever had hurt Marguerite. And he would make them pay.

Chapter Eighteen

"What are you working on?" Marguerite asked. Unbeknownst to Nicolai, she had been awake for some time, watching him where he sat by the window. The bars of buttery morning light fell across his hair and his shoulders in the thin linen shirt, casting him in a burnished glow, like an icon from his homeland. He bent his head over a sheaf of papers, but at her words he glanced up and smiled.

"How are you feeling this morning, my princess?" he said.

"Better," she answered, flexing her foot under the sheet. "My leg hardly aches."

"Then the poultice has done its work." He left the window to come to the bed, leaning over to gently touch her brow. "The fever seems gone, too."

"I had a fine physician," Marguerite said lightly. "It must be the Turin training."

Nicolai laughed. "I see the arrow did not injure your tongue."

"Never. Here, sit by me, show me what you were looking at. Unless it is a secret…"

"Not at all." He slid on to the mattress next to her, helping her sit up against the bolsters. He smelled wonderful, as if he had just bathed with his herbal soap, and Marguerite feared she looked and smelled a mess after her time abed. Yet she could not resist leaning close to him, cuddling against his shoulder like a storm-tossed bird seeking haven.

He handed her the papers. "They are merely lists and designs for the pageant."

Marguerite glanced through them, finding sketches of banners for the green towers—one with three broken hearts, one with a lady's hand holding a man's heart, and one with the same hand turning the heart. There were also costumes, gowns, cloaks, hats, helmets.

And there were lists of characters. Beauty, Honour, Perseverance, Kindness, Constancy, Bounty, Mercy and Pity, to be clad in white. Danger, Disdain, Jealousy, Unkindness, Scorn, Sharp Tongue and Strangeness, in black. Beside every character was inked in a name. "Marguerite Dumas" by Beauty; Lady Penelope Percy, Kindness; Anne Boleyn, Perseverance.

"From what I have heard, Mademoiselle Boleyn should be Sharp Tongue," Marguerite muttered.

"I doubt King Henry would appreciate that," Nicolai said.

Marguerite laughed, and turned to the list of male characters. Love, Nobleness, Youth, Devotion, Loyalty, Pleasure, Gentleness, Liberty, led by Ardent Desire. But Nicolai's name was not among the proposed actors. "Are you truly not going to take a part yourself?"

"Nay, it will be all I can do to keep you wild women in line," he teased.

"There *are* rather a lot of us. It was not kind of Guildford to put this whole business on your shoulders." She laid aside the papers, reaching out to teasingly trace the line of his jaw and throat, dancing her fingertips down the *V* of skin bared by his unlaced shirt. She felt the rapid beat of his heart, the leap of his pulse. "But I think you would be perfect as Ardent Desire."

He caught her hand, holding it still when she would have traced her caress even lower. "Marguerite, you are ill," he said tightly.

"Not any longer, thanks to your fine physicking," she said, pressing a teasing line of light, bird's wing kisses over his cheekbone. "I feel perfectly well."

"But you cannot move your leg until tomorrow. As your physician, I command it."

"Oh-ho, you *command* it, do you?"

"Yes."

"I have never done well at obeying commands. But, of course, if you were to *ask* me, if you were to provide a suitable distraction…"

Nicolai suddenly reached down and caught her around the waist, bearing her down to lie flat on the bed, with him atop her, pinning her down. His lips swooped down on hers, kissing her hard until she was weak and breathless.

"Is that distraction enough for you?" he growled.

"Not—quite," Marguerite gasped. She reached out for him as he rolled away, but he evaded her. He swung to his feet, staring down at her sternly. She had to laugh at him, for he looked so much like her old Italian sword master, Signor Lunelli, who became ever stricter as she became more mischievous.

Nicolai laughed, too, and kissed her quickly on her brow. "Then I will give you the banners to embroider. That should keep you occupied and out of trouble for a time."

"For a day, at least. I suppose I shall have to content myself with sewing, since there will be no swiving."

"Assuredly not."

"How very cruel you are."

"Ah, Beauty, I am not the cruel one," Nicolai muttered. "Here, let me see your leg. The bandage needs to be changed."

"First you refuse me another kiss, now you demand to see my bare leg! Cruel *and* inconstant." She drew back the sheet and the hem of her chemise, watching as he unwrapped the bandage. The wound was red but clean, with no angry streaks heralding a dangerous infection. The edges were neatly sewn together and smeared with the greasy herbal poultice. "How skillful you are, Turin or not. I vow I won't even have a scar at all."

Nicolai dabbed gently at the wound with a damp cloth. "Not like those on your belly."

Marguerite hugged the fabric of her rucked-up chemise closer to her abdomen. Nicolai had kissed her there, touched her, yet he had said nothing of her old wounds before. She had begun to hope he did not notice. "They are ancient scars. I fell from my horse when I was twelve, and was kicked and trod on."

He reached up, slowly loosening her grip so he could raise the chemise. He gently traced the old, uneven pink lines, as if by his touch he could erase them.

She slowly relaxed under his warm caress, leaning back to peer down at her damaged body, strangely removed. As if the scars, the salty tears and hot despair, belonged to someone else. Someone she no longer knew.

"It must have been so painful," he said softly, his Slavic accent heavy.

"After I was carried home, the doctors told my father I would surely not live another day, that I would bleed to death."

"So foolish, to underestimate you and your stubbornness."

Marguerite laughed. "How well you know me, Nicolai. I

do not easily surrender, even to death. I held on to my life by my very fingertips, clinging and fighting. When I had recovered, I was told my womb was so scarred I could never bear a child. Never live a true woman's life."

There. She had said it aloud, for the first time ever. Usually, she dared not even think it. Of all the terrible things she had done in her life, that was the one she was most ashamed of. The thing that made her an unnatural female.

But Nicolai did not turn from her in disgust. He never had, no matter what she told him, what he discovered. He merely gazed up at her, steadily, his eyes dark blue with dawning sadness. His hands still moved gently over her leg, smoothing the poultice over the arrow wound. "And did you believe the doctors? When they were wrong in predicting your imminent death?"

Marguerite shrugged. "I did not, not at first. But I have never conceived. And my monthly courses are never predictable, never without pain." She reached down to touch his hand. "When we make love, Nicolai, you do not have to draw away. There is no danger you will send a half-French bastard out into the world to become like its cursed mother."

"Marguerite…"

"*Non,* it is quite all right, *cher.* I would truly make a terrible mother! Can you imagine what useless skills I could teach a son or, heaven forbid, a daughter?" she said, with a lightness she had never been further from feeling. "How to fight, how to kill and lie—"

"Marguerite." He pressed his fingers to her lips, stilling her mocking words. "You would be a wonderful mother. You would teach your child how to be strong, how to face the cold world and survive, come what may. How to see people for what they truly are."

She shook her head. "Do you perchance have a child, Nicolai?"

He smiled at her. "Not that I know of."

"'Tis a great pity, for you have more to offer a child than anyone I have ever met. I *do* see people as they are, but only their faults. You see their noble traits, too. You believe in their goodness, in the power of friendship."

"How could I not? I have witnessed goodness and love too often *not* to have faith in them."

"And I have never seen them, except in you. Children surely need that goodness, that acceptance, just as they need the weapons to fight the world's cruel battles." She watched in silence as he tied off a clean bandage, his touch so very light and gentle she scarcely felt it. But she did feel nearly overwhelmed by a cold incoming tide of sadness. "You *should* marry Señorita Alva, take her to your Italian farm, and have a vast brood of lovely children with her."

Nicolai laughed. "I doubt Señorita Alva would care for a rural life, far from the Spanish Court. And I am sure she knows nothing of making wine."

"But she would have beautiful babies."

He finished his ministrations, and slid up the bed to take her in his arms. Marguerite leaned her face into his shoulder, holding on to him tightly. "I would be a poor husband to a young lady like her. We would not understand each other at all."

He drew back, gazing right into her eyes. And, for the first time in her life, Marguerite felt that someone truly saw her. Every flaw, every sin, every hope. Saw, and knew.

For that one moment, it was enough to have him see her soul and not just her beauty. Not her sins. It was more than she had ever possessed before.

It was everything.

* * *

"And her headdress! Five years out of fashion, I vow," Señorita Alva chattered. "I wish you could have seen it, Señorita Dumas."

"Lady Monteath looked very pretty, Maria-Carolina," Dona Elena chided gently. The two ladies had come to help Marguerite embroider the banners, keeping her company while Nicolai went to work in the theatre.

Or run away from her. Marguerite could not tell which he was doing.

But she smiled at Dona Elena, glad of their talk, the distraction of the outside world of gossip and fashion. Just in the short time she had been confined in this small chamber, these four walls had become everything to her. She feared she would never want to leave their haven when the time came.

Would never want to leave Nicolai.

She bent her head over the banner, hiding the warm flush of her cheeks. Surely she had not blushed so much since she was a child—she had seen so much that nothing shocked her now. Yet the memory of her words with Nicolai, of the way he held her while she trembled for all she had lost in her life, made her cheeks flame. Made her want to weep.

She had pressed all that despair and anger down so very tightly over the years, locked it away until she thought it no longer existed, no longer mattered. That the hopeful young girl was dead, and there was only the Emerald Lily. But with one touch, one gentle glance, Nicolai set it all flying free again.

Someone, then, did see and understand. Someone knew. And that frightened her beyond anything. Blades and arrows she could face. She wasn't sure she could vanquish someone who saw her as she truly was, scars and all.

She wasn't sure that, in the end, she could vanquish herself.

So, she kept her fingers moving nimbly over the silk, one stitch and then another until a heart took shape. She turned her thoughts from Nicolai to the arrow itself. Was it really only an accident, born of too much wine and merriment, a careless moment? Marguerite rather thought not. She and Nicolai were too far into the woods for someone to just stumble upon them, and the aim was too straight and true.

Unless they had really been aiming for her heart…

Marguerite frowned as she turned the banner over, examining her stitches on the backside. Enemies had tried to kill her before, true, but seldom ones she could not see at all. Who knew of her true purpose here? None that she knew of—the king kept her identity a secret at all times. Only Nicolai knew. And he had been standing right before her when the arrow flew from the shadows.

Would he still have a reason to kill her? Was everything merely a game, one whose rules she had weakly forgotten?

She had to be doubly careful from now on. Their mission here in England was far from complete.

"Is that not so, Señorita Dumas?" Señorita Alva said.

"Hmm?" Marguerite answered. "Forgive me, *mademoiselle,* I was distracted for a moment."

Señorita Alva giggled. "Distracted by thoughts of Señor Ostrovsky, no doubt! Is he not terribly handsome? I wish I would fall ill, so he could tend to me."

"Maria-Carolina," Dona Elena scolded, "Señorita Dumas was gravely injured. I'm sure she has not felt up to admiring anyone's fine looks of late."

Marguerite laughed. "A lady would have to be unconscious not to notice Monsieur Ostrovsky! His eyes are so very, very blue."

"Yet I fear he has no wish to take a wife." Señorita Alva sighed. "It is so very sad."

"I am sure there are many other attractive prospects, especially for such a pretty young lady as yourself," Marguerite said encouragingly. In ladies' gossip could often be found such useful nuggets, as she had discovered with Lady Penelope Percy earlier. "There are many handsome and ambitious young men among Ambassador Mendoza's party. And with Dona Elena as your patroness…"

Señorita Alva made a face, turning away where Dona Elena could not see her. How very much she was like a shyer version of Lady Penelope Percy! Surely young ladies were the same the world over. "They are all so very dour! Even the young ones. It is all prayers and business, all the time."

"Piety and devotion to the interests of Spain is hardly *dour,* my dear," Dona Elena said. "Look at my own husband! And hasn't the Count de Garcia-Baca paid you great attention of late?"

Marguerite listened as they discussed various prospects, gleaning one or two interesting bits of information about some of the men. All the time, her needle flashed and her thoughts turned on one subject.

Who *had* fired that arrow at her, and why? What was she close to discovering?

Chapter Nineteen

The theatre seemed turned into an aviary, full of fluttering, flocking, twittering birds, bright in their silken plumage. Various Court ladies gathered in one corner of the vast room, examining lengths of black-and-white satin meant for costumes as they waited to hear what their roles would be. Anne Boleyn perched playfully on a papier-mâché throne as she giggled with her friends, poking fun at less well-dressed ladies.

Nicolai's gaze swept over the brilliant throng, gauging and evaluating. Which lady would be best for which part? But his attention kept turning back to one lady in particular—Marguerite.

She stood off to one side with Lady Penelope Percy and a few of the other English ladies, leaning on a carved walking stick that was the only outward sign of her injury. She was dressed sombrely, in brown velvet with a high Flemish collar, her hair drawn back under a pearl cap, and her conversation was quiet and subdued. Yet, as always, the light in the room seemed to gather upon her, silver and celestial, drawing everyone to her side.

She smiled serenely at Lady Penelope, self-possessed and calm even at the centre of the chattering storm. Not at all like the woman he had held in his arms as she told him of the youthful accident that changed her life, that turned her from a woman's usual path. Her whole body was stiff then, rigid and trembling with emotion too long suppressed. She gifted him with her secrets, bits of her heart like precious pearls she gave into his hands, before she withdrew again, pulled back into her icy, beautiful façade, that vulnerable, beautiful core hidden.

But he still knew it was there, the old pain, the iron strength that had borne her up through life's trials and made her what she was. What she could be.

Last night, he watched her as she slept in his bed, her face rosy and peaceful with secret dreams, her breath soft as she curled against his side. He remembered how very close he came to losing her before he could even truly find her, how he nearly watched her die before his very eyes. It awakened something in him he thought never to feel again, a tender protectiveness, a fierce instinct to keep her safe, no matter what it might take.

She herself said she had many enemies; she was surely in danger all the time. Her work guaranteed that her life would not be a long one. But he could not see that tiny, flickering flame of beauty in her heart flare out. Not now. Not when they had found each other, even if only for this short time.

Well, he was not without friends—and enemies—of his own. He had spent his life learning to peer behind masks, to ferret out secrets no matter how deeply they were hidden. Surely he could find out who shot that arrow at Marguerite, and protect her from at least one enemy.

She glanced toward him, flashing him a quick, secret

smile. For an instant, her cold façade fell, and she was the woman who kissed him good morning as the sun rose outside their window. A kiss full of gentle hope, bright promise.

Nicolai smiled at her in turn, then banged the tip of his stage manager's staff on the floor. Slowly, the chatter and flutter died away, and all the ladies turned to him, eager to hear what their roles would be.

It was time to get to work.

"And I am to play Kindness!" Lady Penelope Percy enthused, as Marguerite strolled with her along one of the garden paths. "Do you think it a good role, Mademoiselle Dumas?"

"Assuredly so," Marguerite answered. It was the longest sentence she remembered saying since they left the theatre, as Lady Penelope had a great deal of conversation herself. That was quite all right with Marguerite; in her distracted state, she was not feeling particularly voluble.

"Not as fine a part as Beauty, of course," Lady Penelope teased. "*You* will have the highest seat of all! I vow Mistress Boleyn turned quite as green as the castle with envy when she heard. But the costumes will be most lovely, and very attention-getting. Don't you think?"

"Your dark hair will be very striking against the white satin," Marguerite said. "I fear I will merely fade away!"

"Indeed you will not! You will look like an angel, and Anne Boleyn will have even more to be jealous of. At least we do not have to be one of the ladies in black. My sister is to play Disdain, and she is not at all happy. And they gave us a handsome director for once, not that impatient old Guildford! The last time I appeared in one of *his* pageants, he was constantly shouting at me about my posture and telling me not to giggle. Do you think I have such poor posture?"

Marguerite thought the girl could scarcely slouch in her stays and stiff bodice, even if she wanted to. "Certainly not."

"I did not think so. But I will want to look my best for Master Ostrovsky! He seems quite *angelic* himself."

Marguerite laughed. For had she not often thought of Nicolai as an "angel", too? An angel of beauty, of vengeance and anger—and of goodness, too. She had never known anyone like him. Certainly no one else could have coaxed her secrets from her so easily, so effortlessly, and left her feeling so very light. She slept deeply and dreamlessly in his arms, for the first time in many years.

An angel of peace, too, perhaps.

"Have your thoughts turned from the gentleman you once thought handsome, then, Lady Penelope?" she asked.

"Ah, yes, the comte! No, indeed, but I see him so very seldom. All the men are so solemn these days, thinking of nothing but alliances and treaties."

"Alliances and treaties" were surely the only way for England and France to stand against the ambitions of the Emperor, and thus safeguard them all. Marguerite did not say this, though. Lady Penelope seemed not to care about the intricacies of the Holy Roman Empire, and truth to tell Marguerite herself found it hard to focus on faraway threats at the moment. Not with all-too-immediate arrows pointed right at her—and Nicolai Ostrovsky's danger to her vulnerable heart.

"I am sure no one will be thinking of treaties at the pageant," Marguerite said. "Not with you looking so alluring in your white satin."

Lady Penelope laughed. "How right you are, Mademoiselle Dumas! The comte cannot fail to notice me then, even if our faces will be hidden by those gold masks. I will learn to gesture most elegantly. Perhaps you could help me?"

Marguerite remembered the Piazza San Marco, the woman who had played Columbine to Nicolai's Arlecchino. Her every gesture was full of elegance, of playful mischief. Marguerite wondered who she was, what had become of her, what she was to Nicolai.

"I know nothing of theatrical gestures," she said.

"Of course you do! Why, every man here is in love with you already, just from watching you dance. I have heard that Roger Tilney is writing you a sonnet, though it is meant to be a secret. I do not think I have ever had a sonnet written for *me!*"

Marguerite laughed. "And who would you want a poem from, pray tell?"

As Lady Penelope listed a few of her suitors—"Dull men, with no poetry in them"—they turned along another pathway. A page dashed up to Marguerite, handing her a folded note before running off again.

"You see?" Lady Penelope said. "A sonnet already."

"If it *is* a sonnet, it's a rather thin one," Marguerite mused. She broke the seal, a plain red wax with no signet, and unfolded the square of parchment.

"Be wary," the message said, in plain, block letters. "Trust no one. Danger can lurk in unexpected corners. A Friend." Below the stark words was sketched a crude arrow and a coffin.

Marguerite crushed the note in her hand, feeling suddenly icy cold despite the mild afternoon. Her other hand tightened on the head of her walking stick, until she felt the carved wood bite into her skin.

She glanced hastily around, but the page was gone, and no one was staring at her in a suspicious manner. Was the letter-writer one of the "lurking dangers", watching her even now? Biding their time before another arrow was loosed?

"Is it a very bad poem, then?" Lady Penelope asked.

Marguerite made herself laugh. "Very bad indeed! You must count yourself fortunate, Lady Penelope, that you have never been subjected to such."

She tucked the crumpled note into the little velvet pouch at her waist, and managed to walk on with Lady Penelope, chattering about Court gossip as if she hadn't a care beyond badly composed poetry. When Lady Penelope joined another group of ladies, Marguerite excused herself and made her way back to the theatre.

She didn't know what she would do or say once she got there. How could she possibly show Nicolai what was really nothing more than a childishly scribbled little note? What could he do?

But she wanted, needed, to see him. To feel the strange, alluring warmth and light his presence always brought her.

She slipped into the now-silent space. All the giggling ladies had scattered, leaving trails of white satin and gilt crowns behind. From some far corner could be heard the strains of a lute, as someone practised for yet another of the endless entertainments. The song was a sad one, lonely and plaintive amid all this dusty, artificial splendour. Marguerite paused to listen, the hollow in her very centre aching.

As the music died away, she tiptoed to the doorway of Nicolai's room, peeking inside. He sat at a small table in the corner, surrounded by stacks of papers, his pen scratching as he no doubt wrote the final notes on the day's rehearsal. From her shadowed spot, she saw his profile, sharp and elegant, framed by the bright hair he had swept impatiently over one shoulder. His brow was creased in a slight frown, the corner of his lips turned down as if he, too, had heard the melancholy song of the lute. Had felt the soft, cold touch of fate.

Marguerite suddenly longed to weep, to sink down on to the floor in a storm of tears and wailing. She had not cried in so very long; tears availed a person nothing, changed nothing. Life was as it was, a world peopled by the selfish and the cruel, and only by being just as selfish and cruel could one survive. Tears were a weakness. Yet now, that cold hollow contracted painfully, squeezing her heart until she couldn't breathe. Her eyes itched, her throat grew tight with the tamped-down sorrows of years.

She pressed her hand to her stomach and turned away, reluctant to let Nicolai see her this way. To show anyone how she felt. But he heard the rustle of her skirts, and glanced up just as she would have slipped away.

The frown cleared from his brow, and he smiled at her in welcome. "Marguerite!" he called. "You have come to save me from this tedious work, I see."

Marguerite pasted on her own smile, hoping her eyes were not red-rimmed as she turned back to him. "La, is it so very *tedious* to work with dozens of lovely ladies? Most men would consider it a godsend."

"Most men have never had the dubious privilege of trying to herd a wild pack of Court ladies into some semblance of a coherent tableau," he said, holding out his hand to her.

She reached for it, his fingers closing securely over hers as he drew her closer. As his skin touched hers, so warm and strong and *alive*, some of that ice that bound her heart dripped away, melted drop by tiny drop.

She tumbled down into his lap, her walking stick clattering away as she wound her arms around his neck, burying her face in the curve of his shoulder. How lovely he was, her wild Muscovite of the north, with his clean, crisp heat, the softness of his velvet doublet against her cheek! When she was close to him like this, that selfish world fell away, and there was only the two of them. Only their own small realm where nations and politics and names like the Emerald Lily meant nothing. *Were* nothing.

These moments were so fleeting, though, and soon enough there would be no more of them at all. She had to cling close to them while she could. Store them up in her most secret heart, to keep her warm in cold winters ahead.

"'Tis true that we are not real actors," she murmured. "We want only the best, most visible roles for ourselves. Lady Penelope Percy wants to attract fine suitors. We aren't like your Venetian Columbine."

Nicolai laughed. "What do you know of *my* Columbine?"

"I saw her with you, you know. In the Piazza San Marco. She was very pretty."

"How could you tell, in her mask?"

"Well, she had a pretty bosom anyway. *Everyone* could see that, her bodice was so tight."

He laughed harder, drawing her so close she could feel the warm, deep echo of the sound in her own heart. "It is true that once there was a bit of a romance between Masha and me, but it is done now."

Marguerite smiled at the sudden pang of smug satisfaction she felt at that bit of news. "She did not care to be a farmer's wife, then?"

"On the contrary. She married a farmer's son she met there in Venice, and they are taking care of my new property until I can return to it."

"But you are not returning to *her?* Such an arrangement, if the farmer's son is complacent, could be most convenient."

"I am not interested in such *convenience*." He drew her

ever closer, resting his chin atop her head. "You see, I, too, met someone in Venice…"

Marguerite bristled, the smugness quite vanished, but he would not let her go. "Yet another woman?"

"Aye, a woman with hair like moonbeams, and eyes like emeralds under ice. After her kiss—and the kiss of her dagger—I could think of no one else. She haunted me for many months, until at last I found her again."

She laughed, relaxing back into his arms. "You silly flirt, Nicolai Ostrovsky. What happened when you found her, then?"

"She enchanted me all over again. I can see no one else now. I doubt she will ever release me from this spell."

"She cannot." Marguerite glanced up at him, delicately touching the line of his cheek. His skin was like warm, taut satin, roughened with the light golden sheen of his beard. "For she, too, is bound by the spell."

She pressed a quick kiss to his cheek and slid off his lap, going to the corner where his tightrope was stretched across the empty space. "I thought you could verily fly, when I saw you walk this rope," she said, testing its strength with her fingertips. Such a thin, flimsy barrier between a person and the oblivion that always waited below. "I thought it, and you, were magic."

He came to her side, close, so close, but not touching her. "No magic," he said. "Just years of practice. Of cracking my head time after time until I learned not to."

"A lesson some of us never learn. We just bang our head against the same wall time and again, always foolishly expecting a new result." She closed her fist around the rope, feeling its rough fibres on her palm just as she had the edges of that vile note. "There *is* a magic in you, Nicolai. You fly where the rest of us remain earthbound, tied to our old ways, our old mistakes and fears."

She stepped back, reaching down to unbuckle her shoes and kick them away. "Help me up."

Nicolai frowned. "Marguerite, no. Your leg—"

"Please," she interrupted, insistent. She longed to feel that rope under her feet, to feel what Nicolai felt, even if only for an instant before she did indeed crack her head. She wanted it more than she had ever wanted anything—except Nicolai himself.

"Please," she said softly. "I only want to try. You will hold my hand, yes? With you beside me I can never fall."

He studied her closely for a moment. Even though doubt still clouded his eyes, he finally nodded. "Only a few steps, though."

Marguerite clapped her hands, suddenly filled with sparkling excitement. She watched as Nicolai dragged a stool closer to the rope, and took her hand as he helped her up on to it and from there to the rope itself. He held her by the waist as she cautiously arranged her stocking feet, one in front of the other, the rope aligned with her soles as she had seen him do.

"You are a fine dancer, Marguerite," he said. "And this is just like dancing. You must find your core, your centre of balance. Stay straight and strong through your torso, bend your knees slightly. Use your arms, as you would in a pavane."

She took in a deep, steadying breath, tightening the muscles of her abdomen as she drew herself up straight. She imagined she was in a dance, and slowly her wobbles ceased. Her legs felt strong, an extension of the rope itself, and she was still.

Nicolai's touch eased from her waist. "Don't let go of me!" she cried, feeling that balance tilt.

"I still have your hand," he said gently, his fingers secure on hers. "I will always catch you if you fall. But you are standing on your own."

Much to her surprise, she found that was true. She *was* standing on her own, his hand bearing her lightly aloft.

"Now, take a step," he urged.

"A step?"

"I know you can. Remember, like a dancer. Keep that centre of balance, and lift your back foot. Make your movements smooth, not too rushed, and place it in front."

Marguerite nodded, fiercely determined to do just thus. Holding her free hand out, parallel to the ground, she slowly, very slowly, lifted her back foot an inch from the rope. Imagining she was gliding across the dance floor, she stepped to the front, carefully placing her sole on the centre of the rope.

"*Haroshiy!*" Nicolai said, his voice full of admiration. "Very good."

Emboldened, she took another step and another. That cold hollow at her centre filled with a rush of pride and excitement. She could do this! She *was* doing it. That strength at her core expanded and grew, until she was suffused with that golden glow she always sensed around Nicolai.

His hand slid away from hers until only their fingertips touched. She took another step and another, and another, her movements quicker, easier. She laughed, full of delight such as she had never known since she was a child, running free among the fragrant summer vines. This was glorious! Surely she really could fly.

At the end of the rope, Nicolai again caught her around the waist, lifting her from the rope and swinging her around and around in an exultant circle. Her head fell back in delight, and she laughed until tears sprang to her eyes, spilling free.

"Marguerite, *dorogaya,* you did it!" Nicolai cried. "You walked the length of the rope, on your very first try."

As he lowered her to her feet, she leaned her cheek to his chest, laughing and crying all at once. The very force of life itself rushed through her like tiny kisses of fire. "Only because you held me up, Nicolai."

"Oh, Marguerite." His arms held her close. "You held *yourself* up. You have your own wings, and now you have found them."

Her own wings. Perhaps she had, those tiny, tentative hopes that urged her ever forward, urged her toward a goodness she had never known until Nicolai. He gave her that hope, those wings.

But was it all much, much too late?

Chapter Twenty

"What say you, my lord, with your fat face?"

King Henry roared with laughter at the jests of his favourite fool, Will Somers. But the smiles of the courtiers around him were distinctly more strained, the lines of their set, rigid faces full of fear that *they* would be the next to feel the clown's acerbic wit.

Marguerite was glad she sat far down the banquet hall from the king's dais, so she could just watch the spectacle and not be a part of it. She had no wit left, and no laughter, either. Every nerve end was on edge, every sense heightened, after her walk on the tightrope.

In truth, her whole life had been like that rope. One careful, cautious step in front of the other, acutely aware of everything around her. Every hint that a fall could be imminent.

But today she had *not* fallen. And now it was even harder to be earthbound again, to be caught in the gilded cage of kings.

Nicolai was nowhere to be seen at tonight's banquet. Dona Elena and her husband sat at their accustomed places with Ambassador Mendoza, surrounded by their watchful attendants. Yet Nicolai was not among them. Nor was he one of the players who juggled and jested among the guests. The room seemed distinctly darker without him.

Father Pierre, a silent, watchful presence beside Marguerite, placed a sweetmeat on the plate before her.

"*Merci,*" she murmured, nibbling cautiously at its honeyed edges. Ever since the arrow, the strange note, she couldn't help but wonder what lurked around every corner, behind every tapestry. Even—especially—men of the Church could not be trusted.

"Have you recovered from your unfortunate accident, *mademoiselle?*" he asked.

"Yes, quite recovered, thank you. There will scarcely even be a scar."

"They say that the Russian attached to the Spanish party was your physician."

Marguerite glanced at Father Pierre from the corner of her eye, but she could read little from his expression. He just looked as solemn as ever, as if he expected something from her, watched for something. Something she could not decipher or fathom. "So he was. He is very skilled."

"Is he skilled only at physicking, though?"

"What do you mean?" Marguerite asked coldly. She had found the priest to be most irritating on this voyage, and never more than tonight. She still felt the warm, glowing after-effects of her walk on the rope, of flying free in Nicolai's arms. She didn't want it all to be spoiled, not by anyone. It would all fade soon enough as it was.

Father Pierre shrugged, turning away as if he could not bear to look at her any longer. "I just do not know if it is a wise thing to spend so much time with the Spanish and their allies. They are not our friends, Mademoiselle Dumas, no matter how pleasant a face they put on. They are opposed to our mission here, and will surely use any means to stop the treaty from going forward."

Marguerite glanced toward Dona Elena, who was smiling gently up at her husband. "I am not so great a fool as all that, Father Pierre," she murmured. "I know the ways of a royal Court; I know that no one is really a friend." She spoke with steely conviction, but a tiny voice in her mind whispered doubts. Yes, she *had* known that, once; the wily intricacies of Court politics were her very life. But now…

Had she forgotten? Was she lured by Nicolai's passion, Dona Elena's kindness?

"That is not true," Father Pierre said intently, leaning so close she could smell the rustiness of his woollen robes, feel the disconcerting heat of his thin body. She edged away on the bench. "There are always true friends, if you know where to look for them."

"I will remember your counsel," she said quietly.

"I am always here to listen to your concerns, *mademoiselle.* Sometimes the consolations of heaven are the best to be found, apart from all earthly concerns."

Marguerite pursed her lips. She doubted that heavenly concerns were all he—or any man—had in mind. "*Merci,* Father," she answered.

A page stopped to pour more wine into her goblet, and Marguerite seized the excuse to move farther away from the priest. As she turned to engage the couple on her other side in conversation, the doors to the banquet hall opened and a new group slipped inside, unnoticed in the clamour of wine and conversation. Unnoticed by all but Marguerite, that is, for one of the men was Nicolai.

He wore his fine red velvet Court clothes, his hair tied back to reveal the pearl dangling from his ear, the fine gold embroidery on his high collar. The man with him, though, was someone Marguerite had never seen before. She studied him carefully, this unexpected new thread in the tapestry.

He was tall, even taller than Nicolai, and lean with long, coiled muscles beneath his black velvet and leather garments. Straight, shining light brown hair fell over his shoulders, and his handsome oval face, bronzed by a sun that never shone on England, was framed by a close-cropped beard that roughened his youthful beauty. The gaze he swept over the room was a dark, mossy forest green, heavy with a cynical, humourless amusement. His tall black boots, though clean and fashioned of fine leather, were scuffed and worn; the dagger at his belt crowned with a plain, worn hilt.

A man of action, then. But who was he? He did not have the look of an actor about him, as Nicolai did. He lacked that quick, changeable lightness, that golden glow. If Nicolai was her angel, this man was like some lord of the underworld, trailed by dark clouds and ravens.

As Nicolai and the stranger moved into the banquet hall, followed by a few other watchful, black-clad attendants, speculative glances and sudden whispers grew. They had all been trapped together in the opulent prison of Greenwich for too many long days—a new player in the game aroused an inordinate amount of interest.

The men stopped at Dona Elena's table, speaking quietly with her and her husband, seeming to take no notice of all the curiosity they garnered. Yet, if Marguerite had learned anything about Nicolai, it was that he always noticed *everything*.

She slipped from her seat, edging her way around the back wall of the room. She was glad she had worn her subdued russet satin gown and matching headdress tonight, it helped her blend in, move from group to group, listening but not really seen. She reached the corner of the Spanish group, where Señorita Alva sat with her young companions.

"Ah, Señorita Dumas!" she said, gesturing for Marguerite to come closer. "We were just speaking of Señor Ostrovsky's new friend. Do you know him?"

"If you do not, I am not likely to," Marguerite said lightly. "I must admit he is quite handsome. Such a dangerous air! Do you mean that he is not a new member of your own party, sent from Madrid?"

"None of us has ever seen him before," Señorita Alva said. "Esperanza thinks he is a Mediterranean pirate!"

Another lady ducked her head, giggling into her handkerchief. No doubt she was the one who espoused the "pirate" theory.

"Would Monsieur Ostrovsky really introduce a pirate to Dona Elena?" Marguerite asked. She was quite certain Nicolai knew some pirates, as he seemed to know everyone. Bringing them to Court, though…

"It is more likely he is just a merchant, from Venice, perhaps, or Naples," one of the young men said contemptuously. "Hardly worthy of all this fuss."

Señorita Alva said nothing, but the flash of her dark eyes said *she* found him "worthy of the fuss". They went on to speak of other matters, and Marguerite settled down with them to sip some wine and listen—and bide her time.

Soon enough, one of the duke's attendants came by to invite them all to Dona Elena's apartment later for cards and to meet "Señor Balthazar Grattiano, of Venice".

So, he *was* Venetian, Marguerite mused, watching the newcomer where he sat with Dona Elena. He was certainly polite and correct, but his smiles never quite reached his eyes. His handsome face never lit with mirth, but was tense and watchful. Not an actor, not a pirate. Not a merchant, either, she would wager. Who was this Grattiano, and what was he doing in England?

Marguerite did not care for puzzles and surprises.

She excused herself from the others, rising to make her way out of the hall, to see what she could decipher of this new puzzle on her own. As she reached the doors, a sudden sharp tingling pricked at the back of her neck. The same tingling that warned her she was being watched—usually. It had not warned her of arrows in the woods.

She glanced back over her shoulder to find Father Pierre still staring at her. He gave a slight shake of his head, as if to discourage her yet again from talking with the Spanish.

Marguerite spun around, hurrying out of the banquet hall. *Alors,* she thought. If there was anyone she should be warned away from, it was surely the priest himself!

Chapter Twenty-One

"I am glad you have come here, Balthazar," Nicolai said, as he and Balthazar Grattiano walked by the river's edge. So late at night the water was quite deserted. Only the inky wavelets, etched with pale moonlight, lapped along the banks, listening to their words, but it was deeper and more dangerous than it appeared. Far away, as if from some other world, echoed the loud revelry from the banquet house. "Though you may be sorry you did, once you realise the web you have landed in."

Balthazar shook his head. With his black clothes and dark beard, he became part of the night himself, a part of all its hidden secrets. That roiling, bone-deep anger Nicolai had always sensed in him in Venice was still there, just carefully pressed down, concealed beneath his new solemn mien of a ship's captain.

"I was on my way to the West Indies, anyway," Balthazar said. "Marc is sending provisions and trade goods to Mexico by way of Puerto Rico and Hispaniola, and I offered to captain the *Elena Maria* on this voyage."

"And it was merely a simple trifle to stop at Greenwich on your way from Seville, eh?" Nicolai teased.

A small smile touched the edges of Balthazar's lips. "Well, perhaps not so *simple* as all that. But journeying along the Thames is a good lesson, as I hope to captain my own ship soon enough and need the experience. And Marc and Julietta are still a bit concerned about Dona Elena. The word is that the French are being quite ruthless in the interests of their new alliance."

Nicolai thought of the Emerald Lily, of all the other hidden spies who were probably embedded in the French contingent, all over Greenwich. "They are determined, true enough, as they always are. Yet I do not think Elena is in any danger. No matter what happens with this treaty, she and the duke will be going home soon enough."

"It is *you,* I think, who must face the greatest danger."

Nicolai frowned. Could Balthazar have already heard of Marguerite, heard of his feelings for her and the complications they brought? "What do you mean?"

"I mean that when you went to fetch more wine, Dona Elena told me of her great determination to see you betrothed before they return to Spain. You are in grave danger of being a married man, I fear, with a demure Spanish wife to carry home."

Nicolai laughed. "She is a very ardent matchmaker, true. But I am quite equally determined to avoid a wedding."

"So, avoiding the nuptial mass is all that has been occupying you in England?"

Nicolai thought of all that had happened since he came to Greenwich on this unwelcome errand. How could he even begin to untangle it all, to make a coherent tale of it? "That and the fact that I have been put in charge of a pageant featuring no less than sixteen Court ladies."

Balthazar laughed aloud at that news, a sound that seemed

rusty from disuse. "You *are* in danger, my friend! I would rather face the guns of a fleet of Barbary pirates than assign roles to sixteen ladies."

"Ah, but you chose to leave your cosy little wooden world aboard ship and come to Court," Nicolai said. "You have to face a new kind of weapon here. I am in need of an assistant for the pageant, and I think you will be most suited for the job."

Balthazar backed away, his hands raised as if to ward off a deadly curse. "No, Nicolai, anything but that! I know naught of plays and such."

"But you *do* know of women. I saw how they reacted to you in Venice, curled up at your feet like docile little kittens, claws perfectly sheathed. You will be the ideal person to help me herd them safely through the pageant."

Balthazar still shook his head. "I do know something of women, perhaps, considering that romance was my only pastime in my misspent youth. But *sixteen...*"

"Many of them are very pretty," Nicolai coaxed. From the corner of his eye, he caught a glimpse of moonlight shining on russet satin. He turned to see Marguerite hurrying silently along the river walkway. Had she been following them all this time?

Nicolai cursed at his own folly, his own moment of unwariness. It was not like him, or it *should* not be like him, not in such times as these. "Ah, there is one of our fair players now," he said, loud enough for his voice to carry to her. "Mademoiselle Dumas, what a surprise to see you here!"

Marguerite froze in her tracks, and for an instant she looked like an extension of the low wall she half-hid behind. Then she straightened and edged out from the darkness, strolling toward them calmly as if it was perfectly conventional for a young lady to be creeping about the riverside in the middle of the night.

As she emerged into the moonlight, Balthazar's eyes widened. "I do see what you mean, Nicolai," he murmured. "Pretty indeed."

Nicolai suppressed the violent urge to knock his friend down. "That is Mademoiselle Dumas, one of the Comtesse de Calonne's attendants."

"Good eve, Monsieur Ostrovsky," Marguerite said, folding her hands neatly at her waist. "I see I am not the only one who craved a breath of fresh air."

"Indeed not. May I introduce my friend, Signor Balthazar Grattiano? He is newly arrived from Venice."

"Monsieur Grattiano," she said, with a graceful curtsy, holding out her hand to Balthazar. "A new face is most welcome here at Greenwich."

"If only it was a face as lovely as your own, Mademoiselle Dumas," Balthazar answered, pressing a lingering kiss to her fingers.

Nicolai rolled his eyes, but Marguerite just laughed, pleased. "Signor Grattiano has agreed to assist with our pageant," Nicolai said, smoothly inserting himself between Marguerite and Balthazar. She tucked her hand easily into the crook of his arm, as if she had been doing so for years and years.

"Do you require an assistant?" she asked as they strolled on. "You seem to have been doing so very well on your own. It will certainly be the finest, most elegant pageant this poor English Court has ever seen!"

"Only because certain ladies have been unexpectedly compliant with the direction thus far," Nicolai said. "But I expect that will soon change."

Marguerite laughed. "I am sure you cannot mean *me!* Nicolai, you will give Signor Grattiano the wrong impression of me, I fear. I want nothing but the best for this pageant— and all your endeavours."

They exchanged a long glance, and her hand tightened on his arm.

"I am merely here to assist in any way I can," Balthazar said. "But now I must return to the banquet, for I promised Dona Elena I would not be gone for long. She says she wants to hear all about the new Venetian fashions."

"Do be cautious, *signor,*" Marguerite said lightly. "Or you will surely find yourself betrothed by the end of the night!"

"I will pay heed to your kind warning, Mademoiselle Dumas." With a low bow, Balthazar backed away, leaving Nicolai and Marguerite alone by the river.

They stood there in silence for a long moment, and then Marguerite removed her hand from his arm, strolling slowly away with him a pace behind her.

"Your friend has created a great deal of intrigue among the ladies," she said. "They whisper and giggle about how handsome and mysterious he is!"

"Ladies usually do. He was much sought after in Venice."

"Was he? La, but so very many things seem to happen in Venice! I wonder that anyone lives anywhere else. Is he a member of your troupe?"

"You know he is not. He is the captain of one of Marc Velazquez's ships. He says he stopped here on a voyage to the West Indies, to make certain of Dona Elena's welfare."

"Such devoted protectors Dona Elena has. All women should be so fortunate."

Nicolai caught her hand, spinning her back into his arms. She nestled there, laughing, her hands pressed to his shoulders, lightly caressing through the velvet. "You find Baltha-zar handsome, do you?" he growled.

"Not nearly as handsome as *you!*"

"So, you were following us just to gaze at our pretty visages?"

She tilted her head back, staring up at him with wide eyes. "I was not following. I merely needed an escape from the banquet, and when I saw you talking with your friend I didn't want to interrupt."

"Then you were not eavesdropping?"

The hand on his shoulder tensed from a caress into a slap. "I was much too far away to eavesdrop! And I would have been more clever about it, surely. But I do confess to some curiosity about your friend."

"If you come to play cards in Dona Elena's apartment later, I am sure Balthazar would be happy to assuage your curiosity himself."

Marguerite nodded, suddenly serious, like a cloud scudding over the sun. "I will come to Dona Elena's, but…"

"But what?"

"Can I come to your chamber later?" she whispered, though there was no one to hear them. "I want to ask your counsel about something."

Nicolai's arms tightened around her, his every sense suddenly heightened by whatever that light was in her eyes. "Has something else happened? Something like the arrow?"

She shook her head. "Not really, but—I will tell you later, yes?"

"Very well," he said slowly, drawing her closer. "Later."

Chapter Twenty-Two

Marguerite smoothed the note on her palm—*Danger can lurk in unexpected corners.* What did it all mean? She knew she had enemies. Who in the dangerously, precariously balanced world she lived in did not? But why come after her, and why warn her, now? What had changed?

She glanced from the note to the scene outside her window. It was so very dark outside; even the moon dared not show its face now, hiding behind a veil of lacy clouds. The gardens were quiet, just as silence lay heavily over the whole palace. Even all of Dona Elena's *primero*—playing guests had returned to their own chambers, tucked in to wait for the dawn, for whatever the next day might bring, whether resolution, conclusion, or yet more treading in place as King Henry prevaricated. More empty, false merriment.

Marguerite usually did not consider herself to be imaginative or fanciful. She dealt in what truly was, in the real, sordid nature of human beings, not in what she wished to be so. Not in the celestial beauty and perfect love of the poets. But tonight she had the chilling sense that something was shifting out there in that darkness. Some force was creeping in, like a thick Thames fog, and she could not even see it. Could not begin to fight it.

Who had sent that note? What did they know that she did not?

She knew only one person who could help her find the answers, one person who possessed the knowledge and insight of human nature to begin to judge. And if he was the person who wrote it—well, surely she would be able to see it in the clear blue light of his eyes.

Marguerite tucked the note carefully into the pouch tied at her waist, and reached for her cloak, concealing her bright hair under the hood. The corridors were dark, too, filled with unwavering shadows that turned all the rich furnishings and tapestries to menacing ghosts. Filled with cold draughts that made every sigh a threat. But her feet knew the path by rote now, and she sped on her way.

At Nicolai's door she paused for a moment, leaning close to listen. She heard only the faint rustle of papers.

Without knocking, she slipped inside, shaking her hair free from the hood. He sat at his small desk under the window, clad only in a bedrobe of red brocade trimmed with Russian sable, reading by the wavering light of a candle. He glanced up and smiled at her entrance, as if he had been expecting her all along.

And how could he not? Surely he knew now that she could never stay away. That she was always drawn inexorably to his golden light and heat like a moth to a torch. The moth also knew the flame would singe its wings, but could not resist.

"What are you reading?" she asked quietly. "Never say you are working on the ridiculous pageant at this late hour."

"Indeed not," he said. "I have had quite enough of Beauty and Disdain and the others. These are some letters Balthazar delivered."

"Ah, yes, the mysterious Signor Grattiano," she said. She rested her hands lightly on Nicolai's shoulders, peering down at the jumble of documents. None of them appeared to bear official seals, no orders from the Tsar of Russia or the Doge of Venice. "How amusing it was to watch all of Dona Elena's fair damsels flirt so madly with him, and he with them! With not a flash of sincerity in his eyes. He is quite the most serious man I have ever seen."

"He is readying for that journey to the West Indies," Nicolai said, reaching up to touch her hand. "The New World beckons. I doubt he is thinking of flirtation so much as stocking his ship with provisions."

"The New World," she echoed musingly. She ran her fingers through the glistening strands of his hair, thinking of all the tempting possibilities of the wider world. "I have heard it is a vast and empty place, where the sun shines all the time, and the oceans are like sapphires they are so clear and blue. That pearls blanket the beaches, and the silence is perfect."

"Should you like to go there, Marguerite? There are no Court intrigues or satin gowns, no gingerbread or sweet malmsey wine," Nicolai teased.

She laughed. "I should dearly love to sail away from all those things! Except the wine, of course. But I also hear there are fevers and savage natives, and far too many Spaniards littered about. Perhaps the New World is not for me."

"Nor for me, I confess. But it will all suit Balthazar admirably, I'm sure. Perhaps he can lose his ghosts in those tropical forests."

Ghosts. Yes, that was why she was here tonight. She had nearly forgotten in the dream of faraway lands. She feared her own ghosts could not be left behind on any islands, nor in dark castle corridors. She drew a stool up close to Nicolai's chair and sat down, reaching into her pouch to draw forth the note.

For an instant she hesitated. Never had she asked for help before—the Emerald Lily never needed it. But Marguerite needed it. She had to know.

Nicolai frowned, as if he sensed her shift in mood, her doubts and fears. He crossed his arms over his chest, watching her steadily.

"What is amiss, Marguerite?" he said. "Has something happened? Another attack?"

She shook her head. "Not yet. But I received this." She handed the note to Nicolai, her hand trembling. She watched him very closely, studying him for any sign, any trace of guilt.

He read it in silence, studying the block letters longer than the brief words required. She saw no starts or flares, only the faintest flush of angry red under the bronze of his cheekbones. His fingers tightened on the paper, and when he spoke his voice was rough, his accent thick. "You do not know who sent this?"

"It was delivered by a page, and when I tracked the boy down he said it was placed by his pallet, with a note saying to deliver it to me. And the handwriting is not familiar to me."

"You have received no others?"

"Not like that. I have received threats in the past, of course, but they have seldom been couched as warnings! I am most puzzled."

"So, you came to me for help? Or perhaps to discover if I sent it?" He glanced up at her, his eyes clouded and serious.

Marguerite stared back. "Did you?"

"Surely you know me better by now, *dorogaya*. If I wanted to threaten, or warn, you, I would do so to your face. I have nothing to hide from you."

Marguerite saw, *knew,* the truth of that. He did not hide from her. She could no longer hide from him. Or from herself. "I know," she said simply.

Nicolai nodded, and gave her back the note. "Who knows of your purpose here, besides the two of us? The bishop, the comte?"

She shook her head, putting the paper back into her pouch. "No one. King François knows well that the effectiveness of his spies lessens with each person who knows their identity. The comte and comtesse both believe I have been sent to attend on her, though truly I do not spend much time in her company. I think she suspects I have been sent here as someone's mistress! Probably her husband's. She does not trust me."

"And if it was one of the Spanish…"

"They would simply kill me, and toss my body into the river."

Nicolai reached for one of the letters on his desk, turning it over to write on the blank back. He dipped his pen into the inkwell and jotted down "Comte and Comtesse de Calonne." "Who else can we possibly suspect? Tell me everyone, no matter how far-fetched."

They worked over their list for a long time, adding more names, more suspicions, until Marguerite's head whirled. She knew she lived with danger, true. It had been her trade for years. Yet it was oddly disconcerting to see it all written there, in stark black ink.

Her head ached with it all, and she rubbed at her temples. The strange miasma of the night grew thicker around her, a sticky web that wound tighter and tighter until she feared she would never escape it.

Nicolai glanced up from the list, his brow creased in concern. "Are you well, *dorogaya?*"

"Yes, of course. Just tired, I think."

"And not yet fully healed, I fear. I should not keep you up making lists," he said, putting aside his pen and reaching out for her.

"Certainly we should stay up making lists! It is important," she insisted, but she did slip gratefully into his waiting arms. They were like a warm, strong shelter, a place where, for one moment, arrows and warning notes had no place. No meaning. She curled on to his lap, burying her face in his robe's glossy fur trim. "I came to you for help, after all. To use your cleverness for my own ends."

"And I am glad you did," he said, his voice like rough, soothing thunder that moved all through her. Into her, like that cord that bound them together wherever they were. "But also puzzled."

"Puzzled?"

"I thought the Emerald Lily trusted no one. Needed no one."

"She does not." Marguerite drew back to gaze up at him. She touched his cheek lightly, and suddenly it was as if the dark night parted, and, for one shining moment, she glimpsed the bright, hard light of truth. Swifter and more painful than any arrow. Unbearably beautiful. "But Marguerite does. Marguerite trusts only *you*."

And loved only him. That was the burning, blinding truth that struck her heart. She loved Nicolai with all she had. With every fibre of her black-spotted heart and soul. He was all she had thought never existed—beauty, goodness, intelligence, with a heart full of light and humour and honesty. All *she* was not, and did not deserve. Yet that did not stop her from loving him, needing him. Trusting him.

She remembered that night in the Venetian bordello, and

her heart pounded at the thought of how close she came to losing him. How close she came to killing him, her own love! Something had stopped her hand, though, and brought them to this moment.

Suddenly, she felt the hot flood of tears in her eyes, tears that would no longer be suppressed and held back. She pressed her hand hard to her mouth, choking back raw sobs filled with the frustrations, and wants and needs, and loneliness of years. She ducked her head back to his shoulder, praying that he would not see, that he would not glimpse her weakness.

But he *did* see, just as he always saw everything. He hugged her close, so close it was as if they became one. "I will not betray your trust, Marguerite," he said firmly. "And I will not let you die. I promise."

Overcome by his simple, gentle words, she kissed him, pressing her lips hard to his, winding her arms around his shoulders to bind him to her. It was like no kiss before had ever been. It was her spell to hold him with her, so that he would never forget her, never forget what they found here for one brief, perfect moment.

Nicolai groaned, and she felt his embrace tighten, felt him rise to his feet, lifting her with him. She wrapped her legs about his waist, and the world spun and tilted as he carried her to the bed, slowly lowering her to the velvet blankets.

He eased away from her greedy kiss, trailing a tiny, alluring ribbon of caresses from her cheek to her throat, drawing away her clothes. They spoke no words, just watched each other in the dying candleglow as he undressed her and himself. When they were both naked, vulnerable, he slipped back into her arms, and they just held each other in silent, desperate hope. Need.

Marguerite rested her cheek at the curve of his shoulder, closing her eyes as she inhaled his scent with such longing. This man, this moment, was all she thought could never be hers in this life. Now it *was* hers, so fleeting and precious. She had to memorise it all, everything—the smooth, hot feel of his skin against hers, his cool breath on her brow, the way he smelled and sounded and kissed. Then, when this was over and she was alone again in France, she could tuck this moment away like a jewel, like her mother's diamond, and take it out when she needed consolation and strength.

Still caught in silence, Marguerite kissed Nicolai again and again, sliding her fingertips lightly along the groove of his spine, dancing over the tight curve of his buttocks. His penis, already erect, lengthened against her thigh, iron-hard with the same firestorm of desire that burned inside her. That flame of need to be as one.

She spread her legs, welcoming his slow slide into her body. His hands entwined with hers, holding tightly as his movements grew quicker, their breath matched, their heart-beats drumming out the same pattern. It said what they could not—*I love you. I need you.*

Marguerite closed her eyes, her head falling back to the sheets as all her senses heightened. Never had she known such a pure tenderness, such a perfect joining. They *were* one. He was a part of her, and always would be.

Deep, deep inside, she felt the build of her climax, the un-bearable tension that grew and grew. She wrapped her legs tightly around his hips, holding him with her, part of her, until at last that tension snapped, and fiery stars showered around her head. Blue, green, red, crackling with passion. Above her, Nicolai's back arched, his head thrown back.

"Marguerite!" he gasped. *"Moya lubimaya."*

He collapsed to the bed beside her, still holding her hands, his face buried in her hair. She rested her cheek on his shoulder, and, smiling, slept at last. She was safe here. For this one moment.

Nicolai sat on the edge of the bed, lacing up his shirt as he watched Marguerite sleep. How very young she looked as she dreamed! Her face smooth, flushed to a rosy gleam in the dying candlelight, her hands curled delicately against the white sheets. She looked young and soft and vulnerable, open to all the possibilities of life, of being a human on this earth. To all her own possibilities, all the beauty and intelligence and kindness she possessed in her heart.

In her face now, he saw none of the trials she had endured—the death of her mother, a neglectful father, illegitimacy, the loss of her future children. The way unscrupulous and powerful men had used her strength and beauty for their own ends. Here she was just Marguerite, a woman unlike any he had ever known. His sweet, steely *lubimaya*.

In here, with him, as they made love, she could show the hidden side of her heart. Could begin to open, like a summer rose too long furled, seeking the heat of the sun at last. Yet someone out there wanted to cut her down before she could blossom.

Nicolai searched through the pile of her garments until he found the pouch where she stored the note, and drew it out. *Danger lurks...*

So, there was also someone out there who sought to warn her. To put her on her guard. Yet this person was surely powerless in themselves, if they had to write anonymously. They feared for their own life or position. It was all up to them alone, Nicolai and Marguerite. But they alone could be serious foes to any who threatened them.

He had vowed, as he tended Marguerite in her wounded fever, that he would find who did this to her. That he would protect her. Now he sensed that time grew short, that their unseen enemy was closing in. They had to be prepared.

Nicolai put the note away and went to open the clothes chest in the corner. There, hidden among shirts and doublets, was the dagger of the Emerald Lily.

He lifted it out, balancing the hilt in his hand as he watched the candlelight glint on the fine emerald. How very far they had come since that night in Venice, when she tried to plunge this very blade into his heart! Who would have imagined then that he would one day vow to protect her with his life? That she would *be* his very life?

He turned back to the bed. Marguerite still slept peacefully, turned on to her side. She needed her sleep, her strength, to face what Nicolai feared lay ahead. Yet he had seen her fierceness, the true, pure flame in her heart, and he knew she could fight any foe she ever encountered. She would not fight them alone, though. Never again.

Softly, so as not to wake her, he laid the dagger on his own pillow. Its blade glittered against the soft bedclothes, as if it knew it was home at last. It would protect her while he ran his errand, while he gathered their army and drew up battle plans.

But, very soon, more than its thin steel would stand between her and her enemy. Nicolai promised her that.

Chapter Twenty-Three

Marguerite slowly emerged from her dreams, like swimming up through thick, icy water, reaching out for the bright surface even as she longed for the dark depths. She burrowed deeper under the blankets, seeking that oblivious haven of sleep.

But it was gone, and she felt the world close around her again. The chamber was chilly, the tip of her nose above the blankets turning cold. She curled into a tight ball, wondering irritably where the maid was to light the fire. And surely Claudine would send for her soon, to begin yet another querulous day…

Then she remembered where she was. Not her own room, her own bed, but Nicolai's, where she had come to seek refuge.

She lowered the bedclothes, peering over the sheet's hem to see that she was indeed in Nicolai's chamber, but she was alone. The fire was dead in the grate, the candles melted out, and the sky outside the window was charcoal-grey with the faint light before dawn.

No doubt he had just gone to visit the jakes, or fetch more

candles, and would soon be back by her side. Yet Marguerite felt strangely bereft as she slid back down on the bed, cast alone on to a vast sea.

Something had shifted irrevocably last night, something between her and Nicolai, something inside herself. She confided in him, showed him the note, told him her fears, when she had always relied only on herself. Trusted only herself, and not even always that. Yet she had *told* him, and, despite her fears, it felt right. Natural.

Then they made love, so very sweet and profound it made her heart ache to remember. She had learned long ago to keep her heart and mind separate from her body. Last night, in Nicolai's arms, they merged—everything that was hers became his and they were as one.

Now that he was gone from her, she felt the cold again, the uncertainty. Saw the chasm that yawned below her.

And she remembered the tightrope. How thin and ephemeral it was, and yet with Nicolai's help she had walked it. It held her up and set her free.

She pushed herself up against the bolsters, brushing her tangled hair back from her eyes, and that was when she saw it, glinting from the pillow beside her. Her dagger, the one she lost, the one Nicolai stole, in Venice.

Marguerite reached for it slowly, half-fearing that the hilt would burn her fingers. But the steel was cold, still perfectly formed for her hand. An old friend, one she once so relied on. Now she was wary of its meaning.

She hefted it on her palm, finding it still light and well balanced, the emerald gleaming with its summer-green light. It *was* hers, or rather the Emerald Lily's. And the Emerald Lily was a part of her she could never be rid of, just as she could never be rid of her loyalty to France and the king. The

Emerald Lily and Marguerite Dumas were two halves of the same flawed coin, and could never be parted. Even as, with Nicolai, she had begun to dream of other paths, other journeys, her shadow was always with her.

Before she could truly be worthy of Nicolai, she had to cast that shadow away. Even if it destroyed her, too.

Marguerite slid from the bed and gathered her scattered clothing, dressing hastily in the faint light. She added the dagger to the note in her pouch, and enveloped herself in her cloak. The corridor outside the Spanish apartments was empty, with no sign yet of Nicolai returning. Soon enough the servants would be stirring on their early morning tasks, the palace coming to life for another momentous day of kings and their worldly aims.

She was still a part of that, whether she liked it or not. She owed loyalty to her king, and she had to see things through to the end. As for what happened after that…

She did not know.

She hurried out to the gardens, preferring the gravel pathways and fresh air rather than the warren of corridors inside. The breeze was cold and bracing, catching at her cloak like spectral fingers holding her back, pinning her down. She did like the night; she felt she could hide in its inky crevices and never be found again. Even by herself. She particularly liked when it was silent and deserted as it was now, as if she was the only person left in all the world.

For a moment, she wished Nicolai was with her, to hold her hand and share in the perfect, beautiful silence. To dance with her around the slumbering flowerbeds, and make her laugh, make her fly, again.

She hurried around a tall section of hedge, and saw a figure looming in the darkness. She imagined for an instant that it *was* Nicolai, conjured up by her dreams, and her heart gave a glad leap. Then it quickly subsided as she saw that this figure had close-cropped dark hair rather than a golden mane, and was too thin to be Nicolai. She fell back a step, tensing into a battle stance.

Before she could slip away, run off, the figure called out softly, "Mademoiselle Dumas! Wait!"

Father Pierre. Of course it would be him. He had lurked around her ever since they arrived at Greenwich. No, before that, since Fontainebleau. Always watching her, wanting something from her she could not understand. Like a looming black crow, heralding doom.

She went up on the balls of her feet, reaching for the pouch that held her dagger. She was prepared to flee or fight, but he said, "I know it is you. I saw you go to the Spanish apartments, I have been waiting for you to come out."

"You followed me here?" Marguerite said tightly. Under cover of her cloak, she loosened the strings of the pouch, her fingertips touching the cold hilt. "To what purpose?"

"You don't know it, but I have been watching over you for the entire voyage," he answered, edging closer to her in a rustle of stiff woolen robes. It was as if he had the wings of a crow, too, and she felt them closing around her. She fell back another step.

"Your attentions have been hard to miss," she said.

"I had to stay close, to protect you." His eyes shone bright and intense in the dying moonlight.

"Protect me? Or spy on me?"

"Oh, no, no, *mademoiselle! I* was not the one set to spy on you. I am your friend, your true friend."

Her friend. "You wrote the note," she gasped.

"I wanted to warn you of the danger you're in. To keep you

away from the Spanish and their pernicious influence. And yet you ran right to them! You did not listen to me!" His voice still held that taut desperation, laced with exasperation, as if she was a catechism student who just would not learn, would not heed his lessons.

Marguerite drew in a deep breath, tamping down her own flare of angry temper. Anger would not help her here. She made her voice soft and placating, coaxing and gentle. "I am only a foolish woman, Father. I did not understand your message. Of course you were trying to be a friend to me, I never should have expected otherwise."

"I have always been your friend! Always—cared about you. Ever since I first saw your great beauty. I knew you would be different, you would *see*." He drew himself up, shaking his head hard. "But I know the truth now. I know you are not just a 'foolish woman'."

Marguerite shivered in the cold night wind. "What do you mean?"

"I know your true work. I was told. You are a spy for the king."

She tried to hide her surprise, the frisson of betrayal that someone—a priest!—would be told her identity. She even tried to laugh, as if that was only so much nonsense. "La, Father Pierre, but where did you get such an idea! I know only about gowns and perfumes…"

"Stop it!" he suddenly cried, lunging forward to grab her by the arms. Marguerite reared back, trying to free her foot from her long skirts so she could kick him between the legs, make her escape. Yet he held her fast, surprisingly strong.

"Stop it now," he hissed. "You cannot lie to me, for I know your true sinful nature. The Comte de Calonne told me."

"The comte!"

"*Oui,* and what is more, the comte is assigned to kill you. I am meant to be his assistant here. That is why I wrote you that letter, why you must listen to me now."

Marguerite heard a great rushing sound in her ears, like an incoming storm, a tide that threatened to overwhelm her. The ground spun beneath her feet. "You lie."

"Indeed I do not. I cannot lie to *you,* not any longer. Never again."

The spinning grew faster and faster, until Marguerite feared she would faint. A very foolish action indeed, when she faced the news of her execution order. Or was this all a trick?

Through the haze, she felt Father Pierre lead her to a marble bench and help her to sit. He lowered himself beside her, yet not close enough to touch. She could surely flee easily now. But, as she studied him carefully, she found she did not want to flee. Written there, in every tense line of his face, every glint of his eyes, was truth. He did care for her, in his own strange, awkward way. He had sent her that note, struggled with his own nature to come to her and tell her this tonight.

"Tell me," she said. "You wrote me the letter. Why did you not just come to me, if you wanted to warn me?"

"How could I? You would not have believed me."

"I am not sure I believe you now."

His thin, taut face crumpled, and Marguerite saw for the first time how young the priest really was, young as she was herself. Caught up in a whirlwind before they could even realise what was happening, how they were being used.

But was he telling her all the truth? She could never be certain.

"You have no reason to trust me, Mademoiselle Dumas,"

he said. "I have tried to show you that I am your friend, but I haven't done it very well. I'm sorry for that, yet now you must listen to me! Time grows short."

Marguerite watched him as he fumbled inside his robes, coming up at last with a little key. It was shiny with newness, as if it had just been pressed from the original.

He gave it into her hand, muttering, "The comte will be with King Henry all morning after he breaks his fast with the comtesse. This key opens a chest hidden under his bed. Look there, *mademoiselle,* and you will see that I am here to help you."

She closed her fist over the key, yet Father Pierre did not release her hand. He held it tightly in his own cold grip, his whole body fairly vibrating with the force of his desperation.

Marguerite eased back warily. She had surely seen desperate men before, men who would do anything to keep what they had—riches, power. Life itself. But never had she been the focus of such fevered *need.* "What is it you want in exchange for this information, Father?"

He shook his head, still clutching at her hand. "I want nothing for myself, *mademoiselle*—Marguerite! Only your safety. I could not bear it if you were hurt, when I might have prevented it." His voice dropped to a hoarse whisper. "I tried to fight against it, to be true to my vows. But you are so lovely, so…"

He turned away, burying his head in his hands. His thin shoulders heaved on a sob.

Marguerite was suddenly seized with pity. *Pity*—for Father Pierre! Life was truly full of endless turns, she reflected. Unexpected revelations. She had been a fool to forget that uncertainty, to forget that people were ever strange and surprising. Nothing was as it seemed, good or ill.

She laid her hand lightly on his shoulder, feeling the jerk of bone and sinew under her fingers. "Please, do not torment yourself because of me. I could not bear it. You have done a true Godly deed today. You have saved a life, even if one as unworthy as my own."

"Never!" He spun around, seizing her hand again. The fresh tears on his cheeks gleamed. "No one is ever unworthy in the sight of God, Marguerite. You must make a new life, one that befits your true goodness and beauty."

Marguerite thought of Nicolai, of his sunny vineyards under endless blue skies. "I promise you that your good deed will not go unrewarded. I will find a new way, if you will, too."

"I will not go back to Court. I will enter a monastery." His face twisted bitterly, his clasp on her hand tightening. "I have had enough of the ways of kings."

"Yes, I know. I have, as well." Marguerite gently extracted herself from him, tucking the key into her pouch as she rose. If this was some sort of trap, she would know it soon enough. But she did not think the priest had it in him to perpetrate such a deception. "*Merci,* Father. From my deepest heart, I thank you. And I am sorry for so misjudging you."

As she walked away, she could feel his stare following her, full of a lonely craving she understood only too well. The crumbling beneath her feet she sensed earlier, the cracking open of her whole world, grew to a deafening roar. It was falling, falling, destroyed utterly beneath this sudden on-slaught. Her feet ran along the paths, faster and faster, yet even as she ran she knew she could not escape. The old world was gone, collapsing into nothing but fire and ash.

Could anything be built in its place? Would she even have the chance to try, or was her fate already sealed?

Chapter Twenty-Four

Marguerite paced the small space of her chamber, a few steps one direction, turn, a few steps the next. Around and around the bed. The steady rhythm focused her thoughts, her emotions, which were so very scattered and hot when she left Father Pierre. She had battles to plan, in the most vital war of her life. And wars were never won with fevered passions, but only with cold, clear consideration.

Claudine and her ladies had gone to play cards with Queen Katherine, leaving Marguerite behind when she pleaded a headache. In the quiet of her chamber, Marguerite bathed and changed into her most sombre black velvet gown. Her only jewel was her mother's diamond, tucked inside the high collar of the bodice. This was no time for scarlet silks and ropes of pearls! She needed strong armour.

Her next step was reconnaissance. She had to gather her proof, make certain Father Pierre's words were not a trap. She had to find out when her enemies planned to strike next. Then she had to recruit her allies. If, that was, she really had any allies beyond one guilt-addled, overwrought priest.

Marguerite laughed ruefully. Who would have thought

Father Pierre, of the staring eyes and lurking presence, would be her friend in the end? That his "love" would lead him to betray the comte, and his own place at Court? Yet she could not completely trust Father Pierre, either. Even if he told the truth, he seemed too volatile, too unpredictable. What if that tormented guilt led him to confess all to the comte?

And the comte—how did she not see beyond his open countenance, his light-hearted manners and affable ways? He was a fine actor, indeed. Surely he could rival Nicolai if he went on the stage. Perhaps there was more to Claudine's petulance than pregnancy, then.

Marguerite had certainly let her guard down, but those days were past. Forewarned was forearmed, and she would not be defeated now. Not when she finally truly cared whether she lived or died. Not when she had something to live for.

She opened her hand, watching the sunlight flash on the key. The key to the truth? To the future?

She spun around, hurrying from her own chamber and crossing Claudine's sitting room. The tables were scattered with the remains of the morning meal, breadcrumbs and empty goblets of ale. Soon, the servants would come to clear it away and clean the bedchambers, so time was short. She cautiously pushed open the door leading to the comte's room.

The bed was still unaired, the stools and clothes chests littered with discarded garments. After making certain no one was really about, and gauging possible hiding places should she be interrupted, she shoved aside the tumbled blankets and knelt to peer under the bed. There was the chest, just as Father Pierre said. A sturdy, iron-bound container for the most important documents.

She drew it out, sitting down on the floor to examine the lock, hidden by the tall bed. It was an elaborate affair, made in Germany, of the sort that was very hard to pick, even for an expert like herself. Luckily she had her unreliable, priestly ally.

The key soon had the chest opened before her. On top of the contents there were several heavy bags of coins, which she set aside to reveal a cache of letters and documents. The first few were instructions on how to conduct the meetings with King Henry, which members of the English Court were friendly to the French and which to be wary of at all times. Then, at last, she found what she sought.

A letter from King François. It was unsigned, yet she knew the handwriting well. For how many times had she herself received just such a letter?

As for the lady in question, her journey with you is the true test. After Venice, we cannot be certain of her continuing competence or loyalty. Watch her very closely—if she seems to be close to our enemies, if you have any cause to question her loyalty at all, you will know what to do. Accidents do sometimes happen…

Accidents. After she had given her youth, her life, her soul to France and the king, this was to be her reward after one mistake in Venice. An accident, quick, clean. Finished. No more troublesome woman.

She remembered Father Pierre trying to warn her so often, in his own awkward way, not to consort with the Spanish. Not to be their friend, or even to appear so. But Marguerite knew her friendship with the Duke and Duchess de Bernaldez was only an excuse. King François considered she was no longer of use to him, and she had to go.

Marguerite carefully refolded the hateful letter and put it back in the chest. Really, the comte was very careless to keep the message. She had always burned such things. Yet she was glad of that idiotic carelessness. Glad that she could see, written there in stark black and white, that the past was truly done.

As she replaced the other documents, the coins, careful to see that they were in the very same order, she knew she should feel sad. Angry. Furious! All she had ever done, all she ever believed in, was destroyed in one letter. Yet all she really felt was—relief. A growing, wondrous sensation that her chains were at long last falling away, the heaviness lifting so she could soar into the sky!

The Emerald Lily was gone. Only Marguerite was left.

But Marguerite was still in danger. Someone, a very powerful someone indeed, wanted her dead. How could she give up her life when it was only just beginning? When she felt she was emerging, newborn, into a shining new world where anything at all was possible? Even love.

She locked the chest and pushed it back beneath the bed, aligning it exactly as it was before. To save Marguerite, she had to bring out the Emerald Lily one more time. She had to fight with everything she had.

She pressed her palm over her velvet bodice, feeling the sharp outline of the diamond above her heart. The stone warmed against her skin, telling her she was not alone. Never alone. Her parents watched over her. And she had Nicolai now.

"*Maman*," she whispered, as she had not done since she was a child. "Help me now. Protect me with your goodness and love. And with an army well stocked with swords and cannons, if you can send one."

Non—she would not give up, even if no army came. Even if she had to stand alone again. For she truly had something to live for.

* * *

"You have grown rusty in this chilly English air, I see," Balthazar goaded, lunging toward Nicolai with his blunted stage blade. "All this feasting and wenching has made you weak!"

Nicolai laughed, parrying Balthazar's sword, spinning around to meet his blade in a clashing tangle. "If anyone knows the perils of wenching, it would be you, Signor Grattiano."

"Can I help it if the ladies find me irresistible? But I never let them distract me, as it seems you have with your blonde French angel."

"*Bud ti ne laden!* And a fine distraction she is. Far better than *this.*" He kicked out with his booted foot, so swift it was like a bolt of summer lightning, and caught Balthazar in the knee.

Balthazar fell back to the floor, cursing, rolling adroitly to the side to escape the tip of Nicolai's blade. "Foul cheater!" he shouted, his curses turning to laughter. "But then what else to expect from a lowly travelling player?"

"Or from a vile Venetian patrician," Nicolai answered. He tossed aside his blade and reached out to help Balthazar to his feet. Their fight concluded, they sat down beside the newly completed Castle Vert for a companionable goblet of ale.

"'Tis true enough," Balthazar said. "We Venetians are taught from our cradles how to cheat and lie. How to say one thing, so charming, so exquisitely polite, when behind the façades our actions are quite the opposite. Like our canals— smooth as glass on the outside. Fetid and rotten at the core."

"Yet you are leaving all that behind," Nicolai said, pouring more ale. "Sailing over the horizon to the New World."

Balthazar nodded. "For the time being."

"You won't stay on some sunny isle? They say the women there are astounding, brown-skinned and wanton."

Balthazar laughed at the teasing. "And they wear naught but a little scarf all day long. I, too, have heard the myths. It did not take Marc long to persuade me to the wisdom of this voyage."

He took a long sip of the ale, and Nicolai thought how very different Balthazar was from the young, satin-clad aristocrat that he met under such strange circumstances in Venice. So full of unfocused anger and black confusion, so very unhappy behind all his riches. The finery was gone now, replaced by plain black velvet and leather, but the anger still simmered. Tightly controlled, channelled into his new life of ships and the sea, yet there all the same.

Would he find his solace in the tropics? Nicolai sought his own in an Italian farm, but he was coming to believe that true consolation could not be found in any land or place, only in a man's own heart.

And he feared that his heart would soon go to France without him, borne by the white hands of the woman he loved, if he could not find a way to make her stay.

"In truth, Marc had no need to persuade me to go," Balthazar said quietly. "I would have begged him to send me on this voyage."

"What is it you think to find across the sea?"

Balthazar was silent for a moment, studying the false green battlements of the castle. "It is not so much what I hope to find as what I hope to lose."

Nicolai nodded. "Well, I wish you calm seas and a prosperous voyage." He lifted his goblet in salute. "May you bring back a hold filled with Spanish silver."

Balthazar gave a bitter laugh. "So that I may be even richer than ever!"

"There is something to be said for riches, when they are used wisely."

Through the half-open doorway of his theatre room, Nicolai saw Marguerite emerge from the shadows. She was almost a shadow herself, in her black gown, her hair covered by a black cap and veil, yet he knew it was her. No other lady moved like her, with such a light grace. Even as she hesitated, glancing back over her shoulder as if she feared to be followed, there was confidence in her posture.

Balthazar saw her, too, and his eyes narrowed. "There is also something to be said for riches that could buy such a rare jewel."

Nicolai laughed. "Oh, my friend. It would take far more than riches to buy *that* jewel."

"If there are more like that in France, I should forgo the islands and seek out Paris instead."

Marguerite came at last to the door, but backed away, her face pale, when she saw Nicolai was not alone. He noticed she rose up on her toes, as if she would flee, and he wondered with growing concern what made her so skittish today.

"I did not realise you were occupied," she said. "I will come back…"

"No. Marguerite, come in, please," Nicolai said, half-fearing that if she flew away now he would never find her again. He hurried to her side, holding out his hand to her.

She studied it for an instant before she seemed to come to some decision, and slid her fingers into his. "If you are certain I do not interrupt your business."

"Not at all. You have already met my friend Signor Grattiano. He offered to help me sharpen my sparring skills." Nicolai gestured toward the discarded blades.

A half-smile touched her lips. "I don't think you need to

sharpen them greatly, *cher*. You are already a foe to be reckoned with. But I am glad you have not left us yet, Signor Grattiano."

Balthazar gave her a gallant bow. "I will probably remain until after King Henry's great joust and pageant. I'm curious as to how the barbaric English do such things."

"I am sure they are nothing at all to Venetian festivals. The ladies will certainly be most happy to see you there. All the *mademoiselles* and *señoritas* were singing your praises loudly last night."

"You hear that, Balthazar?" Nicolai asked lightly. "As you have already broken all the feminine hearts of Venice and the Veneto, you can now begin on those of London, Paris and Madrid. Not to mention the islands."

"It is a vast task indeed," Balthazar answered. "And one I believe I must start on forthwith. Time grows short. If you will excuse me, Mademoiselle Dumas?"

He kissed Marguerite's hand before departing, only turning to give Nicolai a glance with his brow raised. "Riches indeed," he mouthed. Then he was gone, and Nicolai was alone with Marguerite.

She did seem restless today, moving aimlessly from the castle to his desk to a pile of costumes, fingering a length of white satin, the line of a gold-leaf sword. "So, Signor Grattiano is to stay for the tournament. And for the pageant after?"

"He must have his fill of fine food and beautiful women before those long weeks at sea."

"I cannot believe it will be so soon upon us. It seems we have only just arrived in England! I fear we haven't rehearsed enough."

"There are a few days left. These things always have a way of coming together at the last moment." Nicolai leaned back against the wall, his arms crossed over his chest. "But it is not the pageant that causes your restlessness today."

Marguerite dropped the sword. "*Non,*" she said, giving him a rueful little smile. "I fear not."

"Tell me."

She sat down on a stool, folding her hands on her lap as if to still that fluttering wandering inside her. "I discovered who sent me that warning note."

Nicolai stiffened, every muscle alert, as if readying for battle. "Who was it?"

"Father Pierre."

"The *priest?*"

"*Oui.* Not who we expected, eh? He found me as I was leaving your room this morning and told me everything."

"He was the one who shot the arrow, then? But how…?"

"No, no. He did not try to kill me. He says he cares about me, he only sent the note to warn me, protect me."

"And you believe him?"

"I do now. For, you see, he told me who really did try to kill me. He told me where to find the proof." Her hands tightened in her lap, and Nicolai saw the strain in her eyes, the anger and fear in her pale face. "It was the Comte de Calonne. Under orders from King François."

Nicolai feared he had not heard her aright. He reached out to take her hand, holding her fast. "Your own king ordered your death?"

"I am of no use to him now, after my failure in Venice," she whispered, not looking at him, but at their joined hands. "The comte is to use the excuse of my 'friendship' with the Spanish, with you, to cause me some *accident.* Last time an arrow—next time, who knows."

He felt the white-hot flame of fury crackle to sparkling life inside him. "*Nyet!* This is abominable. You have done nothing but serve your country, your king, at enormous price to yourself. For him to do this—"

"No, *cher!*" she cried. She freed her hand from his, reaching up to frame his face in her cold touch. She turned his burning gaze to hers, and in her sea-green eyes he saw tears. Tears of joy, reflected in her radiant smile. Never had she looked happier, more alive.

Had she gone mad, then? Had the discovery of her king's treachery snapped her mind?

"Oh, *mon amour,* don't you see?" she said. "I am *free.* Free to leave the Emerald Lily, free to be—well, whatever I want. I am no longer bound to a loyalty that never really was. I can be Marguerite, whoever she is."

He knelt slowly at her feet, staring up at her, at that glow in her eyes that kindled one in his own soul, burning away the anger, the flare of battle-lust. He understood her strange joy at last, and it became his own. She was free, and so was he. The ties to the past severed in one arrow stroke.

He turned his head to kiss her hand, her laughter the sweetest music to his ear. "Perhaps free to be a farmer's wife?"

"Oh, Nicolai," she whispered. "Truly?"

"If you think tending vines would make you happy. For us to be together, to make a new life—it would be more than I dared dream."

"*Oui!*" She threw her arms around his neck, kissing his cheek over and over until they were both dizzy with laughter. He held her by the waist, steadying her as she nearly toppled from her stool. "Nicolai, my love, we will make the finest wine in all the Veneto, you will see. Wine fit for the gods! And it will be all ours, our home, we will answer only to ourselves, and…"

Suddenly, like a dark cloud passing over the bright, fragile new dream, she stiffened in his arms. Her clasp tightened around his neck.

Nicolai went cold. "What is it, *dorogaya?*"

"I just remembered. In order to even reach our new home, I must stay alive. I must escape from here in one piece."

"Marguerite," he said urgently, holding her even closer. "There is surely no one more adept at staying alive than the two of us. You have surely eluded death more than once! And I escaped from the dreaded Emerald Lily. Is that not so?"

He felt her swallow hard, nod against him. "That is so."

"Your treacherous king has surely underestimated you, but he has done so for the last time. We are not without friends of our own. We have Dona Elena and her husband, and Balthazar, who could not have arrived at a more fortuitous time. And we have each other. You will *not* die, *lubimaya.*" He whispered fiercely in her ear, "You will not die. Not when I have just found you."

"And I you. I know we can prevail; we are not just vintners, we are warriors, *n'est-ce pas?*" she said. "But how? If we just run now, the comte will track us so easily. He must watch me."

Nicolai sat back on his heels, his mind racing, senses alert. *This* was what he had lived for all these years—intrigue, adventure. The fiery rush of battle and excitement. Once, he had loved it. The subterfuge, the complex games. Now, he only wanted it over, wanted his own life close to the earth and the sun, Marguerite by his side. Their fine wines, their new family.

But he could play one more deadly game. A game where the stakes were greater than any he had ever faced—the life of the woman he loved. Their entire future together.

"I will tell you a tale, *dorogaya,*" he said. "A tale of Venice, of two people named Marc and Julietta, who loved each other and found themselves in grave danger. Yet it was a play, a masquerade, that saved them…"

Chapter Twenty-Five

It was a perfect day for a tournament.

The clouds had cleared, leaving an arch of pale blue sky overhead. The watery-yellow sun shimmered down on the observation stands, hastily constructed and draped with green and gold banners and bunting. King Henry, who had injured his foot playing tennis the day before and thus given up his place in the joust, sat beneath a gold canopy of state, clad in lush purple Florentine velvet and soft black slippers. Queen Katherine sat beside him in her accustomed place, smiling serenely. Pages wove their way through the chattering crowds, offering spiced wines and sugared almonds.

Marguerite studied it all from her place behind Claudine. How merry it all seemed, laughter singing out into the cool breeze, mingling with a lute and tambor, the snap of the banners. So very pleasant, as if treacherous currents could never churn beneath the rich, gold-crusted surface.

She folded her hands in her lap, following Queen Katherine's example as she smiled and smiled, giving no hint of tension or fear. No glimmer that she was anything but a Court lady intent on flirtation and a diverting afternoon of mayhem on the joust field.

The Comte de Calonne was nowhere in sight. He was in one of the tents behind the stands, preparing to compete. Father Pierre was also not among the spectators, though Marguerite kept hearing his words in her mind. *You must make a new life.* She kept seeing his thin, haggard face, lined with such pain and tormented love.

She feared that if she could not summon every ounce of her playacting ability, every inch of her old mask, layer on layer, she, too, would look like the priest, with all her excited fear, her desperate love, writ large on her face.

Was this happening, *could* it happen? Could she make herself free? Or was this merely one of those glistening, ephemeral dreams she pushed so resolutely away over the years? Freedom, love, a family with just Nicolai and herself. Such things were never for her, for poor, bastard Marguerite Dumas. Now, it was within her sight, her very grasp. She felt the shimmering heat of it on her fingertips.

But it was not hers, not yet. There was one more test, one more battle.

Slowly, as if carefree and lighthearted, she turned her gaze to Nicolai. He sat with Dona Elena at the end of the stands, Balthazar Grattiano behind them like a black-clad shadow. They were laughing like everyone else, enjoying the bright day, the sport. Yet Marguerite thought she detected a whisper of tension in the line of his shoulders, the arc of his smile.

Tonight was to be it, for both of them. A new life beginning, or one that was over. There could be no middle ground. All of her training, all she had ever done or learned, led up to this one day.

Marguerite pressed her fingertips to the diamond pendant,

hidden under her crimson satin bodice. It lay warm and safe against her heart, reassuring her as it always did. She did the right thing now. The risk, *any* risk, was surely worth it to be with Nicolai.

The knot of ice in her stomach hardened, spreading its chill to every part of her, steeling her resolve. To win the prize, she could be the Emerald Lily one more time.

The gates at the end of the field opened in a blast of trumpets, a flurry of bright silken banners and flashing lance tips. King Henry's champion, Sir Nicholas Carew, rode forth on his brilliantly caparisoned horse as cheers rang out. His opponent, Roger Tilney, appeared at the other end, Marguerite's red-ribbon favour tied to his lance.

Marguerite clapped, too, adding her "huzzah" to the chorus, merry and flirtatious. But beneath her embroidered skirt, snug against her thigh, she felt the heavy weight of her emerald-hilt dagger.

Nicolai slipped away from the tournament under cover of clashing lances and splintering shields, making his way through the gardens to the theatre. The rooms were silent and darkened, as if they slumbered, awaiting some new drama. Some new tale of love, danger and tragical death.

It was a tale Nicolai had played out countless times, in innyards and banquet halls from one end of the continent to the other. He knew the emotions, the movements, as he knew the back of his own hand. Passion, fear, rage, the cold reality of death. Today's play, though, was all too real.

The love was stronger than he ever imagined it could be. When he looked into Marguerite's perfect eyes, she was all he saw, all he knew. The beautiful, wounded bird with her nerves of iron, her will to fight to the end for what she cared for, what she wanted. He saw her beauty, yes, but he also saw her heart, the heart of a survivor, a seeker—like himself. He saw the tentative, careful hope in her when they held each other, when they talked of new lives, new ways of being.

She was the other half of himself. He had searched for her for so very long. He wouldn't lose her now.

He went to his room at the back of the theatre, the little, precious space where he and Marguerite made love for the first time. Where he watched her silvery radiance burst free at last as she balanced on the tightrope, a shower of star-sparks to set the whole world on fire. He knew then, in that perfect, shining moment, that his heart was hers and always would be. He was her knight, her champion, and she was his.

Now they were close, so very close, to that fragile new dream.

Nicolai examined the Castle Vert, completed in all its green glory, embroidered pennants draped from the battlements, stiffened with little weights. Tonight, after the jousting and feasting, Beauty and her Court would take their places in those towers and be carried into the theatre. The eight lords in their blue satin and cloth of gold, led by the crimson-clad Ardent Desire, would lay siege to them with weapons of oranges and dates. The ladies would rain down rosewater and comfits, but all would end well, of course. The dark ladies of Danger, Disdain, *et al,* would flee, and the others would surrender, dancing away into the night.

Nicolai had choreographed it all, every chasse and flung date, to be a perfect representative of courtly love. He had taught a flock of giggling Court ladies their positions and choreography so there was no chance of a misstep. Yet he would not be here to see it.

All was in readiness, as perfectly put-together as the Castle

Vert itself. The façade of pasteboard and glitter only had to last a few hours, but every step was crucial. Just like Marguerite on the tightrope, they could not look down now.

There was a slight rustle in the doorway, and Nicolai spun around, his hand flying to the dagger at his belt. It was Balthazar, though, who peered into the room.

"All is ready?" Nicolai asked quietly.

Balthazar nodded. "The *Elena Maria* waits for us in London. We can be off on the morning tide, bound for Calais. And the boat will be at the farthest water steps at the appointed hour. Everyone knows their roles."

Nicolai laughed. "I think I detect a hint of diabolic glee in your solemn mien, Balthazar! The Venetian love of intrigue has not quite left you, eh?"

Balthazar grinned. "I lost my taste for politics in my father's house, I fear. But a *romantic* intrigue—ah, now, that I can relish. As long as it is not my own," he added hastily.

"We all think we are immune to love, don't we?" Nicolai said. "We are cynical men of the world, too wise to be caught in that trap. But I tell you, my friend, love is far more wily than we give it credit for. It waits where you least expect it, and lays you low in only an instant."

Balthazar shook his head. "Love dares not lurk where *I* go, I'm certain. And my heart is too hard for Cupid's arrow to find any purchase."

"Is that not what I said in the past? What we *all* say? But I vow, Balthazar Grattiano, even you will one day be taken by surprise…"

Chapter Twenty-Six

"You know what to do, yes?" Marguerite asked Señorita Alva. She stood back to examine the girl's attire, to make certain all her dark hair was concealed under the gold cap.

"Oh, yes!" Señorita Alva said, her eyes shining with excitement. Those brown eyes would be a problem, but surely once she wore her mask and was seated high in the battlements of the Castle Vert, no one would notice. "I toss comfits at the man in red velvet, and pantomime surrender with the other ladies. Then I dance a pavane." She tossed up her hands in imitation of surrender.

"And you don't speak to anyone," Dona Elena said, lacing up Señorita Alva's white satin "Beauty" costume. "You do not leave with anyone but me or Don Carlos. I will fetch you as soon as the dance is done, and get you into your own gown."

"Of course I remember all that!" the *señorita* said indignantly. "I am not a child. Oh, Señorita Dumas, how romantic it all is! I am honoured you asked for my help."

Marguerite smiled at her, trying to appear *happily* nervous rather than just frightened nervous. Señorita Alva had simply been told that Marguerite was eloping with Nicolai, running off to be married under cover of the pageant for fear of French protests.

She had engaged in so very many masquerades before, deadly deceptions that aimed to rid France of her enemies. Never had she performed in a disguise with so much to lose.

But she just hugged Señorita Alva, careful not to crush her white satin. It *was* romantic, she supposed, in some bizarre way. An escape with the man she loved, where before in her life love had been a word never even thought. It would all come off. It simply had to.

Señorita Alva went to the looking glass to tie on her gold satin mask, to examine herself one more time. She was nearly the same height as Marguerite, and had fair skin and a slender figure like hers. In disguise, at a distance, they could pass for each other. Marguerite straightened her own attire, dark brown men's hose and doublet, a linen shirt, hooded cloak, tall, sturdy boots. She took nothing else with her except her mother's diamond, and the Emerald Lily's dagger in the sheath at her waist.

"Are you certain she will be safe?" Marguerite whispered to Dona Elena. "I could not bear that anyone would be hurt because of me."

Dona Elena shook her head. "Carlos and I will watch her at every moment. She will never be alone. You must concentrate on getting away, *querida*. That is all."

Marguerite did not know how much Dona Elena really knew. Nicolai had only told her the tale of how they were in love and wanted to marry, but the French were opposed. But Dona Elena was wise, wiser than she liked to appear, Marguerite suspected. She saw deeply into people, into their hearts.

Marguerite clasped Dona Elena's hand, fearing she would

never again see this kind lady she had come to care for. "You have been so kind to me, Dona Elena. I can never repay you, never thank you enough."

Dona Elena laughed, squeezing her hand in return. "Of course you can! Just marry Nicolai and make him happy. I tried so hard to find him a good wife, and he, the contrary man, went and found one for himself. It is true I would have chosen a Spanish lady, but I can see how you care for each other. How you just—fit together. Like Carlos and me. You will have a good life."

Marguerite laughed, too, but her throat felt tight with tears. "If we can get away to begin that life…"

"Oh, you just leave that to us. Charming, diplomatic obfuscation is Carlos's speciality, he will hold off the French. They won't even know you are gone, with Maria-Carolina in your place. And you can trust Balthazar Grattiano, too. He has not been a ship's captain for long, but my son says he is one of the finest men at sea."

Ah, yes—the enigmatic Signor Grattiano. "Dona Elena, who is Balthazar Grattiano, really?"

Dona Elena gave a little smile. "He is many things. One of them is half-brother to my son."

"Are you saying…?"

"Oh, no, he is not *my* son, though I would be proud to claim him. I promise you can rely on him to get you safely away. He is Venetian, and people say they are born with seawater in their veins. I rather wish he would stay here for a time, so I could look about for a suitable wife for him! Do you happen to have a sister, Marguerite? Or mayhap a cousin?"

Marguerite laughed, a genuinely happy sound this time, and hugged Dona Elena. "I will miss you."

"And I will miss you and Nicolai," Dona Elena answered, patting her shoulder. "But I am sure we will meet again."

Señorita Alva spun around, concealed behind her mask and costume. "I am ready! How do I look? Do I look *French?*"

"Heaven forbid!" Dona Elena said. "But you look enough like Marguerite, I think. Now, we must go. It's almost time to begin."

Marguerite crouched low at the base of a marble fountain, enveloped in her concealing cloak. Her breath ached in her throat, the cold wind bracing, holding her up, reminding her of what had to be done. The pageant would surely have started by now, the castle carried into the theatre with Beauty posing in the topmost battlement.

The comte and comtesse, all the French party, would think that she, Marguerite, was right before them, and that would give her the time to get away. Hopefully, when the alarm was raised, she would be safely hidden in the hold of Balthazar's ship.

She laid her gloved hand over the hilt of her dagger. Soon, soon, she would have no more need of it. The tiny scythe used to slice bunches of grapes from the vine would be her only weapon.

She heard a whisper of movement in the gardens behind her, and she cautiously glanced back to see Nicolai hurrying lightly toward her. He was also clad in plain, dark clothes, his bright hair hidden by a hood, but she knew him by his graceful movements. The moonlight glinted on the sword at his hip. No stage blade this, it was sharply honed and lethal.

When he reached her side, helping her to her feet, he kissed her swiftly, hard, clasping her to him. His lips were warm, reassuring, and she felt a fresh strength flood through her. *This* was surely worth any danger, worth fighting any battle to hold on to forever.

"Is all in readiness?" she whispered.

He nodded. "The pageant is well under way. Señorita Alva does seem to relish being your double!"

Marguerite smiled despite her nervousness. "She is a finer Beauty than I could have been, I wager."

"No one will look for you for an hour or two at least. Come, Balthazar waits for us at the river."

Hand in hand, they dashed through the silent gardens, the only sound their breath in the wind, the grind of their boots on the gravel pathway as they evaded the guards. As they turned to the river, Marguerite saw Balthazar Grattiano in the distance, his small boat moored to the water steps that were usually used by servants and tradesmen and were thus out of sight of the palace. He waved at them, urging them onward.

How very close it was, that little boat, and freedom! Marguerite's cold trepidation slowly turned to a tentative hope. She could almost taste it, as sweet as Nicolai's kiss. Just a few steps more, a few steps more…

"Halt!"

Marguerite froze at the sudden shout, her body taut. The bright hope faded like a rosebud cut down in mid-winter. It had all been far too easy, too simple. She never, ever should have trusted.

She spun about, time slowing around her. It felt like she moved in sticky sugar syrup, muffled, trapped. The blood rushed in her ears, and the scrape of Nicolai's sword emerging from its sheath was inordinately loud. She felt his hand catch her arm, roughly shoving her behind him. Her army, her rescuing knight.

But she was not of the shrinking damsel sort. Marguerite

went up on tiptoe, peering past his shoulder as she drew her dagger.

It was the Comte de Calonne who threatened them, but a comte such as she had never seen before. She had always thought him a kind man, if rather ineffectual in his affable nature. Beset with a discontented wife, sent on this English errand by virtue only of his ancient family name and connections.

She had been wrong, and very foolish, to underestimate him. Foolish indeed, when her life had always depended on judging people's true worth. Father Pierre was right—she was so caught up in her own concerns she failed to see the enemy. How many mistakes she had made on this journey.

But she saw him now. The comte came to a halt several feet away, his sword levelled at them. He appeared to be alone, with no guards to back him up, but he also did not seem to need them tonight. His face was set in marble, an ancient statue of martial Achilles, his sword arm strong and steady. Far from an affable Court buffoon, under the thumb of his wife, he was a solider bent on a deadly mission.

"Monsieur Ostrovsky," he said calmly. "I have no quarrel with you, but if you stand in my way I must eliminate you. I'm very sorry, *très desolé,* but I must obey my king's orders."

Nicolai shook his head, his own sword swinging up in a lazy, graceful arc. "Marguerite is to be my wife. If you quarrel with her, you do quarrel with me."

"Ah, *monsieur,* such a pity!" the comte said sadly. "You seem a sensible man, despite your association with the Spanish. Now I see you are just like every other man, ruled by your cock at the sight of her pretty face. She has been the death of so many men before, do not let her be yours. Give her over to me now, free yourself of her spell."

Marguerite's fingers tightened on her dagger hilt. It felt as if ice cascaded over her skin, her nerves and blood, bringing with it a freezing fury. How dare he insult Nicolai? How dare *he* cast slurs on *her,* on her past, when he was naught but a hired sword himself? A hired sword who stood between her and all she loved and longed for in the world.

She slid to Nicolai's side, stiffening when he tried to push her back. She twirled the dagger lazily over her palm as she examined the comte for a hint of vulnerability. A shift of his stance, a turn of his gaze, anything that could show her the chink in his armour. She couldn't reveal her own.

"You are right, *monsieur* le comte," she said, in her most taunting, most seductive voice. She shrugged the cloak back from her shoulders, letting it pool at her feet as she used the dagger to slice open her doublet fastenings. "Your quarrel is not with Monsieur Ostrovsky, he has merely followed my instructions. Been my tool, you could say, to help me with my mission. Men are such foolish little lambs, *n'est-ce pas?*" With her free hand, she eased aside the doublet, loosened the laces of her shirt to reveal the soft white curve of her bosom. "So very vulnerable to a woman's charms…"

"Marguerite!" Nicolai growled. She shot him a swift glance, praying that in that split second he read her desperate message. *Play along with me,* she pleaded. *Follow my lead.*

His brow arched, and she knew he read her well. They were as one now, an inseparable team. It had to be enough to save them.

"You faithless whore!" Nicolai cried roughly. He dropped his sword close at his feet, his hands coming up as if to close around her throat. She slapped him away with the flat of her dagger, the noise of it against his skin far greater than any sting it delivered, and danced out of his reach. The movement carried her closer to the comte, and closer to the edge of the river, tumbling and murmuring past. From the corner of her eye, she saw Balthazar draw nearer to them, saw Nicolai wave him back.

It was good to have a guard at her back. But the comte would not be easily defeated, she could see that in the cold steel of his eyes, the unwavering line of his sword. He was as devoted to his cause as she had once been, when she was deluded and naïve. The cause of the French king, which had no substance, no loyalty. Not to her, to the comte, not even to the king's own sons, sent away to Madrid as hostages. It would surely destroy the comte, as it had nearly destroyed her. As it might destroy her yet.

"You cannot have imagined I had true feelings for you, Monsieur Ostrovsky," she said mockingly, still slipping, tiny step by tiny step, toward the comte. "Such foolishness! I only needed your friendship with the Spanish to help me get close to them, discover their secrets." She smiled at the comte, putting the full force of her beauty behind it, that dazzling distraction of prettiness she had so often used—and loathed—in the past. Never had she been more grateful for her mother's gift of a lovely face. "You see, *monsieur* le comte, we have the same goal. To see the treaty signed, no matter what. We have each just used our own brand of weapon."

She saw it then, the tiniest chink in his armour. His arm wavered, a mere shiver, but it was enough. He doubted. Was she really the enemy, or was she not?

"Monsieur Ostrovsky has been most accommodating with his information," she purred. "Now he can be eliminated. You came along at just the right moment, comte. How clever you are!"

Nicolai gave a hoarse shout of male fury, and lunged toward her. He was like a clumsy bear, with none of his usual light grace and balance. Such an actor. She ducked, taking one long leap toward the comte and his wavering sword. She remembered what it felt like to walk the tightrope, balancing on the balls of her feet, her core strong, mind focused on only one goal—not falling. She couldn't be distracted, not by Nicolai or by her own fear, not with all she had to lose. She had to rid them of their enemy.

She landed lightly, rolling into a crouch as the comte's blade crashed down. The confusion in his eyes cleared; he knew then that she truly was his foe. But that instant of hesitation had cost him. His arm was not as steady, his mind not as clear. As she came up, she drove her shoulder hard into his midsection, driving him back several steps toward the river. She balanced her dagger hilt in her hand, aiming the blade toward his shoulder. The emerald seemed to glow, her old friend and ally, a part of the woman she used to be. The time that had slowed like syrup rushed forward again, a fevered flood.

Before she could reach her goal, driving the honed steel into his flesh, he kicked out with his booted foot, catching her on her injured leg. The pain shot up her body like heated needles, and she gasped as she stumbled to the ground. The earth flew toward her in that sudden whirl of time.

She heard Nicolai's shout, the pounding of his footsteps. Her dagger caught on the comte's doublet, slicing through satin, linen, to nick his skin, but she could not break her fall. She struggled to find that balance again, to get her feet under her, but she was falling, falling…

"Non!" A shout rang out, sudden and clear. "Do not do this!"

The comte half-spun around, distracted at last, and she heard his muttered curse through that damnable rushing in her head. She saw Nicolai use his foot to kick the discarded sword into his hand, and, in one smooth movement, bury that blade in their enemy's chest.

When she hit the ground at last, she shoved the burning pain away and leaped up again, clutching her dagger. She nearly tumbled back into the river, but someone snatched her arm, hauling her back from the brink.

She shook her head hard, clearing away the fog of battle. It was Nicolai who held her, his arm tight around her waist to keep her from falling again. The comte lay face-up at her feet, Nicolai's sword in his chest. A pool of blood spread slowly around him, over his embroidered doublet, with terrible, black viscosity.

Father Pierre was rigid at the comte's side, staring down at him, expressionless, stunned, as he observed the scene. It was his shout that had distracted the comte for that one crucial second, his shout that saved her life.

Balthazar Grattiano stood behind the priest, holding his own sword, mild curiosity on his face, as if he watched a fairly entertaining pageant.

Marguerite glanced at Father Pierre. The priest's face was stark white, his hand still raised as if in warning. He stared down at the comte, at the blood that touched the hem of his robe.

"*Merde,*" he whispered. "Have I killed him?"

Chapter Twenty-Seven

Balthazar knelt beside the comte, calmly pressing his fingers to the man's cold neck. "Very neatly done, Nicolai," he said admiringly.

Marguerite watched as Father Pierre slowly lowered his hand, wiping it against the black wool as if to be rid of what had just happened. "I think I might be sick," he muttered.

She thrust her dagger hilt into Nicolai's grasp before dashing around the comte's body to Father Pierre's side. She well remembered that feeling from the first time she killed, the first time she saw a bloodied body. She remembered that sour surge in the pit of her stomach, the cold fear of impending damnation. True, Father Pierre had not actually killed, as it was Nicolai's sword that ended the comte's worthless life. But she could understand that he would feel guilty, for shouting out at that crucial moment.

She seized his hand, dragging him away from the body and toward the river just as he lost his supper into the dark, roiling water. When he came up again, she handed him her handkerchief, kneeling beside him in silence as he wiped his eyes. She then saw details she failed to notice in the heated flurry of violence. The priest's face was covered in new bruises, just darkening into purple-and-blue stains. A crust of dried blood covered his split lip and cut chin, and the shoulder seam of his robe was ripped.

"You saved our lives," she said softly, wonderingly. How could she have despised this man? That desperate infatuation of his she had once dismissed had spared her life.

"I have committed murder," he said hoarsely.

"You did not! You merely warned us. You prevented a murder, the only way you could."

He shook his head. "It was my fault you could not make your escape. The comte was not fooled by your double in the pageant, and he suspected I was the one who warned you away. He—I refused to tell him anything! But I could not hold out, I was not brave enough."

Marguerite gently touched his thin, battered cheek. He winced, but did not move away. "He tortured you. A priest of the Church!"

"I could not bear it. I told him you knew of his plot."

"Then what happened?" Marguerite said gently. Perhaps if she could make him talk, she could shake him out of that nauseous haze.

"He locked me in my chamber when it became clear I could not tell him more. But I knew I had to escape! Had to find you, warn you."

"You were very courageous," she said. "How did you find us?"

A tiny smile touched his injured lips. "How else could anyone escape from this cursed palace but by water? I only prayed I would be in time."

"And so you were. You saved us. I can never repay you."

"Just knowing that you are alive, Mademoiselle Dum—

Marguerite. Knowing that you are starting that new life we talked of, that is enough."

Marguerite swallowed hard past the sudden knot of tears in her aching throat. "I *will* start a new life, as a respectable, married lady. And I will never forget what you have done this night." She leaned forward to gently kiss his cheek. *"Merci, monsieur le père."*

He smiled at her. "I would take your confession now, *mademoiselle,* and send you into that new life shriven. But I fear we have no time."

"The priest is quite right," Balthazar said. "If we do not depart now, the tides will be against us."

"And the pageant is surely over by now," said Nicolai. "We won't be alone here much longer."

"Oh, no!" Marguerite cried in a sudden rush of panic. The whole unreal scene of the comte's death, Father Pierre's warning, had lulled her into a dreamlike feeling of being alone in the world. Isolated in their own terrible theatre. But very soon the crowds would pour out into the gardens. They were fortunate no guards had yet been this way. Time was very short indeed.

She leaped to her feet, helping Father Pierre to painfully rise. "What will we do about—him?" she said, gesturing to the comte.

"We must set the scene, I think," Nicolai said, as if he followed her thoughts about the theatre, the pageant. This was just one more masquerade. A vital charade.

He swooped up her discarded cloak, handing back her dagger as he held the wool fabric taut. "Make a slice here and here, rough, as if it caught on some pilings."

After she did as she was instructed, Nicolai swept the cloak through the water until it was soaked, draping it artfully over the banks. Father Pierre suddenly seemed to snap out of his guilty haze, nodding with bright, avid eyes. He added her handkerchief, embroidered with her *MD* monogram, to the displayed cloak.

"Whatever are you two doing?" Marguerite asked, bemused.

"You drowned, *lubimaya,*" Nicolai said. "So very, very sad. And surely the comtesse will think it a lover's quarrel!"

"And then the comte drowned, too," Father Pierre added. "Bravely trying to save his lover's life, yes, Monsieur Ostrovsky? I saw the whole tragic thing, but could not reach you in time."

"And the priest still tried to save you both," Nicolai said. "Thus receiving those hideous bruises. You are quite good at this, Father."

Father Pierre smiled. "I have directed a mystery play or two in my time, *monsieur.*"

"Then you understand the *miracle* of resurrection," said Marguerite. "Very clever."

She stood back, watching as Nicolai and Balthazar pulled Nicolai's sword from the comte's chest and rolled his body into the river, his own blade still in his hand as weight. "When he is recovered, won't that wound be questioned, though?"

"*If* he is found," Balthazar said, "the river will have done its work. A sword wound will be indistinguishable from a fish's meal. I've seen it often; bodies are pulled from Venetian canals every day. And now, fair *mademoiselle,* we really should depart."

Nicolai clapped his hand to Father Pierre's shoulder. "You will always have my gratitude, *monsieur.*"

Father Pierre nodded. "I would do it again, for Mademoiselle Dumas."

Nicolai grinned, taking Marguerite's hand in his. "Then we have much in common."

"Where will you go," Marguerite asked the priest, "after you have raised the alarm of my sad demise?"

"I will leave the bishop's service, go to that monastery I told you of," he said, with a new decisiveness. "It is far away, in Bordeaux, a contemplative monastery where my cousin is the abbot. He will welcome me there."

Marguerite nodded. "Then I will think of you living your life in peace."

"And I will pray that you, too, find such a peace."

Nicolai drew her away, urging her toward the waiting boat. As she stepped down into it, leaving her old self behind for ever, she glanced back to see Father Pierre one more time. But he was gone, and there was only her own battered cloak. The remnants of poor, drowned Marguerite Dumas.

Chapter Twenty-Eight

The coast of England was vanishing in the mist, as if it had
never really been. As if it was an invisible kingdom in a
romance story, and King Henry and Queen Katherine, Anne
Boleyn, Wolsey, Grammont and the Comte and Comtesse de
Calonne were mere characters. Figures in a dream, or night-
mare, that was at long last finished. Now there was only the
sea and sky, the fresh salt wind after long hours in the hold,
the ship's timber beneath them—and Marguerite.

They sat atop a coil of rope on the deck of the *Elena Maria,*
Marguerite's head resting on his shoulder. She had fallen into
an exhausted, relieved sleep as they finally slipped away from
England, and her body leaned heavily against his. Her hair
was tangled, her skin pale in the greyish light, her clothes torn
and stained. She was the most beautiful thing he had ever
seen, ever even imagined. And how infinitely precious was
every breath she drew, every warm touch of her skin to his.

Nicolai drew her borrowed cloak tighter around her shoulders, and she murmured in her sleep, curling into him. The
light gleamed on the diamond that rested against her throat.

She sighed, her fingers tightening on his arm as she stirred into wakefulness. For an instant, her green eyes were unfocused, blurred with dreams and old fears. Then they widened, and she sat up straight.

"Where are we?" she gasped.

"Never fear, *dorogaya*," he said soothingly, drawing her back to his side. "We are at sea."

"At sea? Truly?" She glanced around warily. "Gone from England?"

"Gone entirely."

"Oh, praise the saints!" She laughed, and the bright sound was sweeter than any silvery church bell, any music Nicolai had ever heard. It was not her old, flirtatious, throaty laugh, devoid of humour, but the unbridled joy of a young girl. The song of a bird as it soared from a cage. "Nicolai, we are *free!* Can't you feel it in the wind? Free."

"And so we are," he said with a smile. He could not seem to stop smiling now. All the years of restless wandering, of playacting and deception, of seeking for he knew not what were over.

All he had ever sought was here, in the circle of his arms. She was his home.

"Can the past be gone, just like that?" she said wonderingly. "With the crack of a sail, it is all behind us."

"Shall I baptise you in the sea?" he teased. "It might be a bit chilly, but…"

He pretended he would scoop her up, and she giggled, hitting his shoulder and kicking her legs. "*Non, non!* I feel new-baptised already, *cher,* I promise. I feel—I feel I could do anything. Be anyone."

"And so you can. England is behind us, and France, too. Who do you want to be?"

"I want to be Marguerite. Marguerite Ostrovsky, the old

married matron who works in the vineyard all day and dances all night."

"And so you shall be. As soon as we land at Calais, we will find a priest to marry us before we find transport to Venice. Unless you want to go on with Balthazar to the West Indies…"

"I think I have had quite enough adventure for one lifetime! And so have you. I am for Venice, not the New World." She snuggled back into his arms, nestling her head beneath his chin as they stared out over the waves. "I thought never to see Venice again, after—well, after the last time."

"Ah, yes. The last time. Are you sorry you did not finish the job that night?"

Marguerite shivered. "You must not even talk like that! Our own angel stayed my hand that night." She lightly touched her diamond. "Surely she saved both our lives."

"Then when we reach our home, we will build a little chapel to Our Lady of the Dagger."

"Oh, yes! With candles and a blue glass window. And every time I pray there, I will remember the blessing that was sent to me, despite my sins."

"The blessing we were both given."

Marguerite kissed him, her lips tender, the taste of her full of sweet longing, the brightness of a new day. "I love you, Nicolai," she whispered. "With all I am, I love you."

"And I love you. I always will, Marguerite, come what may."

She drew back, her fingertips lightly tracing his face, dancing over his cheekbones, his jaw, his lips, trailing through his hair. Her eyes were wide and full of wonder, following her touch as if she memorised every inch of him. She gave him a smile, so gentle, full of happiness and—and a strange sadness, too.

She eased away from him, rising to her feet. As she turned to the rail, Nicolai felt a cold, irrational flash of fear that she meant to throw herself overboard. He shot up, reaching out for her. "Marguerite!"

She glanced back over her shoulder. "All is well, *mon amour*." As he watched, she drew her dagger from its sheath at her waist. The grey light glinted across the emerald, the length of its perfectly honed steel. She held it up, staring at it as if mesmerised. As if, for that moment, the past tugged at her, stronger than the ephemeral cord that had bound the two of them ever since they first saw each other in that smoky brothel.

She sliced the dagger through the air, cutting off the past once and for all, and tossed it into the sea. It tumbled end over end, shimmering, dancing, before it plunged into the cold waves and disappeared.

Marguerite stared down where it had vanished, her hands braced on the railing. Nicolai went to her side, sliding his arm around her shoulders.

"The Emerald Lily is truly dead now," she said quietly. "I am free."

"From this day onwards, there is only Marguerite Ostrovsky?"

"Yes, Marguerite and Nicolai Ostrovsky, the eccentric winemakers."

Nicolai laughed, and Marguerite spun around in his arms to kiss him again. Her laughter blended with his, and they clung together in the cold sea wind. "The husband and wife who kiss in public like young peasant sweethearts."

"Who make love in the sunshine, and sing all night!" Marguerite cried. "It will be a fine life, won't it, Nicolai?"

"Oh, yes, *lubimaya*," he said, twirling her aro͡ around. "The finest life of all."

Epilogue

The bright summer sunshine burned down on the tangled rows of vines, turning them to shades of emerald and amethyst, curling in heavy twists and spirals. The scent of rich soil, earthy and fresh and weighty, blended with the sweetness of the grapes, the hot smell of the sun itself.

Marguerite knelt beside one of those vines, inspecting the shoots, pruning the leaves. It had been a good season so far; the grapes were fat and lush, there had not been too much or too little rain. There would be an abundant harvest in a few weeks, fine wines for the seasons to come. Wines that would taste of this land, of the soil and the rain and the sun. *Her* land, *her* wine.

Her home and family.

She trimmed off one of the smaller bunches with her little s⸱ ⸱he, and sat back on her heels to examine her handiwork, ⸱⸱⸱⸱⸱ ⸱ purple of its skin bursting with sugar. She tasted one, ⸱⸱⸱⸱ ⸱eet-sour juice on her tongue.

⸱⸱⸱⸱ ⸱he shade of the rich canopy of leaves, Alek-
⸱⸱⸱⸱ ⸱⸱⸱⸱⸱ her blanket, rocking back and forth
⸱⸱⸱⸱ ⸱ little feet and run. Soon enough

she would, too, Marguerite thought fondly, for she crawled like a very demon now.

Baby Shura had been abandoned as a newborn "on the wheel" at the village convent, and the abbess brought her to them, knowing of their "sad" childless state after over two years of marriage. Shura was nearly a year old now, a beautiful, wilful child with bright hair and velvety dark eyes, with the sweetest giggle and softest little hands. Soon she *would* run, dashing along the fields with the dogs, her laughter drifting behind her like a golden ribbon.

But, for now, she was safely confined to her blanket, the newest puppy asleep next to her.

"Ma-maaaa," she cried, when she noticed Marguerite smiling at her. She held out her chubby, dimpled hand imploringly.

Marguerite laughed, and sat down beside her daughter to feed her one of the grapes. Shura rolled it in her mouth, her little face serious as she absorbed the different flavours, the possibilities of the harvest. A vintner in the making.

Down the slope of the vineyard, Marguerite could see the red-tile roof of their villa, the walls a stark white under the summery light. All the window shutters were thrown open, and the maids were hanging out the clean linens to bleach in the sun. The long table was set up under the shade of the cypress trees, where they would have their dinner later, and nearby was the tiny chapel to Our Lady of the Dagger. Its small blue-green window, the colour of the sea, sparkled.

Her home. Her family.

"Ma-maaa." Marguerite felt a tug at her plain linen smock, and looked down to find Shura reaching again for the grapes. Marguerite laughed and drew the baby on to her lap, inhaling her warm, soap-sweet little girl smell.

"Greedy *petite,*" she said fondly, popping one more grape into the rosebud mouth.

For one moment, she remembered France. Not Paris, not the Court, but her father's château. The way he would take her hand when she was small and lead her through the rows of vines, teaching her all the methods she still employed here. The way he lifted her high, showing her the land, and she instinctively felt that love of place, of home.

All that had been lost in what came after. She had thought never to find it again, and thus had abandoned hope of it. She was no longer Marguerite Dumas, only the Emerald Lily, and longing for a home only brought pain.

But now—now it was hers. All of it. The house, the vines, the child. The husband.

"Is it all a dream, Shura?" she murmured, kissing the top of her daughter's silky head. Shura giggled, and grasped a loose lock of Marguerite's hair in her grape-sticky fingers. "Are *you* a dream?"

Sometimes she feared that was so, especially when she woke in the middle of the night, half-fearing to find herself back at Fontainebleau or Greenwich, caught in the web of kings and plots and endless death.

But then she would see Nicolai beside her, his golden hair spread across their pillows. She would hear Shura's stirrings from her nursery next door, see their moonlit vineyards outside the open window, and she knew beyond doubt that it was real. That love was real, and would not fail her.

Nicolai gave her all he promised that long-ago day on Balthazar Grattiano's ship. The kissing in public, the dancing all night, the lovemaking in the sun. The family and home, the simple life of living close to the earth, on their own terms.

He also gave her herself.

"And how are my beautiful ladies on this fine day?" she heard Nicolai call, and his voice made her heart soar. She stood up, Shura in her arms, and turned to greet him.

He had been working in the fields lower in the valley that morning, and wore a plain white linen shirt, doeskin hose, and dirt-stained boots. He had obviously washed at the well before coming to find them, for his shirt was damp, his tied-back hair glistening with water droplets. The sun turned him all to a shimmering gold, and his wide smile made her smile, too. It always did.

"Pa-paaa!" Shura cried, stretching her arms out.

"*Ryebyonak!* Little one," Nicolai said, swinging her into his arms. He tossed her high into the air, her shrieks of laughter ringing out. "I think you are even more beautiful now than you were this morning."

"She was perfectly happy with her *maman,* until Papa comes near and beguiles her away." Marguerite went up on tiptoe to kiss her husband's bronzed cheek. "Just as he has beguiled me."

Nicolai kissed her, a kiss full of the promise of this summer's day—and all the days to come. Then he lifted Shura to his shoulders, took Marguerite's hand in his and the three of them walked home to supper under the magic of the bright sky.

* * * * *

AUTHOR'S NOTE

The "summit meeting" between the French and English was a real occurrence. Between February and May of 1527, a delegation of the French led by Gabriel Grammont, Bishop of Tarbes, travelled to the Palace of Greenwich to negotiate a "Treaty of Eternal Peace"—"eternal" lasting a few years before conflict broke out again. The negotiations, long drawn out by King Henry to the chagrin of the French, were interspersed with lavish feasts, pageants and tournaments, much like the ones Nicolai and Marguerite attend, but the "Chateau Vert" pageant actually took place in March 1522 at York Place. A young Anne Boleyn portrayed Perseverance.

Henry VIII, Katherine of Aragon, Anne Boleyn, Princess Mary, Cardinal Wolsey, Ambassador Mendoza and Bishop Grammont were all real people, of course, though Marguerite and Nicolai live only in my imagination! When Nicolai first appeared in *A Notorious Woman,* I fell in love with him, and I knew I had to discover what happened to him—and find him the right heroine. I hope you enjoyed their tale!

A few of the many good sources for the time period:

Alison Weir's *Henry VIII: The King and His Court* (Ballantine Books, 2001)

Neville Williams' *Henry VIII and His Court* (Macmillan, 1971)

Antonia Fraser's *The Six Wives of Henry VIII* (Knopf, 1992)

Look for LAST WOLF WATCHING
by Rhyannon Byrd—the exciting conclusion
in the BLOODRUNNERS *miniseries*
from Silhouette Nocturne.

Follow Michaela and Brody on their fierce journey to find
the truth and face the demons from the past, as they reach
the heart of the battle between the Runners and the rogues.

Here is a sneak preview of book three,
LAST WOLF WATCHING.

Michaela squinted, struggling to see through the impenetrable darkness. Everyone looked toward the Elders, but she knew Brody Carter still watched her. Michaela could feel the power of his gaze. Its heat. Its strength. And something that felt strangely like anger, though he had no reason to have any emotion toward her. Strangers from different worlds, brought together beneath the heavy silver moon on a night made for hell itself. That was their only connection.

The second she finished that thought, she knew it was a lie. But she couldn't deal with it now. Not tonight. Not when her whole world balanced on the edge of destruction.

Willing her backbone to keep her upright, Michaela Doucet focused on the towering blaze of a roaring bonfire that rose from the far side of the clearing, its orange flames burning with maniacal zeal against the inky black curtain of the night. Many of the Lycans had already shifted into their preternatural shapes, their fur-covered bodies standing like monstrous shadows at the edges of the forest as they waited with restless expectancy for her brother.

Her nineteen-year-old brother, Max, had been attacked by a rogue werewolf—a Lycan who preyed upon humans for food. Max had been bitten in the attack, which meant he was no longer human, but a breed of creature that existed between the two worlds of man and beast, much like the Bloodrunners themselves.

The Elders parted, and two hulking shapes emerged from the trees. In their wolf forms, the Lycans stood over seven feet tall, their legs bent at an odd angle as they stalked forward. They each held a thick chain that had been wound around their inside wrists, the twin lengths leading back into the shadows. The Lycans had taken no more than a few steps when they jerked on the chains, and her brother appeared.

Bound like an animal.

Biting at her trembling lower lip, she glanced left, then right, surprised to see that others had joined her. Now the Bloodrunners and their family and friends stood as a united force against the Silvercrest pack, which had yet to accept the fact that something sinister was eating away at its foundation—something that would rip down the protective walls that separated their world from the humans'. It occurred to Michaela that loyalties were being announced tonight—a separation made between those who would stand with the Runners in their fight against the rogues and those who blindly supported the pack's refusal to face reality. But all she could focus on was her brother. Max looked so hurt…so terrified.

"Leave him alone," she screamed, her soft-soled, black satin slip-ons struggling for purchase in the damp earth as she rushed toward Max, only to find herself lifted off the ground when a hard, heavily muscled arm clamped around her waist from behind, pulling her clear off her feet. "Damn it, let me down!" she snarled, unable to take her eyes off her brother as the golden-eyed Lycan kicked him.

Mindless with heartache and rage, Michaela clawed at the arm holding her, kicking her heels against whatever part of her captor's legs she could reach. "Stop it," a deep, husky voice grunted in her ear. "You're not helping him by losing it. I give you my word he'll survive the ceremony, but you have to keep it together."

"Nooooo!" she screamed, too hysterical to listen to reason. "You're monsters! All of you! Look what you've done to him! How dare you! *How dare you!*"

The arm tightened with a powerful flex of muscle, cinching her waist. Her breath sucked in on a sharp, wailing gasp.

"Shut up before you get both yourself and your brother killed. I will *not* let that happen. Do you understand me?" her captor growled, shaking her so hard that her teeth clicked together. "Do you understand me, Doucet?"

"Damn it," she cried, stricken as she watched one of the guards grab Max by his hair. Around them Lycans huffed and growled as they watched the spectacle, while others outright howled for the show to begin.

"That's enough!" the voice seethed in her ear. "They'll tear you apart before you even reach him, and I'll be damned if I'm going to stand here and watch you die."

Suddenly, through the haze of fear and agony and outrage in her mind, she finally recognised who'd caught her. *Brody.*

He held her in his arms, her body locked against his powerful form, her back to the burning heat of his chest. A low, keening sound of anguish tore through her, and her head dropped forward as hoarse sobs of pain ripped from her throat. "Let me go. I have to help him. *Please,*" she begged brokenly, knowing only that she needed to get to Max. "Let me go, Brody."

He muttered something against her hair, his breath warm against her scalp, and Michaela could have sworn it was a single word…. But she must have heard wrong. She was too upset. Too furious. Too terrified. She must be out of her mind.

Because it sounded as if he'd quietly snarled the word *never.*

nocturne™

THE FINAL INSTALLMENT OF
THE BLOODRUNNERS TRILOGY

Last Wolf Watching

Runner Brody Carter has found his match in
Michaela Doucet, a human with unusual psychic powers.
When Michaela's brother is threatened, Brody becomes
her protector, and suddenly not only has to protect her
from her enemies but also from himself....

LOOK FOR
LAST WOLF WATCHING
BY
RHYANNON
BYRD

Available May 2008 wherever you buy books.

Dramatic and Sensual Tales of Paranormal Romance

www.eHarlequin.com   SN61786

REQUEST YOUR FREE BOOKS!

Harlequin® Historical
Historical Romantic Adventure!

2 FREE NOVELS PLUS 2 **FREE GIFTS!**

YES! Please send me 2 FREE Harlequin® Historical novels and my 2 FREE gifts (gifts are worth about $10). After receiving them, if I don't wish to receive any more books, I can return the shipping statement marked "cancel". If I don't cancel, I will receive 6 brand-new novels every month and be billed just $4.94 per book in the U.S. or $5.49 per book in Canada, plus 25¢ shipping and handling per book and applicable taxes, if any*. That's a savings of 20% off the cover price! I understand that accepting the 2 free books and gifts places me under no obligation to buy anything. I can always return a shipment and cancel at any time. Even if I never buy another book, the two free books and gifts are mine to keep forever.

246 HDN ERUM   349 HDN ERUA

Name _____ (PLEASE PRINT)

Address _____ Apt. #

City _____ State/Prov. _____ Zip/Postal Code

Signature (if under 18, a parent or guardian must sign)

Mail to the **Harlequin Reader Service:**
IN U.S.A.: P.O. Box 1867, Buffalo, NY 14240-1867
IN CANADA: P.O. Box 609, Fort Erie, Ontario L2A 5X3

Not valid to current subscribers of Harlequin Historical books.

Want to try two free books from another line?
Call 1-800-873-8635 or visit www.morefreebooks.com.

* Terms and prices subject to change without notice. N.Y. residents add applicable sales tax. Canadian residents will be charged applicable provincial taxes and GST. This offer is limited to one order per household. All orders subject to approval. Credit or debit balances in a customer's account(s) may be offset by any other outstanding balance owed by or to the customer. Please allow 4 to 6 weeks for delivery. Offer available while quantities last.

Your Privacy: Harlequin Books is committed to protecting your privacy. Our Privacy Policy is available online at www.eHarlequin.com or upon request from the Reader Service. From time to time we make our lists of customers available to reputable third parties who may have a product or service of interest to you. If you would prefer we not share your name and address, please check here. ☐

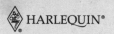
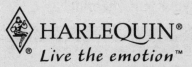

COMING NEXT MONTH FROM

HARLEQUIN®
HISTORICAL

- **WESTERN WEDDINGS**
  by **Jillian Hart, Kate Bridges and Charlene Sands**
  (Western)
  You are cordially invited to three weddings in the Old West this May!
  *Three favorite authors, **three** blushing brides, **three** heartwarming
  stories—a perfect recipe for Spring!*

- **NOTORIOUS RAKE, INNOCENT LADY**
  by **Bronwyn Scott**
  (Regency)
  Her virginity would be sold to the highest bidder! Determined not to
  enter into an arranged marriage, Julia could see no way out—unless she
  could seduce the notorious Black Rake…
  *Harlequin® Historical is loosening the laces with our newest, hottest,
  sexiest miniseries, UNDONE!*

- **COOPER'S WOMAN**
  by **Carol Finch**
  (Western)
  A proper lady should have no dealings with a gunfighter with a shady
  past, yet Alexa is bent on becoming Cooper's woman!
  *Carol Finch's thrilling Western adventure will have you on the edge of
  your seat.*

- **TAKEN BY THE VIKING**
  by **Michelle Styles**
  (Viking)
  A dark, arrogant Viking swept Annis back to his homeland—now she
  must choose between the lowly work that befits a captive, or a life of
  sinful pleasure in the Viking's arms!
  *Viking's slave or Viking's mistress? Annis must choose in this powerful,
  sensual story!*